This is a work of fiction. All characters, organizations and events in this novel are either products of the author's imagination or are used fictitiously.

Cover and map design by Kimberly Monson

The Final Heir

Book I of The Final Heir Trilogy

Jon Monson

Castle Peak Publishing, LLC

For Kim

Other Works by Jon Monson

Chapter 1

S hadows danced among the trees, playing a game unknown to Zahara as she crept through the forest. Mist—dense enough to obscure the mixture of roots, stones, and undergrowth that covered the forest floor—curled around her ankles with each step she took. It was almost as if the vapors were alive, begging her to join in its game with the shadows.

Somewhere above the dense canopy of branches, the mid-day sun was shining. Its light was able to penetrate to the forest floor in shafts—shafts large enough to feed the shadows but too small to provide anything more than a low twilight.

Zahara longed to feel the sun's warmth on her dark skin, but she kept her eyes focused on the trees. The aroma of fertile soil mixed with both dead and thriving vegetation, filling her nose with something almost tangible. With a quiet sniff, she could also pick up a hint of something else, something foreign to the woods.

A sudden breeze rustled the branches overhead, and goosebumps flared across her skin. She wished for more to cover her than just a red, short-sleeved tunic, tan trousers, and leather boots. The clothing was designed for maximum mobility—warmth was an afterthought.

The smallest rustle reached her ears, coming from somewhere off to her right, and Zahara grabbed the hilt of the short sword that hung on her belt. The leather was stiff and new, begging to be gripped by a powerful hand. She kept moving, each step placed with care to avoid even the faintest of sounds.

A twig snapped at her rear, and Zahara spun, pulling the short sword free from her belt in one fluid motion. Through the darkness, a shape emerged from the trees, a long blade swinging through the twilight. Zahara lifted her own sword to block the blow, filling both the sky and her bones with the crash of steel. With a shout, she pushed against the tangible shadow until it relented, retreating back into the darkness of the trees.

The snapping twig had been a warning.

The shadow didn't have to make noise as it moved—she suddenly saw herself as a mouse trying to escape the clutches of a particularly playful cat. She was allowed to feel in control, the possibility of escape a tantalizing dream. Yet she knew the cat would eventually grow tired and finish the game.

Instinctually, she lifted her free hand up to her ear and felt for the *qilada* that was as much a part of her as were her arms or legs. Forged by the First Heirs over three thousand years ago, the chain of white gold was inlaid with rubies and emeralds. The metal pierced the skin in three places and wound its way around her entire ear. She resisted the urge to summon a *kura* and push back the shadows harboring her foe. Instead, she blinked hard, staring into the darkness.

A shape emerged once again, and Zahara lifted her blade in time to block the assault. This time, instead of disengaging, the shadow pushed harder. At such close range, the twilight illuminated the smooth, pale face of a young man. His blue eyes bored into her own, and his blond hair was damp with perspiration.

White teeth were bared in a genuine smile.

Zahara lifted her leg and launched it into the boy's stomach. With a grunt, he fell back in pain. Zahara struck, her sword like a viper. The boy recovered and parried the blow before retreating a few steps, though not far enough to disappear among the trees.

He leapt again, his sword crashing down in an arc. Zahara lifted her own blade just in time, but her feet were unsteady, and the force knocked her to the ground. Her grip loosened with the shock, and her blade fell beneath the blanket of mist. Without waiting for her mind to react, her body somersaulted backwards and launched itself upright. She searched the mist-laden ground for any sign of her blade, but it eluded her.

The boy crashed through the undergrowth in another charge. Unarmed, Zahara leapt out of his path, dodging the sharp steel as it sliced through the air. Knowing she had no chance in her current state, she turned and fled through the shadows.

Her feet carried her through the undergrowth, her honed instincts alone stopping a fall. At her rear, the boy was no longer moving in silence as he struggled to keep up, and the crashing of his passage filled her ears. The sounds grew quieter as Zahara put more distance between herself and the boy, though she knew the silence wouldn't last for long.

Zahara came to a stop, her lungs struggling to fill with air without making enough noise to alert the entire forest. Adrenaline coursed through her veins, and her heart pounded in her ears. She could already feel the bruises beginning to form on her arms and back, though she knew that now was not the time to do anything about the coming pain.

She moved through the trees, trying to keep a map in her head. If she could circle back to the spot of the encounter, she may be able to find her sword. Otherwise, she would need to completely rethink her strategy.

As she neared the spot, her ears perked up—the air felt all wrong. There was no snapping of a twig or sudden movement among the trees to give her opponent away, but she knew he was near. She could feel his gaze tracking her.

Without closing her eyes, Zahara's mind reached out to the buzzing power of the *draod*—the omnipresent energy that fueled all life. Without looking, she could feel the *qilada* on her ear hum as the energy filtered in through the ancient relic.

With her mind's eye, she pulled on that power until thin strands formed. Like hairs spun out of a mixture of gold and silver, the threads glowed in the twilight—a glow visible to only Zahara's eyes. Careful to not make any physical movements visible to the hunter, Zahara began to weave the thin hairs into a familiar pattern.

It was no larger than her hand, but as her mind brought order to the threads of pure energy, the colors began to change. Within a matter of seconds, the pattern was completed, and Zahara finished it off with a tight, complex knot. For a brief moment, the spell hung in midair, its glow pulling Zahara in before the woven energy slammed into her face, covering her eyes.

Immediately, the darkness fled, the dim twilight warming to a bright afternoon glow. Outlines of the trees sharpened, and the mist—while still present—failed to obscure the ground and the obstacles it contained. Less than a dozen feet away, she could see the boy's pale hair and face, his blue eyes staring at her.

Without giving away her newly enhanced vision, Zahara kept on her circular path. She resisted the urge to keep checking on the boy's presence, forcing her gaze forward. Even a single glance could trigger his instincts, making him wary. She needed him docile, arrogant, unsuspecting.

Finding the spot where—just moments earlier—she had tangled with the hunter, Zahara easily found her short sword. Feigning continued blindness, she fell to her knees and felt around the area. Without looking back, she could feel the boy approaching, his silent feet padding along the ground.

Her hand grasped the sword's hilt, and she leapt to her feet in a spin. The blade crashed into the boy's sword, and a small yelp escaped his throat as his unready hand relinquished the hilt. His weapon sang through the air before slamming into a tree, but Zahara kept her gaze focused on the boy as she lifted her blade to his throat.

He looked at her and smiled.

The trees disappeared, along with the darkness and the mist. In their stead, polished walls of red stone stretched well over a hundred feet into the air. High windows allowed light to filter in, more than enough to give Zahara the ability to see. She reached out her mind and undid the knot on her weave. Her eyes returned to their normal, unenhanced state as the threads unraveled and returned to the vast sea of energy.

"Well done," a voice boomed from behind them, but Zahara refused to remove neither her gaze nor her blade from the boy's throat, even as the illusion of the steel blade dissipated, revealing a dull piece of wood.

"You win again, Zahara," the boy said with a shake of his head. "I really thought I had you this time."

"So did I," Zahara finally replied, pulling back and removing her wooden blade from the young man's throat before slipping it back into the scabbard at her waist. "You're a masterful tracker, Ekarath—you should be proud."

Ekarath's smile broadened with the compliment, but he shook his head with even more vigor.

"I think my dad would be more than disappointed," he replied with a chuckle. "He could track a deer in the middle of a storm. I can't even beat a girl half my weight with less than a year of training."

Zahara's stomach squirmed at the words. For one, she was his same height, even if Ekarath did have a lot more muscle packed onto his frame. Second, she wasn't supposed to weave the *draod* during combat training—she hoped nobody had noticed.

"There's no shame for either of you," a deep voice boomed again, and Zahara turned to see an aging gentleman dressed in robes of deep vermillion. A mixture of fat and muscle bulged underneath the thick wool, warning anyone with eyes that the man would not fall easily.

"Of course, Master Kanu," Ekarath replied with a small bow.

Zahara's eye caught the *qilada* wrapped around Kanu's finger—a silver ring shaped like a snake. She could almost feel the energy buzzing from the magical relic, powerful enough to create the forest that had so recently dominated the training room.

Though different in form than the earring looped through Zahara's pierced ear, Kanu's ring had the same purpose—to pull tendrils of energy from the *draod*, forming them into something useful. The man was a master at weaving, especially with Illusion threads, whereas Zahara only had a year of formal training. Of course, she had been training informally for her entire life, but that had only developed her skills to a certain point.

"I'm pleased with the progress that both of you have shown," Kanu continued. "It's not too late for you to join the *Hundiin*, Zahara. You're the only one who can beat Ekarath in a fight."

"I think I'd rather become a mage," Zahara said, her stomach again squirming with guilt. While her father had trained her with the blade, her mother had instilled a love of magic that was insatiable.

"Well, I'm sure Lord Dimitri will be more than proud to promote you tomorrow just the same," Kanu replied.

"Do you really think I'm ready to become a full mage?" Zahara asked, her stomach doing a somersault at the thought. She looked to Ekarath, who looked more than ready to join the elite *Hundiin*, the personal bodyguard that protected the Heir of Segova. But the idea of Zahara earning her own set of vermillion robes, being given permission to practice with the *draod* unsupervised—it was enough to make her dizzy.

"If anyone is ready, it's you," Ekarath said, flashing a smile that made her stomach do a different type of flip.

"Now, I think it's time for you both to get some dinner and a good night's sleep," Kanu said, craning his head to look at the high windows. "Tomorrow is the longest day of the year, and you'll need your wits about you. Today's trial will feel like a leisurely stroll compared to what you'll be facing in the morning."

"Thank you, Master," Zahara replied, giving the large man a bow.

Without another word, Zahara and Ekarath moved toward the large stone doors leading out of the training room. They emerged into a long, windowless corridor, illuminated by dozens of *kura*—white balls of light that floated lazily above their heads. Unlike the hundred-foot-tall ceiling of the training hall, the ceiling in the corridor was much shorter, and Zahara had to take a few deep breaths and force her mind away from the tons of mountain above her head.

"You went easy on me," Zahara said, breaking the silence. Without slowing, Ekarath gave a quick shrug.

"No, really," she pushed, "I heard the twig snap that first time—you could walk through a bramble patch without making a sound."

"I just…," Ekarath began, stopping to look her in the eye. "I don't know. I was about to get you, but I just slipped. I promise it wasn't on purpose—you don't need any help."

Zahara's stomach did a small flip as he placed a hand on her shoulder. She peered into his eyes, pools so deep she could lose herself forever. At that moment, she knew that he was the one to trust.

"Meet me at midnight," she whispered. "On the Boulevard, by the statue of Lord Grogonovich."

Ekarath's eyes shot open wide.

"Oh, not like that," Zahara said, trying to keep the blood from rushing to her cheeks. "There's just something I've got to try, and it has to be exactly at sunrise…on the solstice. I promise that you won't be disappointed."

Ekarath chuckled and shook his head.

"Are you suggesting we stay up all night before our final trials?" Ekarath responded. "You heard Master Kanu—we've got to have our wits about us, otherwise…"

"Do you really expect to sleep tonight?" Zahara asked. "I know I'll be too nervous...so I might as well do something amazing."

"Still, to just ignore curfew and break so many rules..."

"You don't have to come," Zahara said with a shrug as her friend's words trailed off. "You'll just miss out on the greatest spectacle since, well...the Creation."

"Any chance you could be less cryptic?"

"None at all," Zahara responded with a smile before taking off at the fastest walk she could manage, heading down the hallway that would eventually take her to her quarters. She resisted the urge to look back, knowing her friend's curiosity would get the better of him.

As she continued down the dimly lit corridors, her mind went to the ancient book she had recently devoured, hoping it was right.

***

Ekarath watched Zahara disappear around the corner, his eyes lingering on her graceful movements. With her dark Karajaani skin, tight braids, and athletic build, he couldn't help but admire his friend's beauty. Even as her footsteps faded, he couldn't bring himself to move.

"That girl is going to be the death of me," Ekarath finally whispered, shaking his head. For a moment, he considered following the young mage to get some better answers, but he knew it would be pointless. Instead, he went in the opposite direction.

Though Zahara often complained about subterranean life, Ekarath found comfort in the stone walls. True, he had spent the vast majority of his life out in the forest, and there were times he yearned for the feel of rich soil under his boots. Yet there was something just so solid about the red stone.

The hallway led him into a circular chamber, this one much smaller than the one he had just used for training. While this one lacked the complex weaves created by Master Kanu, it did have something a bit more practical: dummies stuffed with straw.

With dinner beginning, the training room was empty. A set of *kura* danced in the air, casting their soft glow on the rack of weapons to Ekarath's right. He took in a deep breath, trying to soak in one of his few moments of solitude.

After tomorrow, his life would diverge from Zahara's—more than he would like. She would live the life of a mage, while he would join the *Hundiin*. Her days would be spent studying the *draod*, while he would be occupied guarding hallways, on the lookout for threats to Lord Dimitri. Their chances to train together would be few and far between.

Of course, that was assuming they both passed their final trials in the morning.

You won't pass anything if you're up all night with Zahara, he thought. He brushed the words away, picking up a bow that hung from a rack, along with a few arrows.

He moved across the room and switched his focus to the row of practice dummies. Lifting the bow and taking a deep breath, he imagined them dressed in the black armor of the Usurper's Horde. He focused all his energy into the bow, forcing the arrow to obey his commands.

The feathers brushed his cheek as he released, launching the shaft across the room. The thud of metal on burlap and packed straw met his ears—a perfect shot in the dummy's chest.

If he didn't pass the final test in the morning, what would happen? Would he be given another chance after a few months? Or would he be deemed too incompetent to join the elite ranks of the *Hundiin*?

Zahara's face appeared in his mind's eye, and he shook his head. The girl was noble, her *qilada* alone worth more gold than Ekarath could hope to earn in a lifetime. If she failed her test, her consequences would be light.

Focusing on the next dummy, he launched another arrow, this one piercing the head. Without wasting another breath, he notched another arrow and let it fly. Within five more breaths, his quiver was empty, and five more arrows protruded from burlap corpses.

With no more targets, Zahara's face once again returned to his mind's eye. He could feel her arms around him still, could smell the mixture of sweat and cloves. Her bright smile wouldn't leave his head as he gathered up the arrows and returned the full quiver to the rack.

"Well, if I'm going to be up all night, I might as well not have an empty stomach."

Chapter 2

Zahara looked around the small, windowless room she had called her own since arriving at the Atsada nearly a year prior. More than half of the floorspace was dominated by a narrow bed, its straw mattress protected by an invisible weave that prevented the material from decay and insects. The spell, unfortunately, did little to make the mattress anything close to comfortable.

At the bed's side, Zahara sat at the small desk formed out of the red stone. Nearly all furniture in the mountain fortress was carved out of the dry, dusty rock. She longed for the feel of fertile soil under her feet, the sight and smell of greenery. She got some sense of it during her training, but there was a stark difference between an illusion and reality. She forced down those desires—they were pointless to dwell upon.

A single *kura* hovered over her desk, casting a soft white glow on the entire room. She had mastered the technique only a few weeks prior, allowing her to study in the dark without using the small ration of lamp oil allotted to a mere apprentice mage. She could tell that the lack of sleep was starting to drag her down, but the extra hours of study and practice felt more than worth it.

She took one last glance at the book sitting atop her desk, hoping the cryptic words—written in an ancient dialect of her Karajaani ancestors—spoke the truth. She had found the tome in a forgotten, dusty corner of the Atsada's library, and she wasn't sure if its neglect was an indication of hidden knowledge or garbage unworthy of proper care.

For the hundredth time since going through the book's promises, doubts crept into her mind. Did she speak ancient Karajaani well enough to follow the instructions? Did the author of this book really have such a deep understanding of the *draod* lacked by everyone else?

"Well, there's no way of knowing until I try it," Zahara whispered to herself before closing the book. She let out a deep breath and opened her door, which swung silently on *draod*-enhanced hinges. In the low light, she could see the delicate threads of Restoration magic strengthening and lubricating the ancient iron, and a wave of pride flowed through her for the work she'd done.

With her *kura* in tow, Zahara crept through the otherwise dark hallway carved out of solid red stone. Just as in her training, she placed each step with care, unwilling to trust her leather boots to be truly silent on the worn floor. The spell—woven from medium threads of Illusion and embedded into the leather—would theoretically eliminate the sound of her footsteps, but her skills at weaving complex illusions were even less polished than the floor she walked on. With her first dozen steps, even the slightest shuffle had failed to reach her ears, but experience had taught her to never place too much trust in an unproven technique.

The thought that she was breaking curfew—in preparation of shattering a dozen other rules—sent a shiver down Zahara's spine. Her brown trousers and red tunic didn't have the same spell as her shoes, and the soft swooshing of the cotton fabric filled her ears. The light umber of her skin practically glowed in the soft light of her floating orb, and she wished her dark hair could be freed from its bun. Yet on a night like this, the last thing she wanted to worry about was a tangle of tight braids getting in her way.

Her feet took her past the usual turn that would take her downward, toward the training grounds near the base of the mountain. Instead, she moved into a smaller tunnel that angled upward. Unfortunately, it also led further away from the edge of the fortress, bringing her deeper into the mountain even as it rose.

She tried to focus on her path forward rather than on the tons of stone and dirt over her head. This deep below ground, the air was moist and heavy, as if it hadn't been disturbed since the Creation. Zahara preferred to spend most of her time near the surface, where windows offered light during the day and fresh air filtered in and out with less rock to impede its movement. These narrow interior tunnels were only useful as shortcuts on a night with too little time.

She lost all concept of time as her feet kept moving in silence. Her ears kept expecting the tap of soft leather on hard stone, but her spell stayed strong.

"Almost there," Zahara finally whispered—hoping the words weren't a lie—before taking in a deep breath. While still heavy and stale, the air held a touch of the rich vegetation that thrived in the fertile plain outside. Her heart leapt at the thought of ending her time in the dank, subterranean tunnel.

She took another hundred steps before the narrow corridor emerged onto a much wider hallway. The Boulevard—as it was called by most of the inhabitants—wound along the mountain's exterior, acting as the main way to travel around the Atsada. While the hallway was carved into the mountain, the outer edge was open to the night air, and a soft breeze met her skin.

Supporting columns stood at regular intervals, doing their best to block the view, but they couldn't stop Zahara from taking in the gorgeous vista on a night like this. The valley below was bathed in moonlight, and the various buttes and spires that dotted the flat ground cast a forest of shadows. A chill rushed down Zahara's spine at the thought of running free and climbing the red rock that burst out of the verdant fields, but she forced her mind back to the task at hand.

With the moonlight streaming in, Zahara focused on the woven tendrils of power that made up her *kura*. Formed of the thinnest known strings of the *draod*, the pattern was complex enough to put a novice to tears. Yet after only a few weeks, Zahara could create the required tapestry in less than a minute. True, it was a minute of intense focus, enough to give her a headache, but she was still proud of her ability. So, it was with a heavy heart that she reached out her mind to a small knot near the orb's base.

With a grimace, she tugged hard on the knot, until it came undone. The threads unraveled, dissipating into an intangible dust before disappearing completely. The *kura* vanished, and Zahara blinked as her eyes adjusted to the moonlight.

Her muscles trembled in anticipation of the road ahead, and her stomach groaned in anger for the time spent in the narrow interior corridor. Zahara ignored both as she looked around for any sign of guards or other midnight wanderers that might question why an apprentice mage was out in the moonlight. The Boulevard was almost quieter than the forgotten corridor Zahara had just left, though she feared even the idea that someone could come around the bend at any moment.

As if in response to that fear, the pounding of feet clad in hard leather sounded around the corner, and a shot of adrenaline coursed through Zahara's veins. Her legs prepared to run, but her eyes darted toward the sound to see a long shadow carved from the soft moonlight. Instead of taking off in flight, Zahara pressed herself against the wall until her ears recognized the harsh gait of a friend trying to subtly announce his coming. As he came into view, Zahara could feel the muscles in her legs and shoulders loosen, the adrenaline dissipating into her body.

Ekarath's smooth countenance rounded the corner—the fact that he was unable to grow a proper beard ate at the young man's pride. His fair skin was practically translucent in the moonlight, and his short blond hair was all but invisible. Dressed in the simple red tunic and brown trousers of the Segovan Army, he looked like the elite soldier he would officially become in a few short hours. In her mind's eye, Zahara could imagine him replacing that red tunic with the blue of the *Hundiin*, speaking his oath to forever serve the Creator and his servants.

"Oh Ekarath, you can't sneak up on me like that," Zahara hissed, stepping away from the wall and keeping her voice at a whisper. "I about jumped out of my skin."

Ekarath leapt at the words, his eyes growing wide. A soft giggle escaped Zahara's throat, despite an attempt to stifle it. With the laughter ringing on the walls of the Boulevard, the boy's eyes focused on Zahara, and a smile spread across his pale face. Zahara's stomach leapt at that smile, though she forced the feeling down.

"By the Creator, you are getting way too good at that," Ekarath said, letting out a breath and shifting his gaze around the wide corridor.

"For a minute, I thought you might be someone else," Zahara responded with a shrug. "You didn't exactly promise to meet me, and I wasn't sure if you'd come."

"Honestly, neither was I," Ekarath replied. "But I knew I would never hear the end of it if I didn't. Is there any way we can still get a bit of sleep before our trials in the morning?"

"Only if you turn back now," Zahara said. "And I know you didn't break curfew just to do that."

Ekarath smiled and shook his head.

"I promise this will be worth it," Zahara said before he could give any more thought to turning back. "If this works, we'll be absolutely famous—it might even help win the war."

"Earlier you said it would be the biggest spectacle since the Creation. Can't you just come out and say it straight?"

"No way—it's way more fun to watch you squirm. You pretend to be grumpy about this, but I can practically see the gears turning in your head as you pretend not to care," Zahara said, motioning for her friend to follow as she began climbing up the Boulevard.

"Remind me again why we're friends," Ekarath said with a soft chuckle as they started walking. Zahara just stuck her tongue out in response, and the two friends trekked in silence.

After several long minutes, Zahara stopped at the base of an unassuming pillar. The archways in this particular stretch of the Boulevard looked just like the rest of the spiraling corridor, but there was a very important difference on the exterior. While most of the Boulevard's edge led to a sheer drop, Zahara had found a small ledge that would allow them to scramble onto the mountainside. They were still far from the top, so the climb would be arduous, but Zahara simply didn't care.

With nothing more than the moonlight to guide her, Zahara pulled herself over the railing, and her feet landed on the slick red rock. The leather shoes made solid purchase on the slope, and she moved to give her friend some room to follow. Ekarath flung himself over without much effort, his unenchanted feet making as little noise as Zahara's.

Zahara smiled at her friend before they began the climb. There was no path, and while it wasn't too steep, there were many times that both of them were forced to crawl on all fours. With the top in view, Zahara looked to the east to see a sliver of grey light peeking over the horizon, and a curse lurched from her mouth.

"That wasn't very ladylike of you," Ekarath said from behind her, and she could hear the laughter trying to escape his throat.

"We need to be up at the top by dawn or this will be for nothing."

"I was wondering why you wanted to start at midnight. This far north—and on the solstice—the sun rises around three."

"I'm from the south, the sunrise doesn't change that dramatically. Ugh, I knew we should have started earlier."

"Well, stop cursing and start climbing," Ekarath shot back, and Zahara refocused on the peak.

The cold light of dawn bathed the red rock in a sea of grey. The cool night air was beginning to relinquish its grip as Zahara pushed her body onto the Atsada's peak. Her legs were burning and shouting protests as perspiration coated her dark skin. Taking a moment to wipe the beads of sweat from her brow, she stopped to admire the view.

Red soil stretched out below for miles until it slammed into the dense flora of the Devna Forest. Fields of cultivated greenery and lush orchards contrasted sharply with the iron-laden soil. The sight was unlike any other she had seen in her seventeen years of life, and a full year of seeing it daily had yet to remove her wonder.

"Still can't believe you made me do this," Ekarath said as he took in a huge gulp of air. "I'm about to be inducted into the *Hundiin*—I shouldn't let myself get bullied so easily."

"Don't think of it as bullying. Just think of it as a favor for your best friend."

"Well, since I'm such a good friend, will you finally tell me why we need to be at the very *top* of the mountain?" Ekarath asked, and he began rubbing his arms. "Please don't tell me we broke all these rules for the view."

"I would have definitely broken more rules for this view, but that's not why we're here," Zahara responded as she tapped the complex earring that looped between three piercings in her right ear.

"Wait, did you bring me up here just to try a new weave?" Ekarath asked, his voice heavy with exasperation. "You know we'll be in so much trouble if we're caught—that is, if you don't kill us first."

"It's not like I'm going to explode the Atsada's peak or anything like that," Zahara said, hoping the words weren't a lie. "Besides, what are they going to do? Kick us out?"

"Exile is always a possibility—though I'd likely face a more severe punishment than you would. Something tells me that neither of us would last very long out there."

"Oh, come on," Zahara said. "I could easily protect you from all the bad monsters with my mystical, scary powers."

Ekarath didn't respond with a smile. Instead, his face grew serious before he opened his mouth.

"What about the Usurper's hordes? Can you protect us from those?"

Zahara's skin crawled at those last words. The Usurper, the Wild Man, the Primal King, the Destroyer of Worlds—whatever you wanted to call him, he was a being of pure evil. He and his armies had taken all of Einar, leaving the Atsada and its surrounding red soil as the last safe haven. She had no idea how long they would be safe, even here. Ekarath must have seen her reaction, because his face softened, and he took a step toward her.

"Please, just let me think," Zahara said, holding out her hands to stop his approach. "That sun is coming up much too fast for my taste, so I need to hurry."

She took in a deep breath and tried to force all thoughts of the Primal King out of her mind, but her eyes focused on the single road—carved out of the red, rich soil—that wound its way across the valley before disappearing into the forest.

Far beyond those trees, across hundreds of miles of rough terrain, rested the charred foundation of her home, along with the bones of her father. Images of that terrible day flashed through her mind's eye, and her legs began to tremble. Zahara let out a deep breath and pushed away the memories.

This is no time to pine for what's lost, Zahara mentally shouted at herself. The sliver of grey light on the horizon was turning into a soft gold, casting a warm glow that made the red soil and green fields give off a magical shimmer.

Zahara reached into her pocket and withdrew a ring of pure silver. For now, it was unremarkable in almost every way, but she gave it a quick kiss for luck before sitting cross-legged on the red stone.

She glanced at Ekarath, who stood with his back to her, staring out over the valley. Even if he were staring intently at her, he wouldn't be able to see what she was about to do—threads of the *draod* were only visible to the mage summoning them. A twinge of guilt slapped her in the face at forcing him up here so early in the morning. Still, she felt no small comfort with his presence.

Closing her eyes, Zahara took in a deep breath and forced everything out of her mind—her exhausted muscles, Ekarath's complaints, images of the Usurper destroying the world.

With those thoughts banished, Zahara focused on the buzzing energy of the *draod*.

In the old tongue, it could be loosely translated as the Power of Creation, but scholars had spent centuries arguing its true definition. Regardless of its real meaning, the *draod* was the energy that filled all of

Einar, and every living thing had a connection to it. Harnessing that energy was no simple task—the *draod* was like a wild animal, and it fought any and all attempts at domestication.

Zahara focused on the energy, and she began directing it through her *qilada*. Relics from the age of the First Heirs, the *qilada* acted as conduits between mortals and the *draod*. Without the earring, she would be nothing more than a teenage girl who knew how to handle a blade.

With her eyes still closed, Zahara used her mind to form the energy into tangible strands, pulling them from the ether and into the mortal world.

With trembling hands, she focused her mind on the thickest of the threads, pulling a tendril of Destruction out of the *draod*. Like the magic it could perform, the thread was unwieldy. The easiest to summon and the hardest to weave, tapestries of Destruction were generally simple—something that came in handy during a duel or battle.

Zahara wove the chunky thread around the silver ring that sat in the palm of her hand before tying the two ends together in a simple knot. It wasn't meant to do anything more than keep the thread from disappearing back into the *draod*.

With one thread complete, Zahara pulled a medium-sized thread of Illusion out of the ocean of energy. Noticeably thinner than the fiery tendril of Destruction, her new thread felt eager to obey as she wove it around the silver ring. With a similar knot, she left it alone before pulling on the thinnest of threads.

Restoration magic was the most complex of the three, and it resisted more than the others. While Destruction threads focused on destroying reality and Illusion was used to change perceptions of reality,

Restoration had the ability to *change* reality. The tapestries that could affect physical properties were complex, requiring intense concentration and skill.

Yet, Zahara had practiced for this moment, and she wound the thread around both the other two threads and the simple ring. Her mind's eye looked in satisfaction at the three strings, each different and yet born from the same source. Unfortunately, while they may be around the same ring, the three types of power were unable to connect, mix, or interact in any way.

Zahara knew if she opened her eyes, the weave would disappear, returning to the sea of energy surrounding her. Most patterns didn't take all her concentration, but this was no ordinary spell.

As the sun rose, Zahara switched her focus to the *draod*. Its energy pulsed, filling the air all around her. It almost felt eager to be used, excited to create magic. Zahara imagined pulling out a thread even finer than the hair-like Restoration.

A tremor swept through the ground, shaking the mountain's peak. A few pebbles around her danced and jumped, creating a sort of music that bounced around her skull. Zahara forced herself to ignore both the shaking and the stones—such quakes were common in the Jabal Mountains, though she had never really gotten used to their frequency. They were just one more reason Zahara hated living underground.

She maintained her focus on the power she could feel but couldn't quite see—threads of energy even thinner than a hair. Her entire body trembled as strands like a spider's silk began to appear. Their light was stronger than the others, nearly blinding Zahara's mind-eye as they grew stronger. Sweat began to bead along her forehead as she began directing the power to wrap around the ring, joining with the other three threads.

The final strand began to resist her, growing stiff and brittle. Her jaw clenched hard enough to break a tooth, but Zahara forced her will on the power as she continued weaving the pattern. Zahara's heart pounded in her ears as she concentrated on the *draod*, the sunlight, and the last remaining knot.

Another tremor rumbled through the mountain—far deeper than the first. While the scattered pebbles did their dance, Zahara could feel the mountain itself tremble. Yet it didn't follow the same pattern as a normal quake, and Zahara struggled to keep her focus. A wave of deep bass met her ears before slamming into her chest, reverberating throughout her entire body.

Zahara's concentration shattered as her mind shot back to the last time she had heard the sound, and her eyes shot open. The woven strands of the *draod* dissipated, returning to the sea of energy. The ring sat in her hand, its sheen in the morning light taunting her.

Ekarath stood with his back to her, looking out over the landscape. The trembling had ceased, but the deep bass still shook the air.

"Please tell me that's not what I think it is," Zahara said, forcing bile back into her stomach as she rose to her feet.

"I think we chose a bad time to leave the fortress," Ekarath said, pointing across the valley. Zahara forced her trembling legs across the peak to stand at her friend's side.

Her gaze traced the route of the single road to the edge of the forest, where a dark shape was spilling out of the mass of trees like an oozing river of shadow.

Even from this distance, she could feel the trembling of armored feet marching in unison. She couldn't see them, but the deep bass of the army's horns continued to hum in the air, rattling Zahara's bones and soul.

Focusing again on the *draod*, she pulled on several strands and created a familiar weave. She finished with a small knot and placed the woven tendrils of power over her eyes and ears. A shock surged through her body as her senses lifted—the landscape became sharper, the sound of marching feet pounding into her ears. With a shiver, Zahara focused her gaze on the black mass spilling onto the red soil.

With her eyesight enhanced by the *draod*, she could make out individual soldiers dressed in black armor of iron and leather. Her ears now picked up the synchronized pounding of feet on dirt, and it sounded even worse than in her imagination. The enhanced sense of hearing wasn't needed to tell her that the sound continued on for miles behind the tree line.

"We all knew this day would come," Ekarath whispered at her side, his voice trembling.

I just hoped that it wouldn't, Zahara thought.

The high-pitched cry of an eagle sounded from above, and Zahara turned her attention to the sky. The silhouette of massive wings filled her vision, and she didn't need any magical assistance to know what she was seeing. With her *draod*-enhanced vision, Zahara could see more detail than she wanted.

The creature's head was covered in brilliant feathers of pure white, which contrasted sharply with its black eyes and gray beak. A set of matching wings extended from the beast's shoulders, flapping in the morning sky before stretching into a glide. Large front claws ended in talons sharp enough to flay a moose, and they were already coated in fresh blood—no mean feat, considering the sun was still rising.

Feathers gave way to a thick white fur on the creature's bottom half, where the body began to shift from a predatory bird to a fierce hunter on land. The powerful hind legs of a lion curled into the body of fur and feathers, ready to bound across the open countryside. While they were currently hidden, claws sharper than swords sat ready to be just as deadly as the talons or beak.

"That blasted griffin," Ekarath spat, pulling Zahara from her inspection of the creature. "If only I had my bow—I'd love to get a good shot at it."

"Your arrow wouldn't get through the shield," Zahara responded.

She was referring to the invisible barrier that separated the Atsada from any potential harm. The spell hovered a mere dozen feet over their heads, and it was the only reason she could fight the urge to run away at the sight both above and below. Danger was coming, but for now, that danger was not immediate.

"I know that, but maybe *he* doesn't," Ekarath replied with a growl. "I mean, just look at him up there—he needs to be shaken up a little."

Zahara knew her friend wasn't just referring to the griffin, and she focused again on the flying monstrosity to see a figure clad in dark plate mail sitting atop the nightmarish creature. While his hands held no weapon, they were covered in thick gauntlets as they grasped the griffin's feathers. A helmet covered the man's head and face, with only two slits for his eyes.

Those slits turned to Zahara, and she could almost see a smile come through underneath the helmet. The man leaned forward, urging the griffin into a steep dive. A scream launched out of the creature's beak that resonated within Zahara's chest even more than the distant horns. The wind rushed through those massive, feathered wings as the creature streaked through the morning air. Zahara stood frozen, her jaw clenched and heart pounding, as the griffin grew large enough that she no longer needed any help to make out details.

She could hear the wind whistling as it was cut by the sharp beak, and the sunlight gleamed on the outstretched talons. For a moment, Zahara could imagine the beast slamming into the barrier that stood between her and the armored tyrant. Her mind's eye imagined the hardened air shattering into pieces, leaving nothing between her and death.

The Usurper pulled on the griffin's feathers, and the beast reared backward. Powerful wings slammed into the air, stopping the descent less than a dozen feet away from the barrier. Those wings kept flapping, and the griffin hovered. For an eternity, Zahara stood with her eyes locked on the tiny slit in the helmet.

The Usurper pulled up his visor, revealing a face that was broad and strong, with a chin sharp enough to slice through granite. Scars streamed across the skin like a hundred rivers fighting for dominance, while the rest of the skin puckered as if fire had ravaged it a dozen times. A wide smile splayed out along that horrible visage, twisting and distorting the scars but revealing a completely ordinary set of teeth.

The man's dark eyes bored into Zahara's soul as the smile grew larger. The Usurper let out a laugh that echoed across the mountaintop, and he gave her a quick wink before urging his mount to rise back into the sky.

Chapter 3

Ekarath grabbed Zahara's arm, her entire body trembling. He could feel the strength in her muscles struggling to keep her upright, and he lent her his strength. From above, a final cry launched from the griffin's throat as it climbed back into the clouds.

The call was enough to destroy the last of Zahara's resolve, and her legs gave out. Ekarath stopped her from collapsing completely, helping her down onto the slick rock. A wave of shivers swept across her entire body, and a sob launched from her throat, followed by tears. Unsure of how to respond, Ekarath sat down at her side, putting his arm around her shoulders.

"It's alright," he said in what felt like a comforting tone. He tried to imagine a father comforting a young child after a bad dream—only this was no nightmare. "Everything is going to be okay."

Zahara continued sobbing for another minute before gaining control of herself. She pulled away and looked up into his face. Even when red from tears, he couldn't see anything but beauty in those dark eyes.

"That was absolutely horrific," Zahara said, swallowing hard. "I'm so sorry for making us come up here."

"There's no need to apologize," Ekarath said. "Besides, now I can say that I've personally laid eyes on the

Usurper, though I'm not sure if anybody will believe me."

"You didn't need to be here for the spell," Zahara said, another sob threatening to break through the words. "I just didn't want to be alone in case...something went wrong."

"Well, there is a bright side to this—it seems unlikely that we'll get in any real trouble for leaving the Atsada. Nobody is going to care about punishing two kids when the Usurper's Horde is knocking on the gates."

Those words made Zahara look back across the valley, and Ekarath followed her gaze to the column of black armor emerging from the dense forest. He knew there were farmers down there, probably already on their way to tend the fields. Would they be able to flee to the fortress in time? Would escaping the Horde now do anything beyond delay the inevitable?

"How long do you think we have before the assault?" Zahara asked.

"Weeks, maybe months," Ekarath replied, tearing his gaze away from the army and directing it toward the Usurper. He and his griffin were already small in the distance, barely visible, even to his sharp eyes. "There's too much protecting the Atsada to just launch an assault..."

Ekarath let his sentence trail off, unsure of what to say next. There was no point rehashing the war that had started before his birth—it was no secret how most battles against the Usurper had gone.

"Let's get back inside," Zahara whispered. "I have a feeling that everybody is awake, and I don't want anyone to worry about us."

Ekarath scrambled upright to help Zahara, but she didn't seem to notice his outstretched hand as she forced herself up. Ekarath simply nodded in response, and the pair began the descent. The red stone was growing warm in the morning sun, and Ekarath knew it would only get worse.

With red dirt smudged on their faces, Ekarath and Zahara climbed back into the covered portico that had been so deserted before sunrise. While still far too early for most residents of the Atsada, the horns had stirred the fortress like a hornet's nest. The Boulevard was filled with a cacophony of soldiers, messengers, and laborers, and the earlier silence was replaced by a buzz of a hundred conversations. Within the fortress, the horns of the Usurper's Horde were almost as loud as they had been on the Atsada's peak.

"I should probably report to Master Kanu," Zahara said, and Ekarath turned toward her.

Ekarath could barely focus on her words. There was still evidence of the earlier tears, but the look on her face was like steel. Without thinking, he wrapped her in an embrace.

"Stay safe," he whispered. "I'll come find you when I can."

The words sent a wave of ice through his own veins, unsure if he had actually let them pass his lips. Unwilling to hear her response, Ekarath pulled away and disappeared into the crowd.

Following the mass of bodies, he descended the mountain fortress until it neared the base. His eyes spotted a familiar side corridor, and he forced his way out of the human river. Within a minute, the world around him was silent.

He entered a small armory—one of the smallest in the entirety of the Atsada. Inside stood three men inspecting their gear, all dressed in the blue tunics and steel armor of the *Hundiin*. A wave of envy washed over him that he would not be able to don the uniform marking him as one of the Atsada's elite soldiers.

Until he passed his final test, Ekarath still wore the red tunic of a regular soldier. With the arrival of the Usurper's Horde, there would be no testing. Yet he forced those thoughts away, knowing his duty was the same no matter his uniform.

He spotted an older officer with greying, short-cropped hair and a muscular build. His face was clean-shaven, and there was no hint of a smile on his lips.

"You're late," Commander Taro barked.

"Sorry, sir," Ekarath responded, bringing his right fist to his chest in salute.

"There's no time for any sort of punishment," Taro said, shaking his head. "And under the circumstances, I can't afford to have you doing penance."

"Of course, sir. Thank you, sir," Ekarath responded with a quick bow. "I'm assuming that duty will postpone my final trial."

"Yes, I'm afraid so. I need someone watching the main gate—with that army approaching, there's a real possibility of desertion. I don't trust those regular soldiers, but I don't want them all feeling nervous with a whole squad of *Hundiin* breathing down their necks."

"Understood, sir," Ekarath responded before giving another salute.

The officer returned the salute, and Ekarath turned to the rack of weapons along the far wall. He considered taking a bow, but the moment seemed to call for sharp steel. He inspected the polished blade, wondering how much time would pass before it would be coated in blood.

Without waiting for the officer to bark another order, Ekarath trotted out into the corridor. For a moment, he considered heading back to the Boulevard, but the idea of pressing against so many people was less than appealing. Instead, he headed deeper into the fortress, into the maze of tunnels that could leave a person lost for years.

He found a familiar set of stairs that wound down into the darkness. Though the steps were lost to his eyes, experience told him that several *kura* would light the way once the steps ended. With a deep breath, he began the descent.

Ekarath could feel the adrenaline still coursing through his veins—he had seen the Usurper with his own eyes. The fabled scars, marred by that terrible smile, burned in his mind's eye, filling the darkness. The cry of the griffin echoed in his ears, accompanied by the man's throaty laughter.

That scarred face had overseen the destruction of millions. The idea that he had come face to face with the most dangerous being in the history of Einar made his legs weak, and Ekarath forced himself to keep moving down the stairs. There was simply no time to waste thinking about the danger that been a mere two dozen feet away, even if the Atsada's shield had acted as a barrier.

He knew that shield couldn't hold forever. While the Heirs had been able to defeat the Usurper's forces on occasion, they had been powerless whenever the monster had come in person. The scarred man riding the griffin had never been held at bay for long.

Ekarath reached the bottom of the stairs, which opened up into a hallway that was indeed illuminated by a few *kura*. Compared to the brilliant sunrise, the light was dim and pale. However, after the pitch black of the spiraling steps, his eyes drank in the soft light.

The corridor took him back to the Boulevard, though he was now near the bottom of the fortress. Here, far from the safety of the Atsada's upper chambers, there were no more crowds. The laborers, messengers, and administrators that had clogged the Boulevard above were absent.

The inclined path ended in a cobblestone plaza filled with a few hundred soldiers. While there were blocks of archers, swordsmen, and spearmen, all wore the red tunic of the Segovan regular army. A single look on their faces spoke of their fear and uncertainty as they watched the Horde spill out of the forest.

The main gate stood ahead, a massive structure of steel and red stone. Stories told of its invincibility, though Ekarath had to believe that without the shield of air around the entire Atsada, the gate would prove mortal.

While the gate and courtyard were at the bottom of the fortress, there was still a gentle slope down to the valley floor. From this vantage point, he still had a commanding view of the approaching army.

Without letting his mind fixate too long on the blocks of dark armor flooding the valley, Ekarath found the nearest officer—a man in his late twenties with short hair, a strong chin, and the standard red cape.

"Reporting from Commander Taro, sir," Ekarath said with a salute. "He sent me to bolster the gate's defenses."

The officer looked Ekarath up and down. While Taro's name wouldn't be widely known among the rank and file, any officer should recognize the second-in-command of the *Hundiin*.

"You certainly don't look like an elite soldier," the officer said with a shake of his head. "But welcome all the same."

"What's the situation down here, sir?" Ekarath asked, ignoring the man's jab.

"Lord Dimitri made an opening in the shield, and we're on watch for refugees," the officer said. "We've already had some of the farmers make their way in. The rest, well..."

Ekarath let the man's words trail off, knowing it was unlikely that anyone else would be making it at this point. Hours had passed since he'd begun the descent, and the sun was well into its trek through the sky.

Shouts sounded from outside, and Ekarath moved his focus beyond the gate. At this distance, he could see two dozen figures dashing for the fortress—men on foot wearing the standard red tunic. These were no farmers, but a patrol that must have been out, caught unaware.

At their rear, ten warriors on horseback were giving chase.

"Poor souls," the officer said. "They're not going to make it."

Ekarath hated to hear those words, but he knew the man was right. While the foot soldiers outnumbered the cavalry, it was obvious they had been running for far too long. There was exhaustion in every movement. It was difficult to see at this distance, but it was likely they had long ago abandoned their weapons.

There was still a good distance between the men on foot and their mounted pursuers. Yet it wouldn't take long for horses at full gallop to catch up. At that point, it would be a massacre.

"Let's do something about it, sir," Ekarath said, turning to look at the officer.

"I have strict orders to stay behind the gate," the officer said, turning to Ekarath with a glare. "We can't sacrifice the whole fortress for a few men, and I'm not about to be ordered about by some *boy*."

Ekarath returned the man's glare, though he knew it would do little good. If he had orders to keep his men behind the gate, there was simply nothing Ekarath could do to change his mind.

"Fine," Ekarath said before pulling the sword from his scabbard. "I'm going."

"You'll stay behind the gate," the officer said, placing a hand on Ekarath's shoulder. "That's an order."

"Your orders are to stay behind the gate," Ekarath said, brushing off the man's grip. "Mine are to bolster the defenses and boost morale. Besides, you can't give me an order—I'm *Hundiin*."

Without waiting for a response, Ekarath took off at a run. He ignored the stares as he dashed through the open gate and down the gentle slope. His feet pounded the hard, red soil, and he focused his mind on the approaching horsemen.

As Ekarath drew closer, his comrades came into focus—he could see their exhaustion, the mixture of dirt, sweat, and blood coating their skin. As he had suspected, the soldiers had dropped their weapons long ago, the spears and swords only serving to slow them down.

This may have been a mistake, Ekarath thought, but he immediately pushed the words out of his mind. He was no regular soldier—he was practically part of the *Hundiin*.

His legs took him past the fleeing soldiers, ignoring the look of confusion blanketed on their faces. Instead, he focused his entire being on the lead cavalryman—a giant brute of a man, clad in black leather and wielding an axe.

Ekarath grabbed the horse's reins, the momentum swinging him upward. His boot slammed into the brute's chest, knocking him to the ground with a thud.

The horse reared onto its hind legs and let out a scream, but Ekarath tightened his grip on the reins and held on. As the horse calmed back down, Ekarath could feel the entirety of the cavalry troop turn its attention to this insane attack.

One down, nine to go.

Without hesitation, he slammed his heels into the horse's ribs, taking off toward the Atsada. He nudged the horse to the right, making a broad circle and—hopefully—leading the horsemen away from his retreating comrades. With a backward glance, he could see that all nine sets of dark armor were now on his tail, their original quarry forgotten.

"Keep running," Ekarath whispered, hoping the Segovans wouldn't stop until they reached the safety of the gate.

His mount's hooves pounded on the hard ground until it began to flatten out. Pulling hard on the reins, the horse came to a stop, danced on its back legs, and turned around to face the Atsada.

"I really should have planned more than ten seconds in advance," Ekarath whispered to himself.

The nine remaining soldiers let out a holler as they approached, clearly convinced that their prey was insane. Ekarath pulled the sword from its scabbard and once again nudged the horse's ribs. He let out a shout of his own as he charged. Eyes widened underneath the dark helmets.

His sword took a man in the chest, slicing through the thick leather cuirass. The force rattled Ekarath's hand, but it knocked the unprepared soldier off his mount. Ekarath kept pushing the horse forward, past the eight men who remained.

That's two. Only eight left.

Shouts sounded from behind, and Ekarath leaned forward in the saddle. Moving his body in time with the horse's pace, he whispered to the beast, encouraging it to keep moving—toward the Atsada and safety.

The whine of a crossbow bolt sounded in the air, the short, black arrow sailing over his shoulder and hitting the ground just in front of him. From behind, he could hear the sharp crack of more crossbows firing, yet there was nothing to do but keep moving.

A thud sounded as a bolt hit the horse's rear, and Ekarath flew through the air as his mount fell to the ground. He adjusted before slamming into the packed slope, managing to roll. Forcing himself upright, he could already hear his pursuers catching up.

Almost instinctually, he lifted his blade. A bolt slammed into the steel, bouncing off the hard surface. The horsemen approached, and Ekarath swung his sword, slicing through the leather straps securing the saddle to the nearest beast. With a shout, its rider fell to the ground, and Ekarath leapt without thought. His sword pierced the leather armor, bringing an end to the man's shouts.

Three down, seven to go.

Footsteps sounded from behind, and Ekarath swung around, bringing his sword up as an axe crashed down. The brute whose horse he had stolen looked down on him, his eyes filled with a fire.

Damn. Make that two down, eight to go.

With a shout of his own, Ekarath pushed back, and the brute disengaged. He lunged at the man's chest, but his blade merely glanced the dark leather as the soldier jumped backward. The black-clad soldier swung again with his axe, but Ekarath parried the blow with his sword before hacking the man's hand clean off.

As the brute howled in pain, Ekarath lunged, jabbing his sword into the man's chest. He let out a soft gurgle and fell to the ground. Ekarath began turning to face whoever was next.

Now that's three down, seven to go. Ekarath was beginning to like his odds.

A bolt took him in the back of his thigh, and he looked down to see the barbed head poking out the front.

Ekarath shouted in pain but managed to stay upright. A horseman rode by, swinging a heavy axe at Ekarath's face. Without command of his brain, Ekarath's arm moved up, blocking a direct hit, but the force knocked him to the ground.

Ekarath struggled to get up, but footsteps sounded.

"You fight with the courage and insanity of a wild beast," a voice said, and Ekarath looked up to see one of the Imperial soldiers descending from his horse. His helmet didn't have a visor, and he could see the pale complexion of a man native to Engarstand. His pale brown eyes almost looked sad as he approached, long sword in hand. "It really will be a pity to kill you."

Ekarath forced his eyes to stay open—if he was going to die, it would not be while cowering. He would face it head on.

A soft whistle sounded, followed by a thud. The soldier's eyes grew wide, and he fell to his knees. He let out a gasp before falling onto his face, a quivering arrow protruding from his back. Around him, the dark-clad cavalrymen shouted in confusion as more arrows rained down.

Ekarath looked toward the Atsada to see soldiers in red tunics charging forward. Some held bows, others wielded swords and spears. They let out a cry that sent shivers down his spine.

"For the Heirs and Einar!"

Around him, two more Imperial soldiers fell. The survivors mounted their horses and ran.

***

With every limb in her body trembling, Zahara made her way up the Boulevard. All around her, men and boys pushed to get by. Fortunately, she wasn't far from her destination, and she was able to get into a small side corridor. She only had to follow it a few hundred feet until she found a now-familiar door.

Most rooms in the Atsada had unremarkable entryways—some were covered by nothing more than a sheet or tapestry. Yet this particular room was protected by an ancient, dark wood. Zahara could feel the *draod* humming from it, and she knew it had complex weaves of Restoration placed into every layer of wood. Letting out a deep breath, Zahara knocked.

"Come in," a voice sounded from the other side, only slightly muffled by the heavy wood. Zahara grabbed the silver knob and pushed the door open.

The room within was larger than most in the ancient fortress, and a few high windows allowed the morning sunlight to stream in. Master Kanu sat behind a rather imposing desk, his face concentrated on a stack of parchment.

"Good morning, Master Kanu," Zahara said with a small bow, and the man looked up from his reading as if he hadn't just told her to enter.

"Ah, Zahara—I'm so glad you made it," he responded in a kind, masculine voice. He removed a pair of reading glasses and set them on the desk before getting to his feet.

Though he was past middle age, Kanu's face was still handsome, with a sharp jaw and high cheek bones. His hair was a light brown, though it was starting to thin out, his hairline receding like a glacier in spring. The poor man only had a few years left before he would need to apply a razor along his scalp as part of his morning routine.

"The Boulevard is a bit hectic this morning," Zahara said, suddenly hoping that she didn't look too disheveled after ascending and descending the Atsada.

"You certainly look like it took a battle to get here," Kanu responded with a laugh, gesturing to her face. "You've even got some dirt smudged along your cheeks."

"Oh, well...Ekarath wanted to get in some sparring this morning," Zahara replied, trying to come up with a plausible lie.

"That boy's far too worried about his initiation," Kanu replied, shaking his head. "That or he just wants to spend more time with you. I have to think it's the latter."

Zahara could feel the blood rush to her cheeks, and her mouth turned into a tight line as she suppressed a smile. She spun away from the man, becoming very interested in the nearest shelf. The entire office was lined with them, the wood sagging under the weight of books and glass jars. She had no idea what the man did all day when he wasn't teaching her, but it had to involve reading ancient text and conducting bizarre experiments.

"What tasks do you have for me today, Master?" she replied, refusing to turn back to the man until she could compose herself.

"Oh, Zahara, just because I've never been married doesn't mean I can't see when two young people are obviously in love," Kanu said, placing a gentle hand on her shoulder. "You can't hide such things from me, even if we've only known each other for a short while."

Despite the storm of emotions inside her, Zahara couldn't help but smile. Kanu was by far the friendliest mage in all Einar, and he was the closest thing she had to family. He'd barely grumbled about taking her in a year ago, and his stewardship had brought Zahara more knowledge than she could have possibly imagined.

"Ekarath is my best friend, the only one I have around here besides you," Zahara responded, turning to look into her master's deep blue eyes. "There's nothing more to it than that. And besides, I think we have a lot more to worry about with the Usurper's horde emerging from the forest."

"Yes, I was sleeping rather well until those horns nearly knocked me out of bed," Kanu responded, moving back to his desk. "I have to imagine we'll be under a tight siege in a few hours. I even thought I heard the cry of the Usurper's griffin at one point."

As the words left Kanu's mouth, images of the Usurper's face flashed through Zahara's mind. Her knees buckled, and she had to grab onto the shelf to keep from falling to the floor. Fortunately, Kanu had already turned his attention back to the stack of papers on his desk and didn't notice. Zahara took in a deep breath, trying to push the image away.

"Oh, I didn't mean to worry you," Kanu replied after a second, and she could hear him set a paper back down on his desk. "Those boys will never get past the barrier. Soon enough, they'll be so hungry and haggard that they'll be running all the way back to Talas. The Usurper isn't any match for the power of Lord Dimitri."

"I'm sure you're right," Zahara said, swallowing hard and turning back around to face her master. The images of the Usurper's scarred, mangled face kept pushing their way into her mind, and she forced them back. "I think I just need some good work to do. That always gets my mind off things like this."

She couldn't tell her mentor what had just happened—it would lead to far too many questions. Just because she wouldn't be exiled from the fortress didn't mean she would avoid punishment for breaking so many rules. The last thing she wanted was to spend her last days cleaning chamber pots.

"That's a good girl," Kanu said. "And you're right, there is a lot of work to be done. I know your final trial was to be today, but under the circumstances..."

"Oh, I assumed that to be the case," Zahara replied. "I just want to be of help."

"Well, if that's the case, I think your talents could be put to use down in the infirmary."

That's almost worse than cleaning chamber pots, Zahara thought, but she didn't allow the words to leave her brain. The doctors and nurses in the infirmary didn't enjoy her presence—probably because she could use the *draod* to heal much more efficiently than their medicines and herbs. But Kanu was right. She would be needed with all the wounded that would likely be coming in. Instead of complaining, she forced a smile.

"That's a good girl," Kanu said with a smile of his own, as if he could read her thoughts. "I know it's not your favorite place, but that's the life of a mage—we serve where we are needed. At least it's better than trying to face down the Usurper and the Horde."

The words made Zahara's stomach squirm, and the knotted face pushed itself back into her mind's eye. Her legs wobbled, but she kept herself upright. Kanu's face fell, and he moved over and grabbed her by the arm.

"Oh my, maybe you should take a break instead," he said.

"No, I'll be fine," Zahara said, shaking her head and gently pushing the mage away. A silence took hold over the room as Zahara contemplated her next question. "Have you ever seen the Usurper...face to face? Up close?"

"That's not the kind of thing many of his enemies see and live to talk about," Kanu replied, shaking his head. "But yes, we came face to face once, a long time ago. It was before he became completely disfigured, and the memory still makes me a bit queasy. People say he hardly even looks human these days."

Zahara thought that last part was a bit exaggerated, but she knew that saying so would lead to uncomfortable questions. Instead, she simply nodded and headed for the door.

"Good luck, my dear," Kanu replied, his voice heavy with concern. "I'll come check on you in a while, just to make sure those simpletons don't drive you too crazy. Oh, and make sure you change before going down. I know the nurses won't want you dressed as a soldier."

"Of course," Zahara replied, looking down at the rather dirty trousers and tunic. Kanu must know she had been up to something, but she appreciated that he didn't say so.

Zahara pushed on the heavy wooden door and emerged into the hallway. The relative darkness—broken only by a few floating *kura*—felt soothing to her mind after the sunlight that filled Kanu's office. Taking in a deep breath, Zahara began her journey that would lead back to the Boulevard and wind down the mountain until she reached the infirmary. Outside, she could still hear the deep rumble of horns announcing the impending doom.

Chapter 4

A low groan awoke Zahara, her body lurching at the noise. Her arms were folded against the cool subterranean air, and she nearly fell out of the rough wooden chair that was not meant to double as a bed. As she caught herself, the muscles in her neck complained about the awkward position they had been forced into after so much labor. Joining the cacophony of minor aches, Zahara's eyes stung as she blinked away the slumber.

She looked around the large, windowless room illuminated by a dozen *kura* floating lazily in the air. Beds lined the walls up and down the room, leaving a wide aisle in the middle for Zahara and the healers to do their work. Despite the appearance of the Horde, most of the small cots were still empty, though a half-dozen of the beds held injured soldiers.

Just like every room in the ancient fortress, the walls of the infirmary were carved out of the mountain's red stone. For a reason that Zahara couldn't fathom, the room where the sick and injured were sent to recover didn't receive any natural sunlight. While the injured eventually left, Zahara spent far too much of her time training in the infirmary, which did little for her feelings about a subterranean life.

There were no decorations to provide color or variation, save a clock that hung over the doorway. Even the clock was utilitarian—with no windows, it would be impossible to even guess the time without the instrument.

A quick glance at the clock told her it was morning. It also told her that just over twenty-four hours had passed since she had climbed the Atsada, coming face to face with the Usurper. A shiver ran up and down her spine at the memory of the encounter, and she forced out images of the horrifying visage.

Her dreams—restless nightmares more than anything else—were filled with that disfigured countenance. Those scars that swirled over pale skin like worms on a decaying corpse in the early morning light had turned into the real thing in the twilight of her dreams. The wink that spoke of a man who didn't care that he was about to launch an assault that would kill thousands repeated every time she closed her eyes. The griffin's cry still resounded in her ears, and her bones felt the weight of the slaughter to come.

The groan that had roused her from those dreams sounded again, and Zahara turned to look at Ekarath's pained face. When she had arrived yesterday morning, Ekarath was already in here, a wound on his leg tightly bandaged. Nobody would tell her what had happened, though she couldn't imagine such a wound coming from an accident.

The doctors and nurses—none of whom were trained with the *draod*—had done what they could. He was even on a mixture of herbs to help him sleep. Though his eyes were closed, the groaning meant his slumber was anything but peaceful.

Zahara redirected her gaze to the wound on his leg. After just a few hours, the bandages were already red with blood, and Zahara began working her nimble fingers to take another look.

The wound was completely open, and there was a greenish tint around the edges. If the herbs had failed, Zahara knew that nothing she had on hand would do any better. Master Kanu could easily take care of the wound, along with a few other mages she didn't know very well, but they were out shoring up the defenses.

Zahara had changed out of her trousers and tunic, and she now wore the white dress that marked her as an apprentice mage, though she had more experience with the *draod* than many of the Atsada's magi a decade her senior. However, the rules here were strict, especially in the infirmary—any use of the *draod* should be under supervision. While she loved ignoring that rule, it would be difficult to do so down here, where the evidence would be irrefutable. Zahara's heart began to pound as she took another look at the infected wound.

Closing her eyes, Zahara focused her mind on the delicate chain that hung from her ear. She could feel the weight of the precious stones, could sense the way the metal glimmered in the soft light of the *kura*. More than anything, she could feel the buzzing power of the *draod* all around her.

She focused on blocking the outside world from her mind and creating a space of perfect tranquility. Ekarath's moaning grew silent; the snores from a large man across the infirmary disappeared. In this moment, there was nothing more than the *draod*.

Raw energy flowed into the earring, turning into something malleable as it coursed through her body. Zahara's hands began to tremble as they pulled on fine threads of Restoration. With eyes still closed, she focused her mind on the power—weaving and interlocking the threads into a thin sheet. The strands crossed and stuck together, growing stronger with each passing second.

She coaxed the woven threads onto Ekarath's thigh, and it began wrapping around the wound like an ethereal bandage. A gurgled scream erupted from her friend's throat, but Zahara forced herself to ignore it—the process of healing with the *draod* was usually a painful one. Knitting skin and muscles back together in an instant was not something the body enjoyed, but Zahara knew from experience that the pain would be worth it.

Zahara opened her eyes to see the infirmary just as it had been. The humming of the *draod* had fled, and the threads of power were gone. She looked down at Ekarath's wound to see a line of tight skin that would usually suggest a recent cut, but one that had mostly healed. This particular injury shouldn't cause any more pain, but Zahara knew there were worse things to come.

Ekarath's groans were gone, and his breathing settled into the shallow, slow pattern of restful sleep. Wiping her hands on the apron, she turned away from the injured soldier to look at the clock.

Standing in the doorway was a man in robes of green silk that hung on a bony frame. His face was an ocean of wrinkled skin, and a long beard of thin, white hair hung down his chest. Despite his frail appearance, Zahara could feel the air tingle with his presence.

Placed delicately atop his head was a crown—a thin branch formed of pure gold.

"Your Holiness," she gasped, falling to the ground in a bow.

"Oh, no need for such deference, Zahara," the old man said with a voice much stronger and kinder than she had expected.

Zahara looked up, and she could feel the blood rush to her cheeks. The old man smiled as she forced herself up, and he didn't say anything as her legs began to tremble. She had never been this close to Lord Dimitri—she had only seen him during festivals when he addressed the soldiers of the Atsada. To have him less than a few feet away was something she had never expected. To hear her own name uttered on his lips felt unreal.

"Don't be scared, child," Lord Dimitri said, moving closer and gesturing for her to take a seat. Zahara didn't need to be given another invitation, and she collapsed into the wooden chair that had so recently substituted for her bed.

"I—I—"

"My apologies for scaring you like this," Dimitri said as he flashed another smile. Those eyes were a cold blue, but they radiated a warmth that Zahara had never seen before. "But I do have some questions for you—a few items I've been very curious about."

He grabbed another chair and brought it over to face Zahara. He looked like a stiff breeze could knock him flat, but his body moved with the fluidity of a young soldier.

"You want to ask me…questions?" Zahara stammered as he sat down just a foot away, his eyes boring into her own.

By the Creator, he knows I climbed to the Atsada's peak.

"First of all, I know all about your little adventure with Ekarath, so there's no need to fear getting in trouble," Dimitri said as he patted Zahara's knee.

"You know? Wait, of course you do. That's what makes you, well…you."

"I assure you there are many things of which I am completely ignorant," Lord Dimitri responded. "For instance, I know that you climbed to the top of the Atsada. I know that you found a ledge that allowed you to jump from the Boulevard onto the mountain side. However, I'm completely ignorant of the most important piece of information—I have no idea *why* you did it."

Zahara blinked hard as she tried to comprehend the old man's words. The fact that she had broken the law didn't even phase the ancient being who had created it. She let out a deep breath and tried to remember the speech she had prepared to defend herself.

"Well, I've been spending a lot of time in the library, getting ready for my final testing," Zahara said, trying to filter her words while still telling the truth. "And I found an ancient text that spoke of the *draod* being at its strongest at sunrise...on the solstice...on top of a mountain."

"So, naturally, you had to test out that hypothesis," Dimitri responded, his smile growing even wider. "Your understanding of ancient Karajaani is commendable."

"You've read the same book?"

"I've tried once or twice, but I've never been good with dead tongues," Dimitri responded with a shake of his head. Zahara couldn't blame him—it had been nearly a thousand years since the old languages had been widely spoken.

"I've always been interested in the unusual," Zahara responded. "My mother encouraged it—I think she found it entertaining."

"She must have been a wise woman," Dimitri said, a touch of sorrow tinging those blue eyes. "Would you mind telling me what you were trying to accomplish while everyone else was still sleeping?"

"Well, I was hoping that if it were true," Zahara said slowly before just blurting out the rest, "I'd be able to make a new *qilada*."

Silence filled the room as the words gushed from her mouth. Nobody had created a new *qilada* since the First Heirs over three thousand years ago. As the words echoed in her ears, Zahara knew how foolish they sounded.

"So, you left the fortress in the dark to do the impossible," Lord Dimitri said, lifting a finger to stroke his thin facial hair. "That would be audacious for someone who has spent a lifetime weaving the *draod*. To see that from a girl who has only spent the past year in training..."

The man stopped and smiled. Then he shook his head with a chuckle.

"You've been training for much longer than a year, haven't you?"

"Y—yes," Zahara stammered before swallowing hard. "My mother taught me everything she knew, starting when I could barely talk. It wasn't quite as formal or rigid as my education is here, but I feel fairly confident in my abilities."

"I have heard many things about your advanced abilities, and I'm quite sure you're ready to be made into a full mage—especially if that weave on your shoes is any indication of your skill."

Zahara jumped at the words—people couldn't see the weaves done by others. Otherwise, what would be the point? Everyone would know what she had done.

"Sorry," she stammered, "did you just comment on my shoes?"

"I can see your mother taught you well, and I hope you have learned a thing or two here," Dimitri said, avoiding her question. "If anyone can have any hope of creating a new *qilada*, I would say it's you."

"When I hear it coming from someone else, I realize how silly it sounds," Zahara whimpered, lowering her gaze. "If Your Holiness can't create a new *qilada*, I don't know what I was thinking."

"Silly? Of course not," Dimitri replied with a small chuckle. "We are facing an unprecedented threat, and I think we are in need of someone who isn't bound by what's supposedly possible. Take a look outside, and you'll see that we're outnumbered by a foe who will not stop until I am dead and buried."

"We all have faith that you'll stop the Usurper," Zahara responded. Lord Dimitri placed a wrinkled, frail hand on her cheek.

"Oh child, you must place your faith in something much stronger than an old man," Dimitri said, pausing as the words hung in the air. He cleared his throat before continuing, his voice cracking a bit. "In fact, I think it's time we placed a fair bit of faith in you."

Those words echoed in her brain, and time slowed for Zahara. She tried to respond, but her mouth couldn't react. Had she heard him correctly?

"You can't be serious. I'm not even a full mage yet," Zahara finally said, but the old man raised his hand to silence her.

"Weaving the *draod* is a skill that can be taught—what can't be taught is the spirit within you," Dimitri said. "In the days, weeks, and months ahead, the fight to free Einar from tyranny will feel impossible. I'm going to be giving you a task, and I need to know that you're committed to keep going, no matter how difficult the path."

The deep rumble of horns sounded outside. Zahara's mind returned to the Atsada's peak—those same horns had announced the arrival of the Usurper's horde, but they had grown silent since then. The smiling image of the evil tyrant filled her mind's eyes, and her muscles again began to tremble.

"I won't rest until the Usurper is stopped," Zahara responded, bringing her eyes to meet the Heir's. "Tell me what you would have me do."

Seemingly out of nowhere, Lord Dimitri pulled out two leather satchels. Zahara could sense the *draod* emanating from them, though she couldn't tell what the weaves were for.

"You will be going on a little journey," Dimitri said. "And you're going to need the proper gear and provisions."

"And I need two bags?"

"Oh, the second is for young Ekarath, here," Dimitri said, turning his blue eyes to the sleeping young man. "You can stop pretending to sleep."

Ekarath's eyes shot open, and his already pale face blanched.

"I'm sorry, Your Holiness," Ekarath responded, shifting into a sitting position. "I just thought it would be—"

"No need to apologize," Dimitri responded. "I was sorry to hear of your injury, but the courage you displayed at the gate yesterday was beyond admirable. So, I'm glad you're here, because I believe Zahara will have need of your skills."

"Where are we going?" Zahara asked.

"To the heart of the forest," Dimitri said. "And from what I've heard, Ekarath knows those woods like the back of his hand."

"That's...almost true," Ekarath said. "I did spend most of my life hunting and trapping in the forest."

"Have you ever met an old man out there named Farban?" Dimitri asked.

"Well, I haven't met him, but I've heard people talk about him," Ekarath said. "Once, I saw him in a village, buying some provisions."

"I need you to deliver this to him," Dimitri said, pulling out a leather-bound book, wrapped in an oil-soaked cloth and sealed with wax. "I've discovered the knowledge we need to take down the Usurper, but I'm in no position to leave the Atsada right now."

Zahara couldn't help her jaw from dropping.

"The knowledge...to defeat...the *Usurper* is in this book?" Zahara asked, unable to believe the words she was hearing. "And you want us to take it to a crazy old man in the woods?"

"People are often more than they appear," Dimitri said.

"Your Holiness," Zahara replied, the words coming out slowly. Questions and incredulity swirled through her mind, battling her desire to serve and to escape the subterranean fortress. Why would he trust two teenagers when there were at least a dozen magi in the Atsada? What could possibly be in that book that would stop the Usurper? Instead, she pushed the thoughts away and lifted her gaze to meet Dimitri's.

"I will do whatever you require," she whispered. "Just point me in the right direction."

"First of all, you need to get out of that impractical dress," Dimitri said with a laugh, handing her the satchel. "I know you won't like it, but you'll be heading deeper into the mountain. You need to be dressed properly."

Chapter 5

M ahzun—the Savior of Man—took in a deep breath of warm, dry air from his position atop one of the many buttes scattered throughout the valley floor. His armored toes dangled over the edge of the cliff as he took in the sight that had filled his dreams for the better part of a decade. Somehow, he had always known the war would end at the Atsada.

The fortress sat nestled in the Jabal Mountains, looking down over the cultivated fields and orchards. Red soil mixing with the verdant plant life was almost blinding, though he could see the beauty in it. More importantly, he could feel the *draod* affecting every living thing. The entire plain around the fortress was almost as saturated in power as the Northern Wilds on the other side of the mountains.

At this distance, he could see the Boulevard winding its way up like a giant corkscrew, along with dozens of other balconies and smaller porticoes. Like a colony of frantic ants, the soldiers of Segova scurried around as if their efforts would mean something.

Above, the sky was a swirl of grey clouds that blocked out the morning sun, muting the red of the soil all around him. A sheet of lightning flashed, bathing the valley in a quick burst of blue light, and the deep rumble of thunder rattled the ground. Mahzun had never imagined this final battle to take place in glorious sunshine, though the cold wind and lightning were likely enough to make his soldiers nervous.

Those soldiers—over a hundred thousand of them—stood in the valley below in pristine blocks that took little heed of the crops they crushed underfoot. They marched and fought like true professionals, though most would be more than happy to return to their homes when all this ended. As the thought entered his mind, Mahzun wished he could share that sentiment.

Banners were lifted at the front of each block, serving as both a simple reminder to the men of where they were supposed to be and of why they fought. Most depicted various beasts—both of the domestic and savage varieties—that acted as the companies' mascots. A normal soldier may or may not risk his life to save a comrade, but all of them would gladly sacrifice anything for those banners.

Footsteps broke Mahzun's reverie, and he turned to see a grizzled and maimed man with the blue cape of a general approaching. Levent had been with the Savior of Man since the very beginning, and his body showed signs that he was ready for retirement. The man's left arm was missing below the elbow, he walked with a distinct limp, and a scar stretched from his left eye down to his chin.

Levent wore the same armor crafted from black steel as Mahzun, though the general's cape was a royal blue instead of imperial violet. What remained of his body was a mass of lithe, sinewy muscles built over a lifetime of hard work and sleeping on the ground. A curved sword hung at his waist, and even the Savior of Man didn't wish to cross blades with the old soldier.

Behind Levent sat a large tent the color of charcoal. The front half was open, allowing the dozens of
officers and couriers an unfettered view of the battle
about to commence. With an army this large, Mahzun
knew he couldn't command everything by himself, and
he was glad for the trust he could bestow upon his
followers.

"Good morning, Your Majesty," Levent said, raising
his right fist to his chest in salute.

Being called "Your Majesty" still didn't sit well with
Mahzun, though he understood the need for the Emperor of all Einar to be given a proper title. He thought
of the names used by his enemies—the Wild Man, the
Primal King.

The Usurper.

As if he were simply using the power of the Heirs.
Neither his allies nor enemies understood the magic
he had been gifted—Mahzun himself didn't fully comprehend it.

"Good morning, my friend," Mahzun finally replied.

"Everything is ready, Your Majesty," Levent said, a
smile creeping along his face.

The words sent a shiver up and down Mahzun's
entire body. He had spent years waiting to hear them
spoken at the base of the Atsada.

"Give the order," Mahzun growled with a smile.

Levent turned to a group of men standing with tubes
of wood over ten feet in length. The general lifted his
good arm, and the men placed their lips to the horns.
Deep, melodic tones erupted from the instruments,
and Mahzun closed his eyes as the sound washed over
him in waves.

"I really hope this works," Mahzun said as Levent
strode to his side. The man refused to look down the

cliff's edge—the drop would surely be the general's end.

"We've both seen what the orchalcium can do, even against the best fortresses the Heirs could build," Levent replied.

"Now we will see what it can do against protections put into place by the Creator," Mahzun grunted before turning to face the general. "If it fails, I'm prepared to do what is necessary."

The words were a reminder that reaching this point had cost the blood of millions. From the plains of Ashgoth to the Gorland Mountains, Mahzun had fought alongside his followers to liberate humanity from the tyranny of the Heirs. He had lost friends and conquered enemies. For years, blood had watered the fields of Einar, an unfortunate yet necessary sacrifice to liberate the land. As he looked over the beginning of this final battle, the cost felt insignificant in comparison to the wonders he would unleash.

The price to be paid had not only been blood, and Mahzun lifted a hand to his once-handsome face. A river of scars masked the boy who had cowered in fear before the Heirs' power and served as a constant reminder of the price he had paid to bring down the old order. He would forever respect those who had made the ultimate sacrifice for the freedom of their brethren, but Mahzun would also envy them. Their suffering was over, while his continued.

Mahzun turned his attention back to the impending battle. Spread throughout the sea of black armor stood dozens of wooden monstrosities that stretched nearly sixty feet into the air. When properly maintained and equipped, the trebuchets could launch a fortress-busting stone over a thousand feet. The ability to kill an enemy from such a distance without resorting to the Power of Creation had changed warfare. It was a change Mahzun was proud to say he had caused.

Today, the trebuchets were loaded with no ordinary stones. Orchalcium—a strange, almost mythical mineral found only in the Arval Mountains in the eastern extremities of his empire—was the day's projectile. Although it had the texture and appearance of normal stone, it burned with more intensity than the finest of lamp oils.

The drone of the long horns continued to fill the air, and the groaning of wood sounded in Mahzun's ears as the trebuchet crews launched the flaming orchalcium into the air. Dozens of infernos flew into the sky, streaking through the air in an arc of oranges and reds. The grey clouds floating just above the valley erupted with the color as light bounced on the drab surface.

An explosion rocked the valley, shaking the ground as the first projectile slammed into the barrier of hardened air and energy. A spiderweb the color of blood stood in the air, as if a glass mirror had shattered. Like the quick staccato of a drum, dozens of explosions followed in quick succession, each leaving their mark on the ancient barrier. While the explosions echoed and bounced around the valley, threatening to bowl over both Mahzun and his army, the cracks in the air widened and spread.

Wherever the orchalcium crashed, those fiery red cracks began to open like wounds on a beast. Almost a hundred bright spider webs appeared on the invisible dome as the charred remains of the strange mineral plummeted to the ground. Mahzun's eyes bulged in disbelief, and his jaw clenched—could the Atsada's powers really be negated so easily?

The trebuchets kept up an orchestrated and steady barrage, with a constant stream of orchalcium hitting the barrier. It gave the crews just enough time to reload and launch without a break in the bombardment. Over twenty minutes passed, and Mahzun grew impervious to the explosions, though his bones rattled with each shot.

The shattered air grew a deep red, and the thin spiderwebs branched out, creating vast chasms in the barrier. A great moan filled the entire valley, and Mahzun's army grew silent. The trebuchets kept up their barrage as the air shuddered.

Light burst out from the cracks, the red glow replaced by an intense white—the kind of power that Mahzun would never be able to replicate. His stomach fell, and he shielded his eyes from light more powerful than the sun.

He knew that this would not be settled so easily. Something created by a false god could not be destroyed without a sacrifice.

"Well, it was a good effort," Levent said. Mahzun could sense fear in the man's voice—the idea to try the mythical rock had been his.

"Do not fear punishment or retribution—I appreciate what you tried to do," Mahzun said, turning to face his old friend. "But I can't allow that sneaky fox another chance to escape. No more tricks, no more games."

"Are you sure?" Levent said, turning to his liege. "There must be some other—"

Mahzun leapt from the cliff, and the rushing wind drowned out the general's response. The forms of his soldiers below grew larger as he hurtled toward the ground. His stomach roiled in protest, and he closed his eyes to better enjoy the moment.

A familiar, powerful cry sounded below him, and his descent was halted abruptly as he slammed into a mass of fur and feathers. Another screech pierced his ears, this one of pleasure accompanied by a hint of reprimand. Aiya never did like her master's theatrics.

You know I don't like that, Aiya's voice shouted in Mahzun's head.

You've told me that at least a dozen times, he responded.

What's going to happen when I'm not able to catch you?

I'll be gone, and you'll be able to return to the Northern Wilds. In short—we'll both be free.

Aiya didn't respond, but she did flap her wings hard enough that Mahzun had to push himself firmly into the white bed of feathers.

The griffin had been with Mahzun since his youth, when he had fled the civilized lands and begun a decade of exile in the Northern Wilds. Together, they had seen the world from a vantage point most people could only dream about. After decades of adventure and war, he was more comfortable clutching the lion fur and eagle feathers than most men were with the reins of a horse.

Of course, it helped that their souls were bound together.

The weave was not particularly complicated, and many members of the high nobility had a beast of the Wilds as a soul-bound, though their creatures were more a symbol of status and wealth. As far as Mahzun knew, nobody in the history of Einar—not even an Heir—had succeeded in binding one of the fearsome birds that nested in the stony peaks of the Wilds.

Mahzun patted his friend's neck and gripped the creature's body with his knees. He crouched low as Aiya's wings began beating faster, lifting the two high into the air. The cold wind rushed across his scarred face, reminding him of what was to come, as Aiya took them away from the world of men. He took in a deep breath of the thin air and looked down on the world below him.

Buttes and spires stuck out of the ground like the fingers of undead warriors striving to rise from their graves. The fields and orchards that had surrounded the Atsada only a few days prior were mostly gone, trampled and torn down for fuel and food. Yet there was still enough of the green to clash with the red soil, something that wouldn't be seen in the density of the Devna Forest to the south.

To the north, the Jabal mountains stretched on for miles, though he could almost see a bit of green on the horizon. He fought the urge to keep flying over the stony peaks until he landed in the paradise of the Wilds—he knew his place was here. The smell of burning orchalcium in his nostrils reaffirmed the need to be present, here and now. He turned his attention back to the Atsada.

A massive gate stood at the mountain's base, crafted from *draod*-laden steel—metal with the Power of Creation pounded into it during the smithing process. Those gates had now stood for thousands of years with no sign of wear, and even in the grey light reflecting from the overcast sky, the metal gleamed. The gate had never fallen, never even taken serious damage.

Until today.

Mahzun smiled at the thought of cracking the gate open, his soldiers pouring into the ancient edifice. For now, the covered portico that snaked around the entire mountain provided cover for the Atsada's defenders. Soon, the Boulevard would propel his army upward, its stone pathway awash with blood and screams.

In addition to the cover provided by the Boulevard, there were dozens of smaller balconies and terraces acting as platforms for archers to rain death on Mahzun's approaching army. The largest of these platforms sat near the top, and it was already occupied by well over a hundred archers, ready to make the Imperial Army pay dearly, should they proceed past the barrier.

A fit of laughter escaped Mahzun's throat, the shrill sound bouncing off the grey clouds that were close enough to touch. Pain unlike any other mortal had ever experienced was coming, but the laughter wouldn't die. After years of dreaming, this moment was finally real.

Why doesn't it feel that way?

Forcing away the thought, Mahzun reached his mind into the *draod*, pulling on the ever-present power, calling for the item that had become both his greatest blessing and his greatest curse—the Eternal Blade. A leather hilt filled his grip, and Mahzun didn't have to open his eyes to know what he held in his hand. The weight of the Blade filled him with an energy he had only allowed himself to experience a handful of times. The Blade pulsed with a warmth that barely hinted at the pain it was about to unleash.

With a throat-rending cry, he thrust the Eternal Blade into the air, and Aiya let out a screech as her wings propelled them higher until they were lost in the clouds. With his vision obscured by the swirling grey mist, Mahzun closed his eyes and focused on the weight of the Eternal Blade. His skin prickled as the *draod* swirled around him, and his mind's eye could see the threads of golden power being pulled into the mortal realm.

The grey clouds began to swirl with the magic, spinning into a vortex of wet, heavy air. Bumps rose up all along Mahzun's scars, and every bone and muscle in his body trembled in anticipation of the coming pain. The knowledge and experience of passing through the trial before did not help—in fact, it only made things worse.

Blue light filled Mahzun's vision as a bolt of lightning struck the extended sword. The power shot into his body, and the bones in his hand threatened to shatter as they clung to the hilt. The Power of Creation filled the Blade, and Mahzun drank it in like a man dying of thirst. His mind disconnected from reality, and he could feel the power of the Blade take over.

Though his muscles protested, Mahzun leapt from Aiya's back. His stomach lurched as gravity took hold, propelling him toward the Atsada's peak. His mind focused on the shield of air covering the vaunted fortress.

The power churned within him, and Mahzun knew there was a fine balance. If he let go too early, there wouldn't be enough energy. If he tried to hold on, the Blade would consume him without any remorse, leaving nothing but a dried husk. Even as his bones approached the point of shattering, he knew there was much worse to come. Mahzun clenched his jaw and unleashed the power at the Atsada's shield.

Lightning tore through his body as he slammed into hardened air, the Blade's tip puncturing the ancient weave of power. The blood in Mahzun's veins became a torrent of fire and ice, ripping its way through his body. His skin threatened to disintegrate into dust. His bones came close to fracturing in a thousand places. The sensation was familiar, and he knew it could be endured. The only question that remained was what would happen when his body could endure no more.

A crimson light spread outward from the Blade's tip, creating a spiderweb along the shield of air. Woven tendrils of the *draod* that had been in place since the Creation frayed and snapped, the energy held within returning to the vast ocean of untapped magic. With a deep groan, the air shuddered as the power raged through Mahzun's body.

Like a glass cloche on the wrong end of a hammer strike, the barrier shattered.

Chunks of untouched weaves larger than most buildings fell from sky, dissolving into nothing as the energy that had sustained them for so long disappeared. Mahzun began to fall, the weight of the Blade pulling him into a dive. Below, he could see the panic of his foe—archers on the largest platform scurried about like ants whose colony had been stepped on by a child. He pointed the Blade at them, praying it would give him enough strength to withstand both the fall and the coming battle.

Talons snatched his feet, and Mahzun's neck almost snapped as his body changed course. Aiya's wings tipped and pounded on the air, pulling up from her desperate dive.

You ruin all my fun, Mahzun thought.

You ruin my health, Aiya responded as she took him away from the battle that should have been his.

While still dangling from the powerful talons, a cheer reached Mahzun's ears. He directed his gaze away from the Atsada, toward the black mass covering the red sand. It was the cry of impending battle.

Not just battle. Impending victory.

From the butte holding his command tent, horns bellowed to announce the command to move forward, and not a single being present could miss what the signal meant. The crashing of armored feet sounded in Mahzun's ears as the straight lines marched toward the fortress.

The trebuchets—still loaded with the mythical orchalcium—recommenced their barrage. Flaming projectiles soared through the air below before slamming into the red stone, blasting away chunks of the ancient fortress. Explosions filled the air, and the Savior of Man looked down with a smile.

Okay, will you let me on your back? Mahzun asked, trying to pull himself up. *I promise to be a good boy.*

Chapter 6

Zahara strode at Ekarath's side through the narrow tunnel, hoping they weren't lost. Despite the boy's experience with the inner hallways of the Atsada and the instructions—written by Lord Dimitri—in his hands, Zahara still wasn't sure if she completely trusted her friend. After all, they had been walking for nearly an hour, a *kura* following them through the otherwise pitch-black corridor.

While bobbing in the air, the orb cast its soft light, creating shadows that danced along the walls. Those walls were rough, as if they had been carved by a complete novice. Even worse, the ceiling was lower than in the rest of the Atsada, giving Zahara the constant desire to duck.

Despite her worries, Zahara couldn't help but appreciate the clothing provided by Lord Dimitri. The Heir of Segova had used his legendary skills to weave threads of Restoration into the fabric, making every article of clothing an absolute work of art. Her grey trousers were thick and strong, yet they breathed as if her legs were bare. Her blue shirt and charcoal cloak felt as if they were part of her, and they moved without making a noise.

Her boots were crafted of solid leather, strengthened by the *draod*, and topped with the weave to dampen her footsteps. Ekarath was dressed in a similar set of clothing, and it felt odd to see the boy walking at her side yet be unable to hear a single noise.

"You seem rather excited to finally have a real blade," Ekarath said, his voice breaking the silence. Zahara looked over with her brow furrowed.

"What do you mean?"

"You've been fingering the hilt of your knife this entire time," Ekarath responded. "So, I thought that must mean you're nervous or you're just really excited to have a real blade."

"Would you believe me if I told you I'm nervous?"

"Of course—I'd be worried if you didn't feel that way. We're escaping a besieged fortress through an underground tunnel to bring a message to a hermit. There's very little about our situation that isn't nerve-wracking."

Zahara responded with a laugh, but she didn't quite know what else to say. She was certainly glad to have her friend at her side for this assignment—the thought of navigating these hallways and the forest on her own was more than daunting.

The two continued in silence, the ceiling slowly descending. Zahara forced herself to take steady breathes, fighting the panic that was trying to take over.

"What was it like?" Zahara asked, the words leaping from her mouth without permission.

"What was *what* like?"

"To actually kill someone," Zahara said, averting her eyes and cursing herself for speaking the words aloud. Ekarath's first real fight was less than twenty-four-hours old, and here she was pestering him about it.

"To be honest, everything happened so fast," Ekarath responded with a shrug that was barely visible in the soft light. "I was so focused on trying to save my comrades and stay alive at the same time. I—I don't think it really hit me for a while what I had actually done. In the moment, it didn't really feel much different than killing a deer or a squirrel."

"Well, I think you were very brave," Zahara said, unsure how to respond. She shouldn't have asked the question, but she already felt sick about the concept. Yes, she hated the Usurper and everyone who followed him. Yet the thought of actually killing anybody didn't quite sit right with her. She just went back to fingering the hilt of her knife.

"I get the feeling this passageway isn't used a lot," Ekarath said, and something in his tone told Zahara that her friend was just trying to break the silence. "The entire corridor has the feeling of being long abandoned, as if the stone itself has forgotten what people look and sound like."

"I wonder if we took a wrong turn..."

Zahara let the thought trail off as the passageway came to an abrupt end. While the ceiling was now just a few inches above her head, the wall ahead held the first piece of decoration she had seen in hours—a tapestry with colors so faded she couldn't tell what it had once depicted.

Zahara looked over at Ekarath to see his broad grin in the soft light. Letting out a deep breath, Zahara reached behind the fabric until her fingers latched onto a solid piece of metal. She let out a small grunt as she pulled, and the latch gave way.

The grinding of stone on iron met her ears, and a hole in the floor opened, revealing a gaping darkness. Cool, moist air drifted upward, mixing with the stale corridor, and Zahara took in a deep breath. If it weren't for Lord Dimitri's assurances, she wouldn't dare trust the gaping hole.

Even with those assurances, she grabbed the *kura* and shoved it into the opening. Its soft light illuminated steps that spiraled downward, eventually disappearing into the darkness. The sound of running water and the faint aroma of algae wafted up the stairs, carried on the breeze, confirming they had indeed found the right passage.

"Follow the water, it will lead you out of the Atsada and eventually to Farban," Ekarath whispered, repeating Lord Dimitri's last words.

"Everything's going to be alright," she whispered to herself before realizing she had said it out loud. In response, Ekarath placed a hand on her shoulder.

"You're the most powerful mage I know," he responded. "We will *definitely* be alright."

Zahara nodded before leading the way, taking that first step into the spiraling staircase. Almost immediately, the staircase revealed itself to be made for one person at a time, making the tight corridors feel luxurious in comparison.

Someone with a wide, muscular frame would certainly struggle in this space, Zahara thought. She smiled at the thought of the Usurper—with his layers of plate mail—struggling down the stairs.

"Can you believe this has been here the whole time?" Ekarath asked, and she resisted the urge to look back as she responded.

"Makes me wonder what else this place is hiding. When we get back, we'll need to dedicate plenty of time to unlocking all the secrets."

When we get back. Zahara winced at those words, but she knew they had to return. Find Farban and pass on the knowledge Lord Dimitri found to defeat the Usurper. Certainly not an easy task, but it shouldn't be a long journey.

The staircase ended, and Zahara pulled herself out of her thoughts. Free of the confined stairwell, the *kura* floated high above her head, its light revealing a large cavern that had been carved over millennia by water, metal tools, and the *draod*. A river took up most of the cave, its dark waters rushing downhill.

The walls were marked by the rough chiseling of hand tools used to widen the corridor, and the ceiling hummed with weaves, most likely in place to stop a cave-in. That ceiling was less than ten feet high, but in comparison to the tunnels they had just left, it felt like more than enough room for Zahara to stand tall.

A narrow path was carved along the bank of the river, though the way was strewn with large rocks. Something about it felt deliberate, as if the boulders were an attempt to disguise the obvious footpath.

"Follow the river, right?" Zahara said, and Ekarath smiled.

"Looks easy enough," Ekarath said, and he gestured for her to lead the way.

Zahara was increasingly glad for the solid boots as she began traversing the rocky path. She forced her mind to focus on the road ahead, knowing that a fall into the river below would mean death.

In the dancing shadows of the *kura*, Zahara couldn't see much of the river below, but the crash of rapids told her all she needed to know. While the fall itself looked to be less than ten or twenty feet, the sharp rocks and swift current would enough to prematurely end her journey.

With the roar of the river and the shadows cast on the walls by her *kura*, time turned into an illusion this far underground. It was comforting to have Ekarath's presence behind her, even if they didn't speak. She could feel his warm, calming energy—a stark contrast to the adrenaline pumping through her veins.

Zahara tried to keep her mind on the path, but there was little to keep her attention. The sealed book in her bag, the siege, the grizzled face of the Usurper: all three took their turn on her mind's stage. It was still so hard to fathom the reality of their situation.

Of all people, she had been given a task by the Heir of Segova—the last of his kind, the only thing standing in the Usurper's way. She most certainly didn't feel up to the confidence the old man had placed in her, though she wanted nothing more than to succeed.

Her mind went to the celebrations that would accompany their victory over the Usurper and his armies. She could imagine breathing free air and returning to her homeland. Yet Zahara knew that dwelling on life after the fight was useless—she needed to focus on not falling into the river.

Resisting the urge to glance back at Ekarath, Zahara tried to focus her mind on the rough path. She wished for the rushing water to quiet, even if it were just enough to carry on a conversation with Ekarath as they descended.

As if in response to her desire, the river's harsh roar did soften, if only slightly. Zahara suspected that a look at this particular stretch of river would reveal fewer rapids, but that was simply based on the noise made by the water.

With the water quieting, a soft tapping met Zahara's ears. Unlike the chaos of the river, this new sound was smooth and rhythmic, as if a troupe of percussionists were practicing in the distance. More than hearing it in her ears, she could feel it in her chest, reverberating in her soul.

She stopped and turned around, her eyes scanning the path for any sign of someone following them. Ekarath gave her an inquisitive look, but Zahara ignored him as she strained her ears. Beyond the continued tapping, there was no sign of trouble, so she gave her friend a shrug and turned back around. Yet as she moved, her mind and ears maintained their focus on the strange noise. The sound grew louder—closer, somehow—as she continued along the river.

Focusing on the *qilada* hanging from her ear, Zahara pulled some fine threads of the *draod* into the mortal plane. She wove them into a thin, delicate weave, though doing so while walking proved to push her skills. It took a few seconds longer than it would have normally, but she put the finishing knot into place and moved the spell over her ears.

The roar of water grew almost deafening, but she forced herself to ignore it, focusing on the peripheral noises. The soft tapping rose above the chatter, though she still couldn't quite tell where it was coming from. As she strained her ears, the sound grew louder.

A thud sounded on the ground in front of her, and she looked down to see a shadow moving in the dim light of her *kura*. Squinting, she made out the form of eight legs on a body the size of a dinner plate. The shape leapt into the air, straight at Zahara's face.

A blade extended from behind her shoulder, skewering the shadow mere inches away from Zahara's nose. A yelp escaped her throat, and she turned around to see the tall, pale form of Ekarath. In his hand was a blade of pure steel, though most of it was now covered by the shadow. Now that she could see it clearly, it was apparent it was no shadow, but the largest spider she had ever seen.

Its body was a dark black, broken by veins of an electric blue running across its body. Large pincers near its mouth twitched, and its powerful legs began to curl inward. The spider let out a high-pitched squeal as a goo ran out of the wound and onto Ekarath's sword.

"Thank you," Zahara squealed, trying to keep her voice down. "What is that thing?"

"This is a *kabut*, a spider fairly common in caves of the Northern Wilds," Ekarath said, flinging the creature into the raging river below. "I've heard of them making nests in the Jabals, but never this far south."

Those words sent a jolt through Zahara's entire body. She knew the Wilds were just on the other side of the mountains, but the stony peaks of the Jabals were meant to protect Einar from the horrors beyond. The idea of *draod*-infused creatures invading made her shudder.

The tapping began again, and she turned around. Squinting beyond Ekarath, she could see dozens of shadows moving along the walls and ceiling.

"I don't think it was alone," Ekarath said, pointing upward.

"Run," she shouted before turning to lead the way.

High-pitched shrieks filled the air, as if the *kabut* could tell their quarry was trying to escape. Zahara pushed herself over the stony pathway, trying to ignore the sound of far too many legs crawling on the stone.

A squeal filled her ears as one fell directly onto her head, its legs tangling in her hair. The creature's tiny hairs scratched at her skin, and she could hear pincers cracking as they tried to make contact. Her hands reacted before her brain could, and Zahara reached up, grabbing one of the legs and flinging it through the air. Behind, she heard Ekarath's blade pierce the thick exoskeleton of another beast.

Ahead, a *kabut* the size of a large dog landed on the pathway, its legs and pincers flailing wildly. Before she could pull on the *draod*, the creature leapt. Its weight slammed into Zahara, knocking her onto her back.

The creature's maw opened, a set of pincers aiming at her throat. Zahara focused on the *qilada* and pulled on a few strands of raw power, barely giving the *draod* any direction. A flash of heat and power slammed into the monster's mouth, knocking it backward with a scream.

Strong, warm hands lifted Zahara to her feet. The screams of the spiders filled the air, and she pulled on the *draod*. Forcing out the noise, she wove thin tendrils of Restoration before finishing the tapestry with a clumsy knot.

A shield of solid air formed around her and Ekarath. The light of her *kura* bounced off the solid air, distorting the view of the outside world.

"Good thinking," Ekarath said. "But what do we do now?"

"Not sure," Zahara replied, shaking her head. "But it's clear we can't outrun them. Even if the path were decent, the *kabut* are too fast."

"But at least they die with a good stab," Ekarath said, and Zahara turned to look at her friend.

Not only was his sword covered in the slimy blood, but so were his clothes and hair. A long scratch extended from his ear to his lip, though it wasn't deep. Hopefully, it was from the sharp tip of a leg rather than a pincer. She had no idea how venomous the large spiders were.

A loud thump sounded above Zahara's head, and she looked up to see another spider the size of a cat. Its legs pounded on the mixture of air and *draod*, trying to break through. It hissed, splattering the shield with a mixture of snot and water.

"Maybe we can hold out here for a bit," Zahara suggested. "Any chance they'll leave us alone?"

"Not likely," Ekarath said, shaking his head.

Another loud thump sounded as a second large *kabut* dropped from the ceiling. Three more approached along the path, their powerful front legs pounding on the air. The shouts and squeals from dozens more filled the cavern.

"Zahara...how powerful is this shield?" Ekarath asked, his eyes scanning the weaves he could not possibly see.

"Strong enough to hold indefinitely, I would suppose," Zahara said. "A least, against the *kabut*."

"And is it a complete sphere?" Ekarath asked, stomping his foot on the ground.

"Of course," Zahara responded. "The weave wouldn't have enough integrity to hold if it didn't connect everywhere. Don't they teach you soldiers anything about weaving?"

"Why would they?" Ekarath asked with a shrug as his eyes continued to scan their little sanctuary. "I'll never be rich enough to have a *qilada*."

"Is that really what you want to talk about in our last few minutes of life?" Zahara asked, shaking her head.

"Oh, I intend for us to live through this," Ekarath said, a smile flashing across his face.

Without another word, he wrapped Zahara into a big hug, his arms completely enveloping her. For a moment, she didn't know how to respond—until Ekarath's legs bent and he threw both of them against the shield.

His body took the brunt of the collision, but her added weight helped knock them off the path. Zahara shut her eyes as the world spun around her, and she could feel a scream erupt from her throat as the ball rolled down the steep bank. With a deafening crash, the orb slammed into the raging water.

For what felt like an eternity, Zahara shut her eyes and clung to Ekarath as the river tossed them like a child's toy. The orb slammed into boulders, sending shock waves that rattled her bones. Water rushed all around her with nothing more than a thin weave of the *draod* separating them from a cold, painful death.

The roar died down, and a solid minute passed without hitting rapids. Zahara opened her eyes and realized she was laying on top of Ekarath. A smile spread across his face, and she scrambled off her friend, taking a seat on the inflexible surface.

While protective, there wasn't much space for both of them. The shape of the air shield smashed them into each other, and Zahara struggled to get comfortable. The *kura* still floated lazily above them, though it didn't give off enough light to make out anything substantial outside the shield.

"Well, that was foolhardy," Zahara finally said, shaking her head. "I wish I had thought of it."

"I had no idea if it would work," Ekarath said with a smile.

"You could have just told me what you were planning," Zahara said. "We could have made that descent a bit smoother...I could have made the bottom a bit flatter."

"Where's the fun in that?" Ekarath shot back.

"You're right. And to be honest, I'm just glad we escaped the *kabut*—I'm certainly not going to complain...too much."

Her body, however, was already complaining, and a headache was encroaching from both her neck and forehead. She forced back the pain, hoping that a little bit of rest would help. Some fresh air and the smell of trees probably wouldn't hurt either.

"I'm glad that at least part of the river is a bit more gentle," Ekarath said, shaking his head and turning around to look forward. "I wonder how much longer until we're out in the open."

As if in response to his inquiry, a light appeared ahead. It was small, little more than the size of a pin. Yet in the pitch black of the cave, it was an obvious sign of the end. A wave of relief flooded through Zahara's body at the thought of being outside again. The light grew larger, and her heart pounded with excitement.

Their vessel hit a boulder, knocking Zahara backward. She braced herself as best she could as they bounced along another set of rapids. She looked to Ekarath for comfort, and the twit was laughing. At a particularly large hit, he let out a holler and thrust his fist into the air.

"I can't believe you," Zahara yelled, shaking her head. "Here we are about to die, and you're having the time of your life."

"Life is meant to be enjoyed," Ekarath shouted back. "Maybe you'll learn that—"

The weave dissolved, and Ekarath's words were lost in a torrent of rushing water. Zahara's lungs filled with a mixture of air and icy liquid, and she could feel the current pushing her down. She slammed into a rock, and the world grew fuzzy.

Something within her said it was best not to fight, though her legs and arms didn't listen. They thrashed, surrounded by cold and darkness. All around her was water and pain.

Her head broke the surface of the water, and warm, fresh air filled her lungs. Strength returned to her limbs, and her mind shot back into action. Still panting, her eyes found the rocky banks of the river, and she began swimming toward it. Moments later, her feet hit solid ground, and she crawled onto the shore.

Zahara's muscles locked up, and she collapsed onto the wet stones. As she breathed in, the scent of wet, rich soil and pine trees filled her nose. The shrill song of a bird sounded in her ears, barely piercing the roar of water hitting stones.

For the first time in a year, she opened her eyes to see greenery instead of red stone, and a bout of laughter leapt from her throat. The crunch of limbs on sand sounded to her side, and she looked over to see Ekarath climbing out of the water.

"You alright?" the boy gasped, his pale hair slicked straight back.

"Nothing a little bit of sunbathing wouldn't cure," Zahara responded, pushing herself up to her feet and moving her limbs to ensure nothing was too badly damaged.

"Well, unfortunately for you, we'll be heading into the forest," Ekarath responded as he copied Zahara—pulling himself up right and checking for broken bones. "That leafy canopy doesn't exactly allow giant sunbeams through."

"I know that all too well," Zahara said, shaking her head. Her mind drifted back to thoughts of home—of the dense, tropical forests of Karajaan. Taking in a deep breath, her soul longed to be among the trees.

"Well, wet or not," Ekarath said, a smile plastered on his face, "I say it's time to get moving. For all we know, an Imperial patrol could be moments away from breaking out of the tree line."

Footsteps sounded on the rocky banks.

"That's a pretty valid fear," sounded an unfamiliar voice.

Zahara looked over to see a dozen soldiers, all clad in the black armor of the Horde. Half of them held crossbows, ready to fire.

"Put your hands on your head and come with us," one of the soldiers shouted. "You're now prisoners of His Imperial Majesty."

Chapter 7

E karath silently cursed himself for being so lax as he complied with the order. At his side, Zahara did the same, though a quick glance told him she was not ready to simply give up. As she lifted her hands, a ball of fire erupted from the air, careening toward the soldiers.

"Go!" she shouted, and Ekarath didn't need further encouragement. As the soldiers shouted and dove to the ground, Ekarath dashed toward the tree cover just behind Zahara. With the weight of soaked clothing, Ekarath pushed himself to move across the open ground. They stumbled onto a narrow trail forged by creatures of the forest—deer and elk from the size of it.

Maybe we should stop and fight, Ekarath thought. Among the trees, they could possibly set up an ambush. He had taken on such a patrol by himself at the Atsada's gate, though this time there would be no allies to save him. Was it simply a squad to be dealt with? Or were there hundreds more nearby?

"Stop," shouted one of the soldiers. The whistling of an arrow filled Ekarath's ears, followed by the smack of iron piercing wood. He looked up to see a short crossbow bolt quivering in a tree—an understandable miss from a rushed archer? Or a warning shot?

Ekarath pushed himself forward, trying his best to keep up with Zahara. Their only hope was that the narrow trail would be too confined for a large group, at least slowing them down.

Despite the years of intense training, his lungs began to gasp for more of the moist, heavy air as he ran. The muscles in his legs pushed hard against the soft dirt, trying to put distance between himself and the soldiers. Something hard hit his ankles, and Ekarath spilled onto the ground.

Looking down at his feet, he saw a rope with heavy iron balls at each end—the preferred tool of slavers within the Usurper's empire. Ekarath reached down and struggled to untangle the ropes as the pounding of armored feet drew near.

"Don't move," a voice sounded, and he looked up to see a soldier approach, crossbow pointed directly at Ekarath's chest. With his stomach falling, Ekarath lifted his hands in surrender.

"That's a good boy," the soldier replied. "Now, get on your feet. We'll find your friend soon enough."

Ekarath pushed himself upright, his skin prickling at the sharp arrow mere inches away. His mind buzzed, trying to think of a way out. Even on his own, Ekarath liked his odds against a few soldiers, but a single twitch of the finger could easily send the crossbow bolt into his chest.

As his mind buzzed, the nearby snapping of branches took his attention. The soldier furrowed his brow at the sound, which was followed by heavy breathing. The ground trembled.

The sound was growing closer, the breathing turning into a snort. He could hear the pounding of feet on the ground move from a walk to a half-run. It was almost as if—

Emerging from the plants and twilight, a creature the size of a bear let out a roar. Instead of a thick coat of fur, it was covered in a green, rough scales. The head was a cross between a lizard and a pig—sharp teeth and yellow eyes, but with a large snout at the end. It walked on all fours, and a curly tail stuck out from its rear.

It let out a deep rumble and leapt onto the armored soldier, who let out a shout and turned his crossbow toward the beast. The bolt flew through the air, slamming into the mass of green flesh before the creature crushed the soldier. Razor teeth sliced through the leather armor, and the man's shout turned into a scream.

Ekarath dashed in the other direction along the game trail, heedless of the branches smacking his face. He ran into Zahara, pushing her in the other direction.

"Ekarath, what's—"

"Run," Ekarath shouted, pushing the girl even harder along the trail. Whatever that creature was, it would not be distracted by the soldiers for long. First the giant spiders, now this monstrosity—he had never seen a creature of the Wilds south of the Jabals. Now he had come face to face with two. As if in response to his fear, the monster let out another deep rumble, and twigs began snapping as it gave chase.

As Ekarath pushed his legs through the dense undergrowth, he knew it was futile to run from such a thing. It would catch them in a matter of seconds. He forced his mind to think through the options. Knowing what had to be done, Ekarath stopped and pulled his sword free. The creature didn't hesitate, showing no sign of fear.

"Come and get me," Ekarath shouted, charging the pig-like lizard. Its mouth opened, revealing razor-sharp teeth covered in blood. Its front claws swiped, and Ekarath leapt. His foot caught on the scaley arm, and he launched himself upward.

As he came down, he slammed the steel blade into the monster's back. It let out a powerful shriek and reared onto its hind legs. Ekarath hung on, his hands maintaining their grip on the leather hilt of his sword. Ekarath's bones shook as the creature went back to the ground, and it began moving in circles in an attempt to remove this unwanted pest.

The air grew hot as red flames slammed into the creature's skin. The monster stopped its movements, looking for the source of the new threat. Ekarath looked up to see Zahara standing far too close, her fingers working on another spell.

A second flame shot from her hands, hurtling through the air before slamming into the mass of green skin and muscle. Ekarath had to close his eyes, the heat washing over him. The beast let out a high-pitched squeal and turned its attention fully to Zahara.

With a shake of his head, the animal charged. Zahara stood tall, her eyes closed and her hands moving quickly to create her strange magic. Ekarath could feel the power radiating from her, could almost see the threads of the *draod* being woven into a complex tapestry.

The energy shot out, a concentrated bolt of lightning instead of a rougher ball of flames. The bolt slammed into the creature's chest, and Ekarath felt the energy swirl through the bones and skin, into his blade. Like the powerful kick of a mule, it knocked him off the monster's back, and he sailed through the air, landing in a bush.

As he worked to free himself from the tangle, he could hear the creature's scream turn into a soft moan. The smell of fried flesh filled the air, combating the fresh scent of pine and leaves. With bones and muscles aching, Ekarath hobbled back to the pathway to see the beast lying still, smoke rising up from its skin.

He moved to Zahara's side, unsure of what to say. It was no beast of the forest—everything about it spoke of the Wilds. A rustling to their right caught Ekarath's attention just as a voice called out.

"That was impressive," a kind, masculine voice said. "It's not every day you see a *sahali* on this side of the Jabals."

Ekarath looked over to see a grizzled face covered in both a beard and plenty of dirt. The newcomer was of an average height for a Segovan, and his skin and frame looked well suited for a life in the forest. His lips formed into a smile, revealing surprisingly white teeth for someone living so far from civilization. Ekarath opened his mouth to speak, but Zahara beat him.

"I'm sorry, but who are you?" Zahara asked.

"What kind of question is that?" the man began as he approached. "How many old coots do you think live out here? Lord Dimitri said he had chosen someone young and powerful; he didn't mention your inability to make simple inferences."

"Wait, you're Farban?" Ekarath asked. As the old hermit drew closer, there was something familiar about that face. "We've been sent to find you."

"I know, and that's why I'm here—though I'm sorry I didn't arrive in time to help you with that monster. For now, we should probably head somewhere safe before we have any more chit-chat. The forest is a lovely place, but I think you've already seen how dangerous it can be."

"Before we set off, how did you know to meet us?" Zahara asked. "Lord Dimitri only gave me this mission a few hours ago."

"As I already said, I can explain fully when we're inside—for now, it's enough to know that your role in world events is about to expand. You're a powerful mage, Zahara. It's almost time for you to become more than that."

Chapter 8

Floating in the sky above the ancient fortress, Mahzun lost track of time. He watched the gate crumble under the onslaught of the trebuchets. He cheered as his soldiers stormed into the fortress itself. Yet how long had it taken? Hours? Minutes?

In the clouds, time had no meaning.

Mahzun looked down on the archers that had been raining death on his troops. He had no idea how much damage they had done, but he knew they would soon be dealt with. It might take hours yet for his soldiers to battle up the Boulevard and reach the top. The Eternal Blade grew warm in his hand, eager to taste blood, and Mahzun looked again at the archers.

"Probably not prudent to attack on our own, right?" he shouted. "We've prevailed against worse odds, but it feels like a shame to risk everything when the end is so near."

Agreed, Aiya responded. *I'm glad to see you gaining wisdom in your old age. Did that last drop rattle something in your brain?*

Mahzun ignored her jab, but he could feel the griffin's hunger growing in her belly. Despite Aiya's words of caution, he knew the smell of blood wafting up from the battlefield was enough to tempt her. Yet after all these years, he knew that Aiya—while not a coward by any stretch—had a strong sense of self-preservation. Moving in to attack all on their own would never be her idea.

The whoosh of an arrow whipping past Mahzun's ear tore him from those thoughts, and he looked down at the balcony. Several of the archers were no longer aiming down the mountain at the assaulting army. Instead, their gazes were drawn skyward, as were their bows. Another arrow fell just short of Aiya's belly, while another clipped her wing. The griffin let out a shout, though Mahzun knew it was more of annoyance than actual pain.

"What insolence," Mahzun shouted. "Don't they know who I am?"

I think that's exactly the reason they're firing, Aiya replied.

"Well then, I don't think we can allow this affront to go unpunished," Mahzun responded. "It would set a poor precedent."

If you insist, Aiya responded with a deep sigh. *I am getting a bit hungry.*

"Oh, I insist," Mahzun shouted. "Let's get you some dinner."

Aiya didn't need much more coercion, and a simple nudge brought the griffin careening toward the balcony. Wind rushed in Mahzun's ears, and his eyes watered as he forced them open. Below, he could see the men scatter, the panic evident in their movements. Shouts erupted—did those men really not expect their crime to slip by unnoticed?

Man and beast slammed into the crowded balcony, and bodies flew in all directions. Mahzun let out a roar as he lifted the Eternal Blade and swung it like a butcher with a cleaver. The finest of metals crafted by master armorers felt like thin foil under his hand, a mixture of the Blade's power and the energy swirling through his muscles.

Aiya joined in the fight, her sharp talons and beak acting as perfect weapons. Mahzun's heart grew lighter at the sight of his old friend grabbing an archer with her massive beak and tossing the man off the balcony to his death. Another archer managed to lodge an arrow into Aiya's shoulder, and the griffin let out a scream of pain before her talons severed the man in two.

In this moment, Mahzun's exhaustion fled. In this moment, he felt none of the worries that had plagued him for so long. In this moment—this perfect moment—there was only the fluid motions of the Blade. There was nothing outside of the death that filled the balcony.

Soon—far too soon—Mahzun found himself alone except for Aiya and the many corpses that littered the ground. A hundred men lay like broken rag dolls on the balcony, its floor covered in their blood. Despite the sight of his enemies brought to justice, the joy that had flooded Mahzun's heart only moments ago transformed into a numb apathy. He turned to the mountain, and his eyes made their way to the Boulevard.

Wait here, he commanded his majestic beast.

Be careful, Aiya responded.

Mahzun simply nodded in response and made his way toward the inner fortress. At the threshold between balcony and the Atsada proper, he stopped for a moment to take in a deep breath. He had waited years for this moment, and it felt far too normal. There should be music playing, at least in his head. Yet there was no orchestra, no band of triumphant drummers—not even a single bard to sing of his bravery.

"No matter," Mahzun whispered to himself. "The tales of this day will be sung for generations to come."

He forced his foot over the threshold, and for the first time, he entered the fortress crafted by the Creator's own hands. He had studied maps and heard dozens of descriptions from prisoners, informants, and traitors. All told him of the honeycomb of hallways that were carved through the mountain, of the various layers of protection. Few had thought to speak of its simple beauty.

The walls of the Boulevard were smooth as glass, a sight he had never seen before in red rock that usually felt at least somewhat grainy. There was nothing to adorn the walls, other than a few orbs that would provide light in the midnight hours. The lack of ornamentation allowed the structure to be enjoyed for what it was.

Mahzun placed a hand to the wall, and he could feel the *draod* tingling within. The amount of power used to carve this fortress out of a mountain must have been immense, and the very stone itself buzzed with the energy. While that power had held him at bay for years and cost the lives of thousands, Mahzun had to give it the respect of a worthy adversary. It was almost a pity that today would be its last.

With tears threatening to burst, Mahzun cleared his throat and kept walking. The map inside his head told him he was close—the balcony itself was near the top, and a trek along the Boulevard would bring the Savior of Man to his destination. But for the sound of fighting far below, the hallway was silent as death. His footsteps cracked on the hard stone, and Mahzun could imagine the joyful slaughter that he was missing out on. With a shake of his head, Mahzun pulled himself out of the image—there were more important tasks at hand.

Mahzun's eyes kept darting around the hallway in search of soldiers, yet the corridor was barren. His bowels spoke of a trick, but so far there was no sign of an ambush, and Mahzun's feet kept propelling him upward.

The Boulevard ended at an imposing set of doors, crafted from an ancient ebony tree. The door itself was an imposing black, and Mahzun could sense the *draod* woven into every layer. While impressive, it was nothing special compared to that at other palaces and fortresses—except for the centerpiece.

A tree was carved from a white gold that glowed without the aid of the sun. There wasn't a single blemish or mark of a craftsman's tool—it was either created by an Heir or the Creator himself. Mahzun's blood boiled at the sight of the Shajarat, the ancient tree that was venerated by too many.

The details were crafted down to individual leaves, and there wasn't so much as a fingerprint to smudge the white metal. To some, it was the absolute centerpiece of the Atsada, while to many, the Shajarat itself was the centerpiece of the world. Mahzun raised a foot and launched it into the tree's trunk.

The ancient gateway exploded inward, and the doors crashed open with a shower of white gold and black wood. A wave of pleasure swept through Mahzun's veins as the dust settled, but that happiness was surpassed by the scene awaiting him within.

A grand hall with ceilings stretching a hundred feet into the mountain gaped before him. The floors here were of a glassy white marble that extended like an ocean, bound only by the walls of polished red stone. Created and sustained by the *draod*, not a single column was needed to support the roof, which peaked in a gentle arch high above.

Yet it wasn't the grand hall that brought such joy to Mahzun's heart—it was the frail old man awaiting him. He sat on a throne carved from an ancient hardwood with the warm tones of a *braza*—a tree only found in the forests of the Northern Wilds. Mahzun had seen six other thrones, all of which had cradled the frames of men and women unfit for the roughest of chairs.

The ancient figure was certainly nothing special—at least, not compared to the fear and awe with which his name was spoken. Green robes hung on an emaciated frame, and a beard of white, thin hair hung down his chest. His face and hands were covered in more wrinkles than a sun-dried grape, and his eyes screamed of exhaustion.

Mahzun's eyes fixed on the old man's crown, a thin circlet formed of pure gold.

"It appears you have won," the old man wheezed, his voice echoing in the empty stone chamber. "And for that, I offer my sincere condolences."

"Condolences? My empire stretches from sea to sea, and from the Northern Wilds to the Tagus Islands," Mahzun shouted, striding forward. "And now my soldiers are pouring through the once-invincible gate of the Atsada. There is nobody left to defy the Savior of Man."

"There certainly is a lot of blood on your hands to give yourself such a title," Lord Dimitri replied, his voice gaining strength as the words left his mouth. "From my calculations, you've destroyed much more than you could have possibly saved."

"An Heir wouldn't know anything about bloody hands," Mahzun replied, spitting on the ground before moving closer to the throne. The Eternal Blade grew heavy in his hand, itching to slice through the old man's skin. "Your kind always left the dirty work to men like me."

"Men like you are the reason the Creator spread power to seven Heirs," Dimitri responded, shaking his head. "It's apparent what happens when a single man obtains all power—can't you see what it has done to you?"

"I see the effects of the Eternal Blade every time I glance in the mirror, every time a child looks at me and screams. I feel it every time my subjects bow to me, avoiding eye contact out of more than just respect," Mahzun shouted as his footsteps brought him closer to the throne. "Ever since I was forced to kill Lord Elandrian, I have been consumed—bit by bit—by power."

"I believe that power isn't the only thing to consume you," the old man said. "Hatred—whether it is justified or not—has consumed you from the inside out. And hatred can't do that on its own. You let it into your heart. You let it destroy a young man who just wanted to save his people."

"At least I wasn't consumed by a lust for power," Mahzun said.

He knew that speaking with Lord Dimitri was dangerous. The Heir with a silver tongue could convince people to fight a lost war, but he wouldn't be able to convince Mahzun of anything. Yet he needed to hold onto this moment, to let it burn into his memory.

"You and the other Heirs never could see your own hypocrisy. You spoke of goodness, you spoke of the Creator—yet you worked only to enrich yourselves. Instead of helping, you enslaved us. You were to be servants of mankind, not its masters."

"Some of the Heirs...yes, mistakes were made," Dimitri replied. "That does not justify waging a war that has killed half of Einar."

"Oh, but it does," Mahzun barked before leaping up the dais and coming face to face with the old man. He lifted the Eternal Blade to admire the way the sunlight bounced off the ethereal steel. "While you give lip service to a false god, I have found a true deity to worship. Unfortunately, my god is harsh, and it doesn't tolerate lethargy."

Dimitri slammed his fist on the wooden throne, and Mahzun jumped, pulling his face back from the Heir's. He looked into those ancient eyes to see a raging inferno along with the strength of a much younger man.

"You meddle with forces you cannot understand," Dimitri shouted. "I know you've experienced pain, and I understand the wrongs committed against you, but you don't have to do this. The Eternal Blade was never meant to be used. You may believe it to be your new god, but it is nothing more than a devil."

Mahzun paused as the words echoed in the hall. Dimitri looked spent, his mouth hanging open and the fire extinguished. A smile spread across Mahzun's face as he again leaned forward.

"That was a very stirring speech. Is it the reason you've spent the past few years hiding in this rabbit's warren?"

The old man furrowed his brow, and a faint glow surrounded him. Around them, the air hummed as the Power of Creation was called upon by an Heir. Dimitri's eyes closed in meditation—something Mahzun thought the old man would no longer need. Before the *draod* could be fully roused from its slumber, Mahzun let out a shout. With all the strength left in his body, he rammed the Blade through the old man's chest.

The Eternal Blade sliced through the wispy frame and rammed into the wood, pinning the Heir of Segova to his throne. Mahzun's shout died in his throat, though it echoed and bounced on the stone walls. A single look at Dimitri's face confirmed the man was no longer in the mortal plane.

Mahzun couldn't count the times he had played this moment over in his head. The speech had changed each time, but he had managed the core aspects, though he knew the following weeks would find him wishing he had said so much more. After all, this was the most important moment in history.

This was the moment that mankind became free.

He had expected one with the power of an Heir to resist death, to struggle and cling to life. Yet, Lord Dimitri died just like the hundreds of others Mahzun had killed, with no sign of life in those limbs. There was very little blood on his clothing, as if he had already withered and had simply been awaiting death.

With trembling hands, Mahzun yanked on the Eternal Blade, ripping it free from both the throne and the corpse. The quasi-solid sword disappeared, returning to its place within Mahzun's soul, and the room's silence grew deafening. In that quiet, the Savior of Man couldn't tear his gaze away from the lifeless face that had given him years of sleepless nights.

"Even united, the Heirs—with all their power—couldn't stop me," Mahzun said. The words swept through his entire being, and a smile sprung across his lips. "I will admit that you put up a magnificent resistance. However, your time oppressing the peoples of Einar has come to an end."

He grabbed the old man by his silk robes and tossed him off the throne. If there had been little blood on his clothing, there was even less on the throne. Mahzun's smile threatened to split his face as he took a seat on the ancient chair. His gaze swept across the room, trying to imagine it filled with adoring subjects.

Like a swarm of flies on rotting flesh, those subjects flooded the room, only their faces held no adoration. There were women in silk dresses covered in filth, and delicate perfume mixed with the odor of decay. Gentlemen in fine suits of silk and wool stood among them, stony faced and unmoving. He saw soldiers dressed in the uniforms of all seven Heirdoms, and more children than he would have liked. All bore wounds given to them by the Eternal Blade.

Those wounds had killed them.

Their deaths meant he was never truly alone.

But giving a speech to those he had killed was better than giving a speech to nobody at all. He knew they wouldn't respond. Neither cheers nor boos would accompany his words—for that, he was grateful.

"I'm very pleased to announce that the last remnants of resistance have been wiped out," Mahzun said, his words bouncing on the stone walls and floor. He settled further into the throne, lifting his left leg on the armrest and slouching like the teenage Mahzun had so often done. He imagined a goblet of wine in his hand, and he took a sip.

"For too long, the Heirs have ruled over you in the name of their false god. Well, it's time to leave the old ways behind. Many of you may not be comfortable with the new order—my advice is to lay low and blend in. Traitors will be crushed. Citizens will be left alone."

Mahzun stopped to take another imaginary sip and grimaced. Couldn't his imagination conjure up anything better?

"Some of you may ask what I'll do now that the world is free. My answer is that the pathetic figure at my feet is far from the last creature that would enslave Einar. I will spend my time rebuilding when I can and hunting down all those who would see the world descend back into slavery."

Mahzun paused for the words to take effect. The assembled aristocrats that existed only in his mind didn't respond—they just stared at him with blank faces. Not a single smile could be found among the crowd.

"I would love to delight you all with a much longer speech, for I know that my words must glitter like diamonds in your dark existence. However, I will leave you with the knowledge that your best resistance was not enough to keep Einar in the chains of fear and superstition. The world is free," Mahzun shouted, leaping to his feet before his voice grew to a barely audible whisper. "The world is mine."

Chapter 9

Z ahara's mind burned with questions as the old trapper led the way through the trees, winding through trails even more obscure than the one they had just left. Yet his demeanor had not allowed for those questions to be uttered. Instead, she just continued following, occasionally looking back at Ekarath for reassurance.

It took a full hour to reach a small hut built from wooden planks and disguised with branches. There was no window giving visual access to the interior, and Zahara could barely make out an entrance. Yet the old man moved a few branches and opened a door, motioning for them to enter.

The interior was lit by a single lamp that flickered in the darkness. As Zahara looked around, it was about what she would have expected: a small cot, a rough wooden table, and a single chair were the only furnishings. The wooden walls were completely unadorned. However, there was a small hum that resonated within her chest that spoke of the *draod*.

"Now, I'm sorry for so much mystery, but there's a lot happening in the forest," Farban said. "It's certainly no place to stand around talking."

"You apparently know me already, but you don't seem familiar at all," Zahara said as she strained her eyes in the low light.

"We've never been officially introduced," Farban chuckled in response. "But Lord Dimitri shared his plan with me weeks ago, though he didn't give me all the details."

"Lord Dimitri sent us with a book for you," Zahara said, removing the pack from her back. "He said he had found the secret to defeating the Usurper."

"Did he, now? Well, he's probably right, though not in the way you were expecting."

Farban took the journal and broke the wax seal that bound the waterproof covering. He flipped the book open and smiled.

"May I ask what's in there?" Zahara asked. "Lord Dimitri seemed to think you would know what to do with it."

"You haven't looked at this?" Farban asked, and Zahara and Ekarath both shook their heads.

"I'll admit I was curious..." Zahara began, but she didn't quite know how to finish her thought.

"Well, I'll let you satisfy that curiosity," Farban replied, opening the book and handing it to Zahara.

The page was blank.

Zahara flipped through the thick ream of papers, looking for something—anything—that would indicate a path to victory over the Usurper. Yet there was nothing.

Zahara didn't quite know how to respond. She had faced two different monsters from the Wilds, she had been nearly captured by the Usurper's soldiers. She had looked death in the eye and kept going—all for supposed knowledge. Her brain just couldn't process that it had all been for a blank book.

"What was that old man thinking?" Zahara asked, handing the empty book to Ekarath. The young man flipped through the pages as well, though his face didn't betray any of the thoughts flowing through Zahara's mind.

"Well, I'm glad to see that you two are either fantastic actors or terrible spies," Farban replied, shaking his head as he took the book from Ekarath.

"What do you mean?" Ekarath shot back, and Zahara placed a hand on his shoulder.

"Is there more to this book than meets the eye?" she asked.

"Things are rarely as they seem," Farban said with a wink before snapping the book shut. "Come with me—I can most likely unlock this girl's secrets."

Zahara looked around the small room, wondering where else they could go. There were no stairs indicating a second story, no trap door for a cellar.

"Follow you where?"

"Despite appearances, I'm not just an old man living by himself in the forest."

With a soft chuckle, the hermit moved the rough wooden chair, and Zahara noticed an old rug covering the floor. A low hum of energy filled the air, and the rug evaporated into the void. Instead of revealing solid floor, Zahara's eyes took in a set of stairs leading underground.

"Follow me," Farban said before descending. He didn't look back, and Zahara found herself alone with Ekarath.

"Well, we've already come this far," Ekarath said with a shrug.

"If he wanted to do us any harm, he already could have," Zahara responded with a laugh. "I guess we should see what his cellar looks like."

The steps were formed of solid stone, and she could feel the threads woven into them, though she couldn't tell their purpose. Many parts of the Atsada were infused with the *draod* to stop the decay of time—a strange requirement for a hut's cellar. A sudden end of the steps also forced an end to these thoughts, and Zahara turned her focus back to the present.

She followed a narrow corridor until it turned a corner, unveiling a world that was in every way the opposite of the small, cramped hut. Instead of packed dirt, the floors were a polished marble that gleamed in the light of a dozen *kura* that hung on wall brackets. The walls were a mixture of polished stone and stained wood, decorated by tapestries, oil paintings, and shelves laden with books and scrolls.

The room's center was dominated by a sturdy table, upon which a map was spread. Dozens of pins were stuck to it in various points, though Zahara was still too far away to discern much else.

"Welcome to my most humble abode," Farban said, lifting his hands and gesturing to the magnificent, subterranean structure.

"This is...wonderful," Zahara replied, trying to find the correct word. While she could appreciate the craftsmanship, there was no disguising the moist, stuffy air that came with living under ground. A year in the Atsada had left her clamoring for life in the sun.

"For decades, I've been acting the part of a crazy old hermit while fulfilling my true role as Lord Dimitri's spymaster," Farban said. "From the forest, I've kept an eye on the war, the plots against Dimitri's life, and anything else that goes on. It's rather handy being dismissed as an eccentric old fool living in the middle of nowhere."

"Well, you must have missed that huge army marching through the forest, because we were all taken by surprise," Zahara responded, immediately regretting the harsh words.

"I sent word well before the Usurper arrived at the Atsada," Farban responded, a smile taking up his entire face. "If you didn't know about it, that must mean Lord Dimitri and his staff didn't think the news was worth sharing with the rank and file."

"Why would they keep that such a secret?" Zahara asked.

"To stop a panic," Ekarath responded before Farban could do so. "And to make sure nobody deserted—it's hard making an escape with the Usurper's horde surrounding the place."

"Now, this boy shows at least some promise," Farban said, slapping Ekarath on the back. "Even if you're obviously not a mage, you seem to have a sharp mind."

"I was to be inducted into the *Hundiin* the day the Usurper arrived," Ekarath responded.

"Ah, so that explains why you took on an adult *sahali* with nothing but a sword. You elite guards always seem to have more heart than brain."

"As much as I would love to keep discussing every aspect of our lives, I think we should focus on the reason we're here," Zahara said, gesturing to the leather tome in Farban's hands. "You mentioned being able to unlock its secrets?"

"Well, there are always risks with sending written notes," Farban said. "We often use code, but it's not necessarily the best method..."

Farban trailed off as he placed the book on the table. His hands moved swiftly, creating a spell. A tiny flame appeared in his hand, dancing just above the skin. He held it close to the first page, and Zahara's jaw dropped as words began to appear.

My dearest Zahara,

If you're reading this, then I hope it means you have found Farban. Give heed to his counsel and advice—he is much wiser than he appears. His words will guide you to great heights and (I hope) victory over the Usurper.

It is with a heavy heart that I tell you there is no hope in the coming battle. The Atsada will fall, and I—along with far too many others—will leave the mortal plane. Though the battle is lost, hope cannot be allowed to perish.

I wasn't lying when I told you I had found the secret to defeating the Usurper. The secret is a young woman who doesn't believe anything to be impossible. The secret is someone so passionate about magic that she has devoted her life to its study.

The secret is you.

I do not know exactly when my life will end. If all goes according to plan, you will be my successor. Farban will guide you in this journey of discovery, for he was instrumental in my own.

Take courage. In the coming months, all hope will feel lost. In those dark nights of the soul, remember that you were chosen for a reason. May the Creator bless you and your endeavors.

—Lord Dimitri, Heir of Segova

Zahara's heart pounded harder with each word her eyes took in. She could feel the strength in her legs threaten to give out, and her knees began to wobble. The thick book suddenly felt very heavy in her grip as her muscles trembled.

She looked up from the words to see Farban beaming at her. There were tears in the old man's eyes, and she had to blink away those forming in her own. Her vision spun, and she put the book down on the large table.

"My scouts reported that the Horde was readying its assault this morning," Farban said, clearing his throat. "I don't expect any more reports until tomorrow, but I'm afraid that it's only a matter of time until you become the Heir of Segova."

"But...how? Why? I..."

"I'm missing something," Ekarath interjected, his brow furrowed. Zahara gestured for him to grab the book, and his eyes began scanning the ornate script.

This can't be happening, Zahara mentally screamed. She was a low-born noblewoman with barely a year of formal training. She wasn't even a full adult. The only time she had seen the Usurper had left her ready to vomit and faint—there was no possible way she could face the monster in battle.

Zahara found the nearest chair and lowered herself onto the sturdy wood, as if the weight of her coming responsibilities had become physical. She could hear Lord Dimitri's chuckle in her mind, could picture his kind smile. Farban still smiled at her as Ekarath finished reading the note.

"I can't really say I'm surprised," Ekarath said as he wiped a tear from his eyes. "I mean—yes, this is all very surprising. I didn't expect the Horde to attack so soon, and I certainly didn't expect Lord Dimitri to just admit defeat. Though if he's going to choose a successor, I can't imagine anyone better than you."

"I think we might be forgetting something," Zahara said. "If Lord Dimitri dies by the Usurper's Blade, doesn't it stop his powers from passing on?"

Before the war, there had been seven Heirs, as had been decreed by the Creator. For millennia, their powers had passed onto a successor upon their deaths. Yet being killed by the Usurper's sword had stopped those powers from being passed on.

"That is what has happened with the others, but I wouldn't doubt Lord Dimitri for even a second," Farban replied.

Zahara couldn't quite say she agreed. What had the old man been thinking? Did he really expect a seventeen-year-old girl to take his place?

"And...what do I do once I become the Heir?" Zahara asked, not exactly sure how to form the question.

"That's why you've been sent to me," Farban said, his smile somehow growing even wider. "What better place to train you than here? When the time is right, you can reemerge into the world, giving hope and light to all Einar."

The soft chime of a bell filled the room, and Zahara looked up. On the far side of the cellar, a series of brass bells hung on the wall. There was no string or rope, but one of them moved, sending its clear note into the air.

"Those are just my perimeter alarms," Farban said without looking up from the map. "Each one is connected to a weave out in the woods. If something gets too close, the bells ring."

"So, should we be worried?" Ekarath asked before Zahara could do so.

"Probably not," Farban replied. "The bigger the ring, the more movement there is out there. Something that little is likely to be a rabbit or a badger. Now, we should start thinking about training Zahara."

"She's already quite good with the *draod*," Ekarath said. "Almost better than most of the old magi in the Atsada."

"It will be a little different once Dimitri's powers pass," Farban replied, his gaze moving back and forth between Zahara and Ekarath. "For example, you won't need that *qilada* any longer. As an Heir, you'll have a connection to the Power of Creation that a normal mage can barely imagine."

"I will admit that sounds nice," Zahara said, trying to think of the spells she could try. The thought brought her back upright, though she could still feel the heaviness in her chest.

Across the room, a second bell chimed, this one louder than the first. Zahara furrowed her brow and looked to the old spymaster, but he didn't seem to even notice the sound. His attention had turned to the map that took up the large table.

"Now, I've got a few other mages with teams of saboteurs spread throughout the forest," Farban said, pointing at one of the pins in the map. Zahara was not familiar enough with Segova in general and the forest in particular to know where they were. "I think we could meet up with a few of them here. We could help disrupt the Usurper's supply lines while you get some solid experience."

A third bell chimed, followed by a fourth. This time, the noise was sufficient to rouse Farban from his study of the map. Within seconds, over a dozen bells were ringing. The sound filled the room, bouncing off the stone walls and echoing in Zahara's soul.

"What does it mean when all of them go off at once?" Zahara asked, her voice barely rising over the alarms.

Farban turned, his eyes and face growing dark.

"It means we're surrounded."

Chapter 10

An explosion rocked the underground chamber, knocking bits of dust and stone from the ceiling. Zahara ducked under her arms as the debris rained down, unsure of what to do next. Instinctively, she began pulling threads of Destruction out of the *draod*, weaving them into a simple flame—enough to give a nasty surprise to anyone trying to enter.

Her ears picked up the crackling of fire feasting on the timber of the hut above. While there wasn't yet any smoke invading their underground sanctuary, she could smell the burning wood. Sweat began to bead along her forehead; whether it came from the heat or her own nerves, Zahara was unsure.

A strong hand secured her shoulder, and Zahara turned around to see Ekarath looking into her eyes. He lifted a finger to his lips and withdrew his sword.

"I think whoever followed us has more than just swords and crossbows," Farban whispered, joining them. "An explosion like that could only come from a powerful weave—there's at least one mage up there."

Zahara shuddered at the thought of facing someone with decades of training. It was one thing to spar under the watchful eye of Master Kanu. It was something else entirely to face a fully trained mage who would have no qualms about killing her.

Heavy footsteps sounded above, the noise colliding with the cracks and pops of the flame. Those were soon joined by the deep rumble of voices—not exactly shouts, but they were certainly not whispers.

Letting go of the destructive weave she had been planning to use, Zahara instead pulled on a few threads of Restoration. With a quick weave and finishing knot, she placed the familiar spell over her ears, and the world grew louder. She had to block out the sound of the fire above, but the voices quickly came into focus.

"I know they came in here," a deep, husky voice growled.

"Well, I don't see anybody now," a second voice responded.

"Maybe they died in the blast," the first man said.

"There would be bodies," the second man shot back. "Or at least something left. If they got away, we are going to be in—"

"It appears you've been fooled again," a third voice sounded, this one much higher than the first two. Instead of the growling bass, it was a harmonic baritone that rose above the ambient noise. "I don't appreciate being disturbed to chase down ghosts."

"Of course, Your Grace," the deeper voice responded.

Your Grace? Zahara had never heard such a title, though the Usurper had spent years spinning society in all directions. Whatever the title meant, it was obviously a sign of deep respect—nobility, at the very least.

"Now, if you'll excuse me, I have an entire province to be governing," the aristocratic voice said with a scoff, and Zahara let out a sigh of relief—whoever had followed them didn't expect the little hermit shack to hold a luxurious bunker. "Again, next time you—"

The man's words cut off, and Zahara furrowed her brow. She looked over to Ekarath before remembering that her friend wouldn't be able to make out the conversation. Yet a glance at Farban told her the hermit had also enhanced his hearing. His skin was pale, and his lips were pursed in concentration.

"What's wrong, Your Grace?" the soldier above asked.

"I feel...something," the aristocrat responded, the words moving at a glacial speed. "It's almost as if..."

As his words trailed off, the air began to hum with power. The false ceiling at the top of the staircase shuddered, cracking under the weight of a powerful spell. Zahara's stomach tensed, and she reached for threads of Destruction. At her side, Ekarath lifted his sword, and Farban began to move his fingers in a silent dance.

The ground trembled, and the ceiling above the staircase cracked. Large chunks of stone fell on to the stairs, shattering into small fragments as they bounced to the ground. Zahara could now see sunlight streaming through the large opening, could feel the heat of the fire.

The snap of a crossbow filled the air, and a bolt slammed into the wall just behind Zahara. With a yelp, she dove to the ground as the air filled with arrows from the soldiers above. Yet within a matter of seconds, the assault ended.

Footsteps crunched on the mixture of solid marble and scattered dirt. Zahara looked up to see dark figures moving into the dimly lit cellar, swords drawn. Pulling herself into a crouching position, she pulled yet again on threads of Destruction.

She leapt to her feet, bounding through the smoke and dust. With a jump, Zahara unleashed a bolt of lightning, and it slammed into a soldier's chest. He fell with a thud, his leather armor hitting the marble floor.

A shout filled the air, and Zahara spun as a second soldier rushed toward her. Without time to weave another spell, she dove and rolled past the man. Springing back to her feet, Zahara slammed her dagger into the man's back—the steel pushed right through the thick leather and into flesh.

A gurgling sound escaped the soldier's mouth, and as Zahara pulled her blade free, the body slipped to the ground. A shudder ran through her entire frame—despite all the months of training, she had never actually killed someone. For what felt like an eternity, she couldn't pull her eyes away from the soldier as he gasped on the floor.

Footsteps sounded to her left, and Zahara turned to see a brute of a man bearing down on her. A wicked axe was raised above his head, and there was fire in his eyes. She needed to move, to do anything—yet her mind was stuck on the writhing figure at her feet.

A sword blocked the man's axe as it began to swing down, and Ekarath appeared at her side. With a grunt, the boy launched the much larger man backward. The sharp crack of steel shattered the fog in Zahara's mind, and she was able to push the dying soldier out of her thoughts. Pulling on threads of Destruction, she launched a bolt of lightning into the thug's chest, and he fell to the ground.

Shouts from above filled the air, followed by the pounding of more armored feet on the stone steps. Zahara began pulling on the *draod*, weaving threads from the ocean of energy. At her side, she could feel Farban doing the same—two magi preparing a rain of fire for the ordinary soldiers.

Zahara finished her knot and launched an inferno, filling her vision with a mixture of blue and red flames. Men screamed before falling to the ground. More shouts sounded from above, and Zahara began moving her hands to gather up even more energy.

Her arms froze into stiff boards, and the ephemeral threads dissipated. She tried to speak, but her jaw was clamped shut. Unable to turn her head, she could barely see Farban in the corner of her eye—the man looked just as imprisoned as she was. She tried kicking her legs, but they were completely unresponsive.

The *draod* hummed all around her—a weave of air turned solid. Her body was more than capable of moving, but it was encased in a mixture of magic and air strong enough to stop her from doing so.

A single set of footsteps sounded on the stairs, and Zahara moved her eyes—the only part of her body still mobile—to the sound. A man dressed in robes of royal blue descended into the darkness. With a flourish of his hands, a *kura* appeared above his shoulder, illuminating the scene.

The man's head was shaved bald, his skin light enough to be almost translucent. It certainly glowed in the white light of the *kura*. His face was rather handsome—a strong jaw and a firm nose spoke of someone whose power and authority extended well beyond his ability to weave the *draod*. His pale blue eyes moved between his three prisoners before scanning the entire room.

"Look at what we have here," the man said, a smile coming across his face. "I've been combing the entirety of Segova in search of the brains behind our little rebel friends. It turns out, I just needed to find an old hermit—is that really what you've become, Farban?"

"It's a better fate than a lapdog," Farban spat at the man. "Tell me—how long of a leash does the Usurper give you? Was it worth betraying your friends to gain the title of Governor?"

Zahara's mouth would have dropped were it not for the woven air that secured her. The man standing before her was Governor Pavel, the man in charge of occupied Segova. She had heard rumors of both his power and cruelty. Beyond that, she knew little of the man.

"You and I were never friends," Pavel whispered. "I'll admit that some sacrifices made for the Cause have been painful. However, I'll have nothing but joy at seeing you hang from the end of a rope."

Pavel wove his hand, and Farban's response was muffled beyond comprehension. Zahara couldn't be sure, but it seemed likely the man had just placed a gag of woven air over the hermit's mouth. Before she could give it any more thought, the aristocrat turned to look her in the eyes.

"And it appears we have a bonus," Pavel said, lifting a hand to Zahara's ear. While his fingers touched the *qilada*, his eyes remained fixed on hers. "Such a thing of beauty."

Despite the bindings, her body managed to shiver. There was a look in the man's eyes that said he wasn't referring to the earring. After a moment, he shifted his gaze to the powerful relic.

"This is a very powerful tool for such a young and delicate girl," Pavel said.

His hand began unclasping the jewelry from the three piercings. It had been years since she had removed the *qilada*, and her ear immediately began to itch at the absence. Holding up the golden chain and jewels, the man flashed a smile at Zahara.

"You've done the Empire a great service," he said before his eyes flashed with a dark fire. "The gold from selling this relic will find its way into the province's coffers." Zahara instinctively reached out for the *draod*, but its familiar hum was gone. Without her *qilada*, she had no way to access the power.

At Pavel's side, one of the soldiers spoke up.

"Your Grace, what should we do with them?"

"Bring the girl to the palace," Pavel replied. "As for the other two—well, now that we'll have a flood of slaves and prisoners from the Atsada, it will be instructive to have at least a few executions."

Zahara's head spun with the words. A flood of slaves and prisoners from the Atsada? Was the man simply confident of the Usurper's victory in the impending battle? Or did he know something she didn't?

"Oh, I know that look on a woman's face," Pavel said, his smile growing even larger. "Have you not heard? The Atsada fell to the Imperial Army just a few hours ago. His Imperial Majesty killed your pathetic Heir with the Eternal Blade—bathed it in his blood. The war is over."

Chapter 11

A warm, summer breeze welcomed Mahzun home as he clung to Aiya's mixture of fur and feathers. It had taken all night, but the griffin's powerful wings had traversed the skies between the Atsada and the Imperial capital of Talas. Below, the city's lights burned in the night—the streetlamps and lanterns from individual windows combining to form a glow visible for miles.

Mahzun leaned forward, and Aiya let out a screech that rang in the night air. The rhythmic pumping of her wings ceased, replaced by the rushing wind as the two descended from their lofty height. The ocean of lights grew closer, and Mahzun forced his eyes to adjust.

The city was built into perfect squares, and he knew that wide streets and boulevards offered ample room for the many mule-drawn carts, horse-drawn carriages, and pedestrians. Most of the streets were lined with connected buildings that rose three to four stories into the air. Depending on the neighborhood, those buildings could be occupied by a single noble family or a hundred commoners. As he soared above the streets, he could smell the mass of humanity and the associated waste.

At the very center, the Mount of Creation dominated an entire city block. All four sides of the mountain were sheer, while the top was as flat as a table. Roads had been carved out of the rock, and even at night, Mahzun could see a stream of lantern-guided wagons moving back and forth along the switchbacks.

Unlike the rest of the city, the Mount's top was largely free of buildings. The Creator had mandated it stay a refuge, and the Heirs had turned it into a lush park filled with tree-lined pathways and fountains. However, at its center sat the Creator's Palace, which he had of course renamed to the Imperial Palace.

The building was formed out of pure white stone that rose five stories into the air. Delicate arches lined the top floor, creating a covered portico that allowed for open-air strolls. Domes capped with pure gold rose out of the four corners, while out of the center grew an ancient tree that stretched toward the sky.

Orders of magnitude more majestic than the carved depiction on the door to Lord Dimitri's throne room, the Shajarat was large enough to be seen from almost everywhere in the city. Its bark and leaves of pure white glowed in the light from both the moon and the sun. For thousands of years, it had stood as a symbol of the Creator, its beauty outshining even the efforts of the Heirs. People from across Einar made pilgrimages to see it; fallen leaves were dipped in wax and sold as souvenirs across the Empire.

It made Mahzun sick.

You're getting worked up, Aiya's voice sounded in his mind.

I'm fine.

So, you just pulled out my feathers for no reason?

Mahzun looked down at his hands to see that they were indeed full of white feathers. Letting out a deep breath, he relaxed his hands and forced his mind away from the tree before Aiya landed on a stone plaza near the palace's entrance. Despite her size, the griffin's soft paws landed with barely a sound. Without hesitation, Mahzun leapt off his friend's back. His feet slammed into the ground with a crack that echoed throughout the garden. He never could match Aiya's grace.

The call of mating crickets filled the warm night air. He took in a deep breath of air perfumed by the flowers and ferns that filled the gardens. While the aroma was pleasant, it merely masked the smells of life that filled the city streets. He would need to experience that in the morning.

May I leave? Aiya asked. *I'm hungry, and unless you want me to eat random residents, I'll need to make my way out of the city to find game.*

"Didn't you get your fill of Lord Dimitri's soldiers?" Mahzun asked, choosing to use his voice instead of just his mind.

How about you fly through the night and tell me if you're hungry afterwards.

"My apologies," Mahzun responded with a deep bow. "You have my thanks for your friendship and service. Once the celebrations are over, we'll head to the Wilds for a little break."

The griffin gave a small bow in return before launching back into the air. Her wings created a whirlwind in the garden, and Mahzun lifted an arm to protect his face from the dirt and leaves that swirled around him. Letting out a sigh, the Savior of Man turned toward the palace.

From the ground, the building took on a new level of majesty. The white granite absorbed the glow of the Shajarat, while the golden domes on the four corners reflected it. Hundreds of windows faced him, though many were dark and unused.

At the front entrance stood two guards. The men weren't dressed in the dark armor of his legions. Rather, they wore gaudy tunics with yellow, blue, and red stripes. Their heads were covered by flat hats instead of helmets, and their hands wielded long pikes.

Mahzun had little respect for these soft sons of nobility that didn't want to fight in the real war. Their fathers used a mixture of wealth and connections to get them into the city guard, where their only real duty was to look good and maybe clear drunks off the street. As he grew closer, the two men snapped straight at the sight of their sovereign.

Before he could react, the doors opened, and a woman strode out of the front entrance. She wore a dress of deep teal that came down just shy of her feet, with long sleeves covered in a golden embroidery that stretched from wrists to elbows. White silk covered her neck and hair, though a few dark locks did poke out. Her face was long, and it tapered into a strong jaw and chin, while dark brown eyes were accented by fine make up lining the exterior.

A large feline with obsidian fur followed at the woman's heels. Even on all four paws, its head reached the woman's waist, and Mahzun knew the strength of an adult *namura* all too well. After all, he had personally fetched Sasha to be the woman's soul-bound all those years ago.

Fortunately, the quills that covered its back were laying flat at the moment, though that could change in the blink of an eye should the soul-bound detect a hint of danger. Mahzun pulled his attention away from the *namura*, focusing on the woman's eyes.

Those eyes widened as they fell on Mahzun's face.

"You used the Blade again," she said, as Mahzun began climbing the stairs.

"I didn't think anybody would notice a few more scars," Mahzun grunted.

He reached the top of the stairs and pulled on the doors. He didn't want to have this conversation in front of the two guards. Their loyalty was always suspect in his mind, and their tongues would loosen up after a single tankard of ale.

"Do you have good news, then?" the woman asked before slipping through the door.

"Oh Lorna, I was hoping to surprise everyone."

Mahzun chuckled as he looked around the entrance hall. The walls rose four stories before coming together in an arched ceiling. Arched alcoves were spaced throughout the long corridor, which had once held marble statues. Most were of the Heirs, and those were now little more than rubble. The ceiling itself was painted with depictions of the Creation and various scenes throughout history. Mahzun ignored those, choosing to focus on the cracking of his boots on the polished marble floor.

"You can't keep me in the dark," Lorna shot back, raising her eyebrow. At her side, the *namura* hissed, sensing its master's feelings of impatience and frustration. If those sentiments mounted, Sasha's quills would burn a dark orange before shooting off like darts.

Even without the *namura* threatening him, Mahzun knew Lorna was right. While he had been off conquering Einar and destroying the Heirs, she had been the one keeping the empire running. While he had been dealing with the danger of warfare, she had been playing the even deadlier game of politics. Lorna was practically the Empress without a crown. Her ferocity and keen intellect kept the politicians in line and the troops fed.

He stopped to look the woman in the eyes. She was a full head shorter than him, which meant she towered over everyone else. Those eyes were not used to looking up at someone, and he could see the irritation it caused.

"He's dead," Mahzun said, unable to keep the smile off his face. "The Heirs' time oppressing our people is over."

Lorna shuddered and closed her eyes. She took in a deep breath before a smile spread across her face and she embraced Mahzun. Her arms wrapped around his torso, and her face pressed against his breastplate.

"After all these years, it's hard to believe we've won," she said as her embrace threatened to pop Mahzun's ribs, even with his steel armor. "I have a feeling that somewhere, our parents must be very proud of us."

Mahzun winced at the words. They rarely spoke of their shared parentage, especially where others could hear. He looked around for any sign of someone, but the entrance hall was empty at this late hour. The Emperor was to be a man without attachment, without weakness. A beloved older sister was both.

"Gather the Elder Council," Mahzun said, pulling away from the embrace. He began moving again—there was far too much adrenaline coursing through his veins to sit still. "I want to make the announcement to them before word leaks out."

"Are you aware of the hour?" Lorna asked, her eyebrow shooting up. "Laborers might be starting their day in an hour or so, but I've never met a nobleman willing to get up so early."

"I left the Atsada without celebrating," Mahzun growled, looking over at his sister without stopping. "I cut short the moment I've been dreaming about for years, just so I can make sure the announcement doesn't have time to be shrouded with rumors. Those old relics can have a single night of sleep cut short."

Lorna nodded her head. She knew as well as he did that the Elder Council was filled with snakes just waiting for a sign of weakness. If they got word of Lord Dimitri's death, some might make a run for it. Or worse.

"I'll make sure they come," Lorna replied. "Though it will take an hour—maybe two—before I can have them assembled."

Lorna stopped at a side hallway, and Mahzun knew it was time to part ways.

"Make sure they come to the Grand Hall," Mahzun said. "And have the servants set up that platform in front of the Shajarat."

"Of course," Lorna said with the smallest of curtsies. "While that's being done, I suggest using your time to clean up—you look and smell like a man who needs to spend a week in the baths."

Mahzun let out a chuckle at his sister's words, and he couldn't disagree. He knew his smell was a mixture of sweat, dirt, blood, and griffin.

"I'll head to my rooms," Mahzun replied once the laughter died.

"Do you remember where they are? You've hardly spent a week here since moving in."

"I'll find my way," Mahzun replied. "You get going—I don't want anything to delay the esteemed members of the Council."

Lorna simply nodded and turned on her heels. Her slippered feet barely made a sound as they carried her down the hallway. Mahzun continued down the main entrance hall, trying to ignore the finery as he walked.

He couldn't say he liked the idea of living in such an ancient and luxurious structure, but it was expected for the most powerful man in Einar. Yet there was too much history in this building—too many memories of plots and schemes to gain or maintain power. Worse, he had spent years talking about freedom and equality. Living in a palace like this didn't agree with that message.

His footsteps echoed on the marble walls, breaking the nocturnal silence. He ignored the expensive tapestries and rugs that served as decoration and to dampen the echo. His exhausted legs led him down a side corridor and up a grand staircase to the apartments that had been set aside for his use. In the year since conquering Talas, those rooms had largely sat empty.

"The war is over," Mahzun muttered, unable to feel the reality of that statement.

There would be no more winters spent on campaign, no more battles to be fought. It was time to settle in and rule over Einar—time to implement his vision for the oppressed people. As much as his bones ached from years of fighting, his head pounded in dread of the politics awaiting him.

The large room was filled with the finest of luxuries he would have expected—after all, Lorna had been the one in charge of decorating the palace. Soft carpets were spread throughout the large room, and Mahzun stopped to remove his heavy armor. Ahead of him sat three low couches around a wooden table. He didn't know when he would ever host a group in his bedroom, but the setup certainly looked comfortable.

To his left, a gilded bed dominated the other half of the room. Four wooden columns rose into the air, stopping just short of the ceiling. Sheets of silk and a mattress filled with soft down beckoned him. After a life spent sleeping on the ground, he didn't know if he could fall asleep on such softness.

A doorway on his right led to the baths. Now stripped of his armor and covered in nothing more than dirty under clothing, he made for that door. He entered just in time to see three young women make their way out of the back door, which was used only by servants.

His eyes took in a room larger than most houses. Granite columns lined a pool larger than his bedroom. Steam rose up from the hot water drawn directly from a spring underneath the ancient edifice. His nose picked up the scent of rose and lavender—hardly the aroma of a fierce warrior.

He removed the filthy and sweat-stained shirt and trousers, placing both on the ground. He stepped down into the hot water, and the scars covering his body cried out. Gritting his teeth, Mahzun sat down into the water and ignored the pain. The water around him was already turning brown, and he began rubbing his skin to get the dirt off.

Moving away from the edge, he dove underneath the water. For the first time in months, he was immersed in warmth—there was no biting wind, no sleet pounding from above. He had usually tried to wash with a rag and bucket of water while on campaign, but destroying the Heirs had dominated his entire consciousness. Now, he could just allow himself to float in the hot, scented waters.

His long hair floated in the water, the first time he'd washed it in weeks. As he emerged from the pool, it hung over his face, and he forced it away from his eyes to see a green smudge standing at the pool's edge. Mahzun wiped the rest of the water and hair from his eyes, and the figure crystallized into Lord Dimitri.

"I didn't summon you," Mahzun barked. "Go back to where you came from."

Just as with all figments killed by the Eternal Blade, the deceased Heir of Segova responded with a dead-eyed stare. There was no flinch at the Emperor's barking command, no sign that Mahzun was even heard. That ancient frame looked just as ready to collapse as it had in the Atsada. Yet unlike the others who came and went upon command, the old man stood firm.

"Fine—I don't care if you watch me bathe. Enjoy the show, old man."

Swimming back over to the edge, Mahzun grabbed a stiff brush and a bar of soap. He did his best to ignore the silent apparition as he began working on all the visible dirt, knowing he would never get all of it. Anyone with real wealth had personal body servants to wash them, and he knew one of the girls who had just left would be happy to do the job.

"If you insist on staying, it would be nice if you would at least lend a hand," Mahzun said, lifting the brush toward Lord Dimitri. The man's eyes didn't even blink.

"Maybe I should get one of those servant girls to help," Mahzun whispered as he went back to scrubbing the grime from his legs. What would his commanders think if word got out that the Savior of Man didn't even bathe himself? That would be worse than everyone knowing their dread sovereign saw the victims of the Eternal Blade on a regular basis.

Satisfied that his stench would no longer clear a room, Mahzun pulled himself from the hot pool as Lord Dimitri maintained his silent vigil. He had bathed in front of other men countless times while on campaign, but most of them had the decency to not stare. Ignoring the old man, Mahzun grabbed one of the towels set out for him and focused on the soft, warm fibers. He wrapped it around his waist before striding back into the bedroom.

White underclothes of a soft linen and a set of violet robes sat awaiting him on the bed. The silk was the finest he'd ever seen, and he quickly dressed. Next to the linens sat the Imperial Crown—golden leaves formed into a half circle. He placed it on his head and turned to look at himself in the mirror.

Even if he hadn't used the Eternal Blade, his skin would still resemble leather after years in the sun. The scars that snaked across every inch of his body certainly didn't improve his appearance. Yet he wasn't trying to woo a young woman; he was trying to reforge the world into a better place.

"Does this remind you of your crown?" Mahzun said, turning to face Lord Dimitri. "I really should have taken it—an opportunity lost, I'm afraid."

Silence was again the response. Mahzun knew it was pointless, but for some reason he enjoyed speaking with his fallen foe, especially with the knowledge that he wouldn't talk back.

"I could get used to your silent stare. Do you plan on sticking around?"

A knock sounded at his door, and Lorna entered without waiting for a response.

"Who are you talking to?" she asked, her gaze scanning the room.

"Just myself," Mahzun replied with a chuckle. "I must have spent too much time on my own out in the Northern Wilds."

"We all do it," Lorna said before her eyes focused on her brother. "Oh good, you look...presentable."

"I'm glad you approve. Can you smell me from across the room?"

"The elders are assembling," Lorna continued, ignoring his attempted joke. "They're all very curious about being roused from their beds."

"This will be worth their time and sleep deprivation," Mahzun snarled, more at the absent old aristocrats than his sister. "They probably expected me to die assaulting the Atsada."

"There have been rumors of it throughout the city," Lorna said. "Every day you were gone, people speculated. I'm sure there will be celebrations when the people see your return."

"And just as many who will begin plotting—including the elders," Mahzun growled. "Are you sure I have to keep them around?"

"I suggest you do for now," Lorna replied. "They have a control over the city that we don't. Of course, now that you're no longer spending every waking moment out hunting the Heirs, we could reevaluate the arrangement."

"Good," Mahzun said as he straightened out his robes and headed toward the door. "Because these old politicians think they can do as they please. I'll teach them that a new world has been born."

With his words hanging in the air, Mahzun strode out of his bedroom. The hallways were still empty as the grey light of dawn streamed in through arched windows. Lorna jogged to keep up.

"Have you thought this through?" Lorna asked.

"What do you mean?" Mahzun said, slowing his pace to look her in the eye.

"This isn't a battle you can just charge into. The elders are used to playing subtle games against each other."

"I don't need to play games," Mahzun said, picking his pace up again. He wanted to get this over with—the bath had done wonders, but he needed a few hours of sleep. "I have the Eternal Blade."

Lorna didn't respond, and Mahzun quickened his pace even further so she would have to focus on keeping up rather than pestering him with questions. His feet took him through the palace halls while his mind was involved in how he wanted to break the news. He forced his thoughts back to the present as they reached the main entrance hall again.

At the far end, an arched entrance marked the demarcation between the entrance hall and the central atrium. Even from a distance, he could see the white trunk of the Shajarat illuminating the circular chamber that both surrounded the ancient tree and acted as the palace center. Just as he'd requested, a platform was set up at the base of the ancient tree, and chairs were arranged in a half circle facing it.

A murmur of hushed whispers reached his ears as he approached the entrance. Without slowing, he passed the two soldiers standing guard, who stood up a bit straighter. As he entered, the whispers grew silent, and all eyes turned to him.

The Elder Council was a group of twenty-five elected officials from each of the city's sections. In this current group, there were fourteen men and eleven women. Each member was advanced in years, though still young enough to have the energy required to represent a section of the city. All were old enough to have grey hairs, but most used various dyes to keep them hidden.

Mahzun strode past the group without sparing them a glance, focusing his gaze on the massive tree. Thirty grown men clasping hands would barely be able to wrap around the base, and the ancient branches reached into the sky. It was an impressive sight from outside the palace, but at this range, it was breathtaking.

Taking care to keep his gaze forward, Mahzun slowed his pace. He could feel twenty-five sets of eyes on him, and he was determined to not return their gaze. He approached the massive tree and leapt onto the platform before turning to face the assembled elders.

As he faced the old aristocrats, Mahzun's blood began to boil. Even at this early hour, the men wore fine suits and robes. The women were dressed in expensive silk, velvet, and furs. Without exception, each member of the Council wore a *qilada* either as an earring, necklace, or ring—the more prominent, the better.

"I know that you are all questioning this nocturnal meeting," Mahzun began, pausing to let his voice bounce around the hall. All eyes were fixed on him, and he could feel the mixture of hatred and fear radiating from them. "And I know how you all value sleep. This morning, I come bearing urgent news from our campaign in the north that I felt warranted your immediate presence."

Mahzun paused to let the words sink in, though they had probably guessed that much already. His presence in the city must mean some sort of development in the war. With news coming in daily, the entire Council could likely guess what he was about to tell them.

"Far too many of our brave soldiers lay dead at the base of the Atsada," Mahzun continued. "Their blood will mix with the red soil of that valley, making it a holy site. Yet their sacrifice has not been in vain. On a glorious, stormy afternoon, I set foot in the throne room of the Atsada."

A wave of murmuring swept across the Council. More than one face lost all color.

"To get there, I called on the power of the Eternal Blade once again," Mahzun called out, silencing the elders. "She is an unforgiving master, and I bear the scars to prove my dedication to the people of Einar."

He lifted a scarred hand in the air, though nobody in attendance was ignorant of the pain he had suffered. A decade of fighting had decimated Einar, though Mahzun doubted that any single person had suffered as much as he had.

"While the blood of thousands waters the soil, there is one man's blood that matters more than all others," Mahzun said, his voice growing stronger with each word.

He paused to allow his voice to echo in the chamber. Expressions of fear and anger grew on the faces of those assembled, and it lifted Mahzun's heart.

All of them wanted to see his failure.

All of them wanted the old order restored.

All of them knew what he was about to say, and they feared it.

"In the Grand Hall of the Atsada, this man's blood bathed the Eternal Blade," Mahzun cried out. "The last of the Heirs has gone to his eternal rest, while his bones will remain enthroned in that magnificent chamber. They will stand as a warning to all who would enslave Einar and resist the Eternal Blade."

As he said those words, he summoned the ancient artifact, and the sword appeared in his hand. The ethereal metal shimmered in the glow of the Shajarat, but Mahzun forced his gaze away. He looked back to the Elder Council and cleared his throat.

"The Age of the Heirs is over. The Age of Man has begun. And in the coming weeks, the entire city will celebrate Einar's newly won freedom."

The men and women of the Council took in the news with straight faces. He had shocked them with word of his victory, but they weren't about to give anything else away. Mahzun smiled as he summoned his next words.

"And on the first day of celebrations, in front of my adoring subjects, I will remove the one thing that still separates the oppressed from the oppressors," Mahzun called out. This time, he could see surprise enter the elders' faces. He had already destroyed the Heirs. What else could he do?

"Without the power of the Heirs to protect it," Mahzun said, pointing the Eternal Blade to the tree, "I will destroy the Shajarat."

Chapter 12

Ekarath's bones ached after three full days of jostling in the back of an open-air cart, and his wrists were raw from the hemp rope lashed around them. The sights, sounds, and smells of the forest were much less exhilarating as a prisoner. The fine greenery looked drab to his eyes, and the days had stretched into eternities.

His eyes found Zahara sitting across from him, her face giving little insight to her feelings. She was bound just as he was, and her wrists looked nearly as enflamed.

At Zahara's side sat Farban, who looked far worse. Their captors had been overjoyed to find the man who had been coordinating the guerrilla war, and he sported a number of bruises and cuts.

To the west, the sun was setting, casting an orange glow that filtered in through the dense canopy. Long shadows flitted throughout the trees, catching Ekarath's eye, telling of both potential danger and wonders if he could find a way to escape the cart. Yet he knew that was impossible.

A contingent of over a hundred soldiers rode on horseback, both in front and behind their cart. All wore the mixture of black leather and steel, and all carried long pikes as they rode. He could see swords at their sides, and most also carried small crossbows on their backs. The escort was certainly a force he did not want to deal with, even if he could get his hands free and holding a weapon.

Their captors had made it very clear that Farban's execution was to be the highlight of the coming festivities celebrating the end of the war. Ekarath could practically feel the noose around his neck, and he fought the urge to scratch at it.

Ekarath looked ahead to see the southern edge of the forest, the trees giving way to the settled fields and villages of Segova. The highway would soon be lined with once-prosperous farms and orchards, though he suspected that many would still be abandoned or under-worked.

Memories of his time spent in those villages flooded his mind—selling rabbits to a baker in Ilieth, catching the eye of an innkeeper's daughter in Holthen. These almost brought a smile to his face before they were replaced by the bitter realization that those days were gone.

"How much longer until we stop for the night?" Zahara whispered, nudging Ekarath with her foot.

"Probably soon," Ekarath replied with a shrug. He looked over to see a glint in the young woman's eyes. Something told him that she would rather die than simply give up.

Ekarath's thoughts drifted to the wagon that rode just ahead of their own. Within, it held chests filled with the books and maps that had dominated Farban's secret war room. Of course, it also held the *qiladas* belonging to Farban and Zahara—any plan forming in his friend's mind must revolve around getting those back.

Those plans would change if Zahara could access her powers as the Heir of Segova. Though he understood little about the *draod*, he knew that only the Heirs could wield it without help. The woman sitting across from him was Dimitri's successor—theoretically, that meant she didn't need a *qilada* to destroy their captors.

He had not dared to say anything to Zahara for fear of being overheard, but he was dying to know what she was thinking. The soldiers watched all three of them with sharp eyes—though he could sense a bit of extra staring directed at Zahara. Most of the soldiers had been on campaign for a long time, and the sight of a beauty like her could do strange things.

"What do you know about Governor Pavel?" Zahara whispered.

"Well, he used to be part of Lord Dimitri's inner circle, but he went over to the Usurper just before Talas fell," Ekarath responded. "He's now the governor of Segova and head of the Elder Council."

"He's certainly a powerful mage," Zahara said with a nod.

"You don't know the half of it," Farban's voice cut in, and Ekarath looked over to see the man's eyes open for the first time that day. His voice sounded as weary and beaten as his body looked.

"The man's a natural when it comes to weaving the *draod*," Farban continued. "He lives and breathes power, which is the reason he went over to the Usurper. If it weren't for him, we could have held Talas."

"Wait, I haven't seen him since being captured," Zahara said, furrowing her brow.

"He rode on ahead," Ekarath responded. "I heard some of the guards talking about it—apparently the Usurper has already returned to the city, and he didn't want to be left behind. Now that the war's over, there's going to be a whole new sort of battle for him to wage."

Orders were shouted from the front of the column, and the cart shifted course into a field of green alfalfa. Soon, much of it would be flattened by the soldiers. The smell wafted into Ekarath's nose, and he wished the soft ground could be his bed instead of the stiff wood of the cart. He knew the only escape would be a brief moment to relieve himself under the watchful eye of a guard. Then it would be back into the cart for a dinner of water and hard bread.

As the cart came to a stop, the soldiers began to make their camp for the night. Horses were led away from the tents, free to graze on the soft grass. Within minutes, the sound and smell of cook fires filled the air, along with food far more edible than what the prisoners were going to be given. One of the soldiers, a man he had nick-named Stinky, came to open the back of their cart.

"Come on," he grunted. "One at a time. The girl first."

Stinky was large in every aspect—his height was greater than Ekarath's, and his heft was immense. While his strength was evident, there was a lot more than just muscle weighing down the soldier's frame. His leather armor was obviously made for a much smaller man, and the ties that held it together strained under the pressure.

His skin was a caramel color, marking him as a native of Yoruba on the eastern edge of Einar. A scraggly beard covered much of his face, and he scratched at it while eying Zahara.

The look in Stinky's eyes made Ekarath's blood boil as Zahara descended from the cart. He forced himself to sit still as the soldier accompanied Zahara for her bathroom break. Ekarath stiffened as Stinky caught up to Zahara, placing filthy hands on her shoulders.

"Look beautiful, if you're tired of hard bread, I'd be happy to set up a...*trade* for some better food," he growled, moving to get in front of her.

"No, thank you," Zahara responded. "I'm actually rather fond of stale bread. Ekarath might be open to a trade, though I'm not exactly sure he has what you're looking for."

"Oh, you think you're real funny," Stinky said, drawing even closer. "I prefer women who don't talk so much, but since we're all the way out here, you'll do just fine."

Stinky grabbed Zahara by the wrist and pulled her in close. Ekarath rose to his feet and struggled against his bindings as Zahara's fist slammed into Stinky's armored stomach. The soldier let out a soft grunt that was free of any real pain.

"You do have some fight in you," Stinky said as he yanked on Zahara's arm, trying to pull her further away from the camp. "I like that more than the talking."

Ekarath leapt off the wagon, landing hard on the flatted grass. Hands still bound, he sprinted across the field and lowered his shoulder into Stinky's hefty frame. His bones rattled as both he and the soldier collided with the ground.

At this range, the smell of Stinky's breath was overpowering—a mix of garlic and ale that had never been swept away by a toothbrush. Ekarath forced down the vomit as he used his bound hands like a club, slamming fists into the man's face. Before he could land a third hit, strong arms grabbed him from behind, peeling him off the overweight soldier.

Stinky leapt to his feet, blood pouring from his broken nose, but he quickly focused his gaze on Ekarath.

Without hesitation, the large man balled up his fist and swung it into his face. Stars swam across his vision, and the world spun.

"Ekarath!" Zahara shouted, her voice distant. Ekarath shook his head, readying himself for the second blow. Through the din, an authoritative shout lifted above the murmuring.

"What's going on here?" a man shouted, and Ekarath looked over to see the exact opposite of Stinky.

The newcomer wore the same black armor as the soldiers, though his shoulders were draped in an indigo cape marking him as an officer. The officer was tall and lean, and he moved with a lithe grace that spoke of hardened muscles underneath his armor. His face was sharp, and his square chin was clean-shaven, despite the difficulty of doing so while traveling. Eyes the color of steel flashed under his short, greying hair that spoke of a lifetime of military service. Stinky's eyes widened at the sight of his superior, though his cronies kept a tight hold over both Ekarath and Zahara.

"I asked what's going on, soldier," the officer again shouted, stepping toward the man. "Governor Pavel gave us explicit instructions to ensure the prisoners' survival."

"I know that, sir," Stinky growled in a deep voice, "but the boy crossed me."

"Oh, and so you thought an unauthorized beating was acceptable?" the officer said, bringing his face closer to Stinky's. "We all saw you trying to take liberties with the girl when you know the Governor wants her brought directly to the palace."

While that wasn't news, those words still sent a shock down Ekarath's spine. Stinky tried to stammer a response.

"Well, I—"

"Drop the boy," the officer said to the other soldiers, his eyes narrowing.

The soldiers complied, and Ekarath pulled himself free from their loosened grips. The officer's face scrunched up, and he turned his gaze to the soldiers and prisoners.

"Our prisoners—and most of Einar, for that matter—have been raised to believe that the Emperor is nothing but a tyrant and that all who follow him are vile beasts," the officer shouted, and Ekarath could tell the man's words were meant for more than the soldiers. "We all have to understand that the war is over—there are no victors and vanquished, only brothers and sisters who now have to pick up the pieces to build a better Einar. Lording ourselves about because our side won will only lead to further resistance, and resistance will only lead to an early death."

For a moment, Ekarath found himself wanting to believe in the officer's vision for the future. The war was an ever-present part of life. The idea that there might be some sort of peace appealed to his soul, but then he thought about the conversation with Lord Dimitri.

In the days, weeks, and months ahead, the fight to free Einar from tyranny will feel impossible. I'm going to be giving you a task, and I need to know that you're committed to keep going, no matter how difficult the path.

The Heir's words rang in his ears, and he knew there could be no peace—not for him, at least. Despite the words spoken by the Imperial officer, he had seen firsthand what evils the Usurper was capable of performing. Words of peace offered by victorious soldiers couldn't change that.

Most of the soldiers were looking down at their feet, but Stinky let out a sneer.

"Those are nice words coming from a coward who sat back while real men did all the fighting," Stinky shouted, turning to look at his comrades. "And now that the fighting's done, do we get to enjoy ourselves? No, we have to keep doing the hard work while others sit back and enjoy the spoils."

"Stand down, soldier," the officer snapped, rounding on Stinky. "One more word, and you'll make the rest of our journey in chains."

"I'm done taking orders," Stinky shouted back. In a flash, the soldier whipped his sword from its scabbard, slamming it into the officer's stomach. Those grey eyes bulged with shock and pain before his knees buckled. As Stinky withdrew his blade, the officer fell to the ground.

"I'm in charge now," Stinky shouted. "We kill the mage, I get the girl, and we're going to sell the boy once we get to Talas. It's time to show our enemies the price of fighting."

A cheer erupted from the soldiers, and Stinky turned on Zahara. The glint in his eyes and the smile on his face left no doubt as to his intentions. Before anyone could react, Ekarath leapt onto Stinky's back.

"Get off her," Ekarath shouted, slipping his bound wrists over the soldier's beefy neck. With all the strength left in him, he pulled, choking off the man's air supply.

As a gurgle escaped Stinky's throat, something hard crashed onto Ekarath's head. Once again, his vision blurred, but he kept his focus on the fight. Strong hands grabbed him by the shoulders, pulling him away from the gasping Stinky.

"Just for that," Stinky said, taking in huge gasps in between words, "I'm going to kill you first and make her watch."

Zahara screamed, and Ekarath's blood boiled. A jolt ran through his body, rattling the bones and stiffening his muscles. A low hum filled his ears, drowning out the shouts of soldiers. The smell of campfires and food disappeared, along with any feelings of hunger that had ravaged his body.

Grey clouds began to form in the sky, creating a swirl of various hues of black and grey, dancing like serpents preparing for a fight. A sheet of lightning flashed, and a roar of thunder cracked the sky. The shouts of joy from Imperial soldiers turned into screams.

A gust of wind snatched Ekarath from the ground, and his stomach spun as he flew a dozen feet into the air. Bits of dust and chunks of grass swirled around his vision as the wind lifted him higher. His eyes picked out glowing threads pulsing with an energy he had never imagined. Without giving any cerebral command, Ekarath's hands began to move, weaving those strands into a complex pattern.

From below, a single voice rose above everything else.

"Get the boy," Stinky shouted, and Ekarath could sense the soldiers' response.

In the corner of his eye, Ekarath could see some of the soldiers remove the small crossbows slung across their backs. With the rapidity of trained warriors, they launched the projectiles into the whirlwind. Yet Ekarath didn't flinch as the bolts screamed through the air before slamming into a solid barrier and falling back to the ground.

His hands finished a weave, and it hummed before turning into a bolt of lightning, striking the ground near the horses. Their screams filled the camp, hooves pounding into the dirt and tall grass, struggling against the ropes that kept them tethered.

"Kill him," Stinky shouted, though his command was nearly drowned out by the wind and the rising shouts from both soldiers and horses.

Ekarath's hands finished another weave, and a second bolt of lightning descended from the clouds, slamming into Stinky. The ground exploded, sending a shock wave through the camp, knocking soldiers to the ground. Where the beefy soldier had stood was now little more than a smoking crater.

A new shout rose above the noise—feminine, strong.

"For the Heirs and Einar!"

Ekarath's vision constricted, and he fell into a world of darkness and thunder.

Chapter 13

E karath opened his eyes to see the last star disappear as night gave way to the dawn. He was covered in a thick blanket and supported by a bed of straw atop the hard wood of a wagon. The sweet aroma of straw mixed with burning firewood and simmering porridge. Ekarath lifted his head over the wagon's side and looked over to see the stooped figure of Farban tending to a small pot hanging above a flame. At his side sat Zahara, who was nursing a small bowl of food.

His stomach growled at the smell, and Ekarath's muscles trembled as he forced himself up. He took in a deep breath of the cool morning air and climbed out of the wagon without realizing his feet were bare. He was dressed in the same clothing he'd worn out of the Atsada, which was now covered in straw and dirt.

"Oh, thank the Creator," Farban called from the fire, waving him over. "I was beginning to think you were never going to wake up."

While a thousand questions were buzzing through his mind, Ekarath decided that having some food in his howling stomach would have to come first. Without waiting for another response, he stumbled across the matted grass that separated him from the fire's warmth. Sitting on a rock near the flames were his boots and some fresh socks.

Zahara set her bowl down and pounced, wrapping her arms around his neck and nuzzling her face into his shoulder. An electric shock ran through Ekarath's body, and he struggled to catch his breath. He returned the embrace, his muscles finding strength as they squeezed Zahara.

"Don't kill the poor boy," Farban said with a laugh, and Zahara pulled away. "You must be starving."

Farban handed him a piece of soft, fresh bread. With trembling hands, Ekarath snatched it from the man and took a bite. After days of stale scraps, this practically melted in his mouth, and he closed his eyes to enjoy every second. The old hermit let out a laugh, bringing him back to the moment.

"What?" Ekarath asked, the words muffled by a mouth full of soft bread.

"It's just the first time I've seen anyone eat plain bread with so much gusto," Farban said.

"Well, it makes sense after being unconscious for so long," Zahara said.

"How long have I been out?" Ekarath asked, looking around. It was morning, so he had at least slept all night. From the look of things, they were camped on the edge of a small wood—nothing like the massive forest they have just left—in a field of green alfalfa.

"We've been traveling for two days," Farban replied with a shake of his head. "One more, and I was going to start getting really worried."

Ekarath mentally backpedaled at the words, and images of the dreams that had consumed him for two full days flashed in front of his mind's eye. He could remember the lightning streaming through his bones, threatening to break them. There were flashes of men flying through the air or being turned into little more than dust. The flashes were accompanied by screams and the smell of burning flesh. Everything was foggy, but he could remember enough to haunt his dreams for decades to come.

"What...what could have possibly done that to me?" Ekarath asked.

"How much do you remember?" Farban asked in response.

"I remember...enough."

"I think we have some explaining to do," Farban said, gesturing for Ekarath to take a seat. "You both might want to sit down. I haven't given Zahara a full explanation yet, though I'm sure she's figured out a lot of it."

"It will be good to see if we've come to the same conclusions," Zahara said, taking a seat at Ekarath's side.

Ekarath noticed her ear once again held the *qilada*. Whatever he had done, it must have been enough to destroy or run off all their guards, giving Zahara and Farban time to raid the wagon that had held their ancient relics.

"Well, to be blunt, I believe there was a mistake when Dimitri declared a successor," Farban began. "Instead of choosing Zahara—the accomplished, ambitious mage—he somehow passed on his powers to Ekarath."

"In short, you're now the Heir of Segova," Zahara said, finishing the old hermit's thought.

"That...that's impossible," Ekarath stammered, and he could feel the blood drain from his face. His vision blurred, and the world began to spin.

"You summoned a lightning storm that killed all our captors in less than a few minutes," Zahara said, placing a hand on his knee and peering into his eyes.

"You didn't so much use the *draod* as much as it used you."

The memories grew sharper in his mind, their color growing more vibrant. The smell of burning flesh filled his nostrils, and the cries of terror flooded his soul.

"But I've never even held a *qilada*, let alone used the *draod*," Ekarath said, shaking his head. "The letter from Lord Dimitri, it was addressed to Zahara, not me. It's simply not possible. I'm a warrior, not a mage."

"I wish you could have seen yourself—your eyes glowed like molten gold, and your hair turned into a brilliant white," Zahara said. "A whirlwind snatched you up into the air, and for a moment, I thought you were going to be taken away from us. I've never experienced anything like it in my entire life, and I've been weaving the *draod* since before I could talk."

"Zahara, this is supposed to be *you*," Ekarath stammered, barely able to get the words out. Her lips pursed, and she looked away.

"I know," she said without looking up. "But we have to live with what is, not what should have been. Otherwise, we could spend our entire lives in paralysis."

Ekarath could tell from the tone of her voice that she only half-believed the words. She wouldn't admit—even to herself—that she was upset, but her soul was obviously in turmoil. For a time, she had been prepared to take the weight of the world on her shoulders. He had prepared himself to defend her to his dying breath. Now, everything was upside down.

"I know this is a lot to take in," Farban said, his voice filled with reticence, "and I want to give you time to absorb it. However, there are a number of things we need to discuss."

Blinking hard, Ekarath forced himself to look up at the spymaster.

"How do we really know I'm the Heir of Segova?" Ekarath asked. "What if it was just a weird coincidence?"

Farban laughed in response, and Ekarath lifted his hands to study the power they supposedly held. Beyond the exhaustion, he felt no different than he always had. There was no electric hum running through his veins, no extra strength in his muscles. He felt like Ekarath, and nothing else.

The Heirs were semi-divine beings, second only to the Creator. Lord Dimitri had held an aura of wisdom and omnipotence like nobody else. There was simply no way that a trapper from northern Segova could join such an illustrious group.

"Heirs have a connection to the *draod* that a mage can only dream of," Farban began, his hands rubbing across his thick beard. "Beyond the ability to command the Power of Creation without the need for a *qilada*, they can see weaves and tapestries woven by others."

Farban pulled out a golden ring and slipped it onto his finger. The old hermit closed his eyes, and a low hum filled the air. Ekarath's heart nearly stopped as his eyes took in the sight of milky white threads appearing from thin air. Farban's fingers moved quickly as they wove the power into a complex spell that made Ekarath's head spin. It took several minutes, but he tied the final knot and opened his eyes.

"Did you see all that?" Farban asked.

"I saw you weave a spell," Ekarath whispered, the realization hitting home as the words sounded in his ears. "Though I have no idea what it does."

"We'll get to that later," Farban said, shaking his head. "The important thing is that you can see the tapestry. Beyond the Heirs, nobody can see weaves created by someone else."

Ekarath examined the complex pattern of milky threads. There was a pulse to them, almost as if the spell itself were alive. At one end, his eyes found a small knot. Without fully understanding, his mind reached out and tugged on the loose strand.

The knot came undone. The pattern began to unravel, as if the threads were just waiting for Ekarath to set them free. The hum of power grew louder in his ears until the entire tapestry disappeared, leaving no trace that it had ever existed.

"Well, that was unexpected," Farban said, blinking hard.

"What?" Zahara interjected. "What happened?"

"Ekarath...he untied my finishing knot," Farban said, his words coming out at a glacial pace as if he had forgotten how to speak.

"Is that not okay?" Ekarath asked, looking from Zahara to Farban. Both sets of eyes were wide, and even Zahara's dark skin looked a little pale.

"I just didn't know an Heir could do that," Farban replied, clearing his throat and shaking his head. "I always believed that a tapestry could only be undone by its creator."

"As strange as it is, there's no doubt that you are the Heir of Segova," Zahara said, her voice cracking as she spoke. "If your thunderstorm wasn't enough, this proves that the Heirs are not gone. And as long as there is an Heir, hope is not lost."

Silence settled in as those words hung in the air. Ekarath wanted to say the obvious—that there was little hope if the Heir of Segova couldn't do what was required. If Lord Dimitri was unable to defeat the Usurper, what hope did Ekarath have?

"How does this end?" Ekarath asked, breaking the silence.

"You defeat the Usurper," Farban replied. "Or you die, and the world is placed under the yoke of a tyrant."

Those words slammed into Ekarath's stomach with as much force as the revelation that he was an Heir, and he wanted to retch. Life had always been on the verge of ending, from starvation, illness, or war. Yet it had always been his own life at risk—the idea that all Einar turned on his actions sent a shiver up and down his spine.

"Wow, thanks for that," Zahara said, casting a glare at the spymaster before turning back to Ekarath. "Look, we're going to teach you. The Usurper thinks he's won, that the war is over. He won't be looking for the Heir of Segova, because he thinks the power's been extinguished. In a few years, you'll be ready to take him down."

"And as we all saw, the *draod* has a way of protecting a new Heir until proper training takes hold," Farban responded. "Before Lord Dimitri—and all the other Heirs, I guess—knew how to fully weave the *draod*, there were times that the power had to step in."

Ekarath didn't respond as he let the words process. Was it possible that he could confront the Usurper on his own, without waiting years to learn? Would the *draod* kick in and do something a fully trained Heir couldn't?

"I know that look," Zahara said, snapping him from those thoughts. "You're thinking of doing something foolish."

"I wouldn't test the Power of Creation again," Farban cut in, a smile on his face. "It can be a fickle servant. It protected you once, but it won't stop a fool from being cut down. The *draod* would be happier handing the power of an Heir on to another rather than trying to protect someone with no sense of self-preservation."

"Wait, what did you say about handing the power over to another?" Ekarath asked. "Could we do that? Hand it over to Zahara?"

Both Farban and Zahara took a moment to respond. Ekarath sat waiting, the silence humming in his ears.

"I don't think that's the best option," Farban finally said. "You could make her your successor, but the only way to pass it on is to...well, die."

"There has to be a way," Ekarath said. "The Heirs are full of secrets. You didn't even know that they could unravel spells. I—"

"New topic," Zahara said, cutting him off with a glare. "What do we do next? We can't hide in this grove forever, and I don't think your subterranean fortress will be safe."

"You're right," Farban said. "And I've been thinking about that. Ever since the retreat to the Atsada, I've been in charge of the guerilla war. Most of our leaders are actually located in the very heart of Talas, just blocks away from the palace. I think it's best that we join them there."

"You can't possibly be serious," Zahara shot back before Ekarath could say anything. "The Imperial City is the last place we should hide the only hope for Einar."

"I'm deadly serious," Farban responded. "Where is the last place the Usurper would look for an Heir? If he does somehow discover what Lord Dimitri did, he would comb the entirety of his empire. But his own home? That would be unthinkable."

Ekarath had to admit the old man made a good point. Still, the idea of entering any large city made his stomach churn. Entering the largest city in all Einar? That felt suffocating.

"Not to mention that we'll need allies," Farban continued. "And I have plenty in Talas, along with the resources to properly train Ekarath and keep an eye on current events. It wouldn't do us any good to emerge from hiding in a few years only to discover that the Usurper's done something crazy like exterminating everyone."

Ekarath looked at Zahara, but she sat with lips pursed, evaluating the spymaster's arguments. He certainly didn't have anything to counter Farban's points.

"I don't love the idea of entering Talas," Ekarath finally said, forming the words as slowly as he could. "But I do think Farban is right. Zahara, what do you think?"

"I think it's crazy," she said, shaking her head. "But I can't think of anything better."

"Then it's settled," Farban said, jumping to his feet. "Let's pack up camp—assuming we don't get attacked by bandits or another Imperial patrol, we can be at the city gates in just a few days."

"Just a few days ago, I felt ready to become a bodyguard to Heir Dimitri," Ekarath said, rising to his feet. "Hard to believe I'm now the Heir who needs protection."

"For now, let's just concentrate on getting to the city," Farban said. "One thing at a time."

Chapter 14

Mahzun rolled his shoulders, unable to get comfortable—he wasn't sure if it was his wool suit, the wooden chair, or the fact that he was surrounded by hundreds of aristocrats. Music from a thirty-piece orchestra filled a ballroom from the marble floor to the gilded ceilings three stories high. Marble statues lined the walls, a mixture of historical figures and creatures of the Wilds.

Letting out a small growl, Mahzun tugged at his clothing. The jacket was darker than obsidian, and intricate patterns were embroidered with gold on the sleeves and collar. While the jacket and pants had been tailored just for him, the men in Talas liked their clothing far too tight. Mahzun's shirt of white linen wasn't uncomfortable, but the coat was trying to squeeze the life out of him. Meanwhile, the pants bunched, and he was constantly readjusting.

"You really should relax," Lorna whispered at his side. "We are at a party, after all."

Along with the music, the scent of a dozen varieties of food and perfume filled the air. The plate in front of him was crafted from pure gold, and it held a roast pheasant stuffed with fruits and spices. The dead bird sat untouched while the wine in Mahzun's goblet was gone, and he wanted more. He couldn't spot the difference between an excellent vintage and tavern swill—he just knew the dusty beverage was the only way he could survive this display of insanity.

"Are parties in Talas a time to relax?" Mahzun responded in a whisper. "I always thought of them as a time to scheme or begin an affair."

Lorna scowled and looked around to see if anybody had heard, but there wasn't a single person within earshot. At her side, the *namura* hissed at Mahzun. While most aristocrats with a soul-bound didn't bring it with them to social events, Lorna's was an exception. Even though her identity as his sister was a little-known secret, she was the Emperor's steward. That position meant she needed constant protection from a trustworthy source—nothing was better than a lion-sized cat bound to Lorna's soul by the *draod*. Fortunately, there was nobody else at their table to threaten Lorna or her *namura*.

Their table was large enough to seat a dozen guests with ease, and it felt comically empty with only Mahzun, Lorna, and the cat. Their host had intentionally placed the Emperor on a raised balcony at the far end of the ballroom with a set of stairs between him and the ballroom floor. He knew this was supposedly meant to be the place of honor, but to Mahzun, it just meant he had to sit up straight. More than anything else, Mahzun felt like he was on display.

On the floor below, couples danced to the music with intricate footwork. Mahzun had never taken the time to enjoy the high arts, but he did enjoy the music filling the room. It was too bad most of the guests weren't content to merely sit and enjoy.

The women wore dresses that were so impractical, he would have thought them to be a form of torture. The men wore suits of grey and black—very little to distinguish one from the other. Most looked similar to Mahzun's, and he began to wonder how much he could influence the city's fashion now that he would be attending more functions like this.

"You could at least try to hide your boredom," Lorna said. "People may not be able to hear your complaints, but everyone can see you're miserable."

"I already hate being here," Mahzun replied. "There must be some reason for me to go back on campaign—a pocket of stubborn rebels, perhaps?"

"It's only been a few days," Lorna replied with a chuckle. "There can't always be enemies for you to conquer. We both knew the war would either end in boredom or death. Would you have preferred the latter?"

"At this point, I'm beginning to wonder. Maybe the Heirs were just bored of this life, and they allowed me to win. I didn't defeat our old oppressors—I mercy-killed them."

"You're one of the few people in this entire building who isn't having a good time," Lorna said, gesturing to the hundreds of aristocrats below. "Maybe if you tried, you could enjoy yourself. I'm sure there are dozens of young girls down there who would be thrilled to dance with the Emperor."

Mahzun directed his gaze again to the ballroom floor. Except for the space set aside for dancing, the rest of the grand hall was filled round tables seating a half-dozen aristocrats each. Most were engaged in conversation, and he could see more than a few quick glances in his direction.

"We both know these people barely tolerate me," Mahzun said, shaking his head. "Besides, I'm a full decade older than any of those pretty, young things down there."

"That has never stopped the aristocracy before," Lorna replied. "Older men often take younger wives. They need scions to take their name and place. In fact, that was going to be one of the first things on your list, remember? You need to have at least one strapping youngling to take the throne."

"I haven't forgotten about that," Mahzun replied before letting out a deep breath. "I was just hoping you could give me some time to get used to things. It's not as if romance has ever been at the top of my list."

"I don't think it's even been on your list," Lorna shot back before placing another small bite into her mouth.

"And I would appreciate it if you could keep it off my list for a little while longer."

"You have weeks, not months of bachelor life ahead of you," Lorna said with a smile. "And I've already arranged for a private dance instructor—I'm expecting you to dance at the next ball."

Her eyes shifted back to the ballroom and that smile disappeared. Mahzun turned to see what had distracted his sister, and his own smile fled.

A middle-aged aristocrat was climbing the steps to their balcony—the first to do so. His head was shaved bald, and he wore a suit of dazzling white and red. On his finger sat a ring of gold—obviously a *qilada*, yet it was the smile on his face that made Mahzun most uncomfortable.

"My dear Emperor," the man said as he reached the top of the steps. He gave a rather short bow before taking a seat at one of the empty chairs facing Mahzun. "I do hope everything is to Your Majesty's liking."

"You throw a wonderful party, Lord Pavel," Mahzun replied.

Hakan Pavel was Governor of Segova and head of the Elder Council, though he was two-thirds the age of its average member. Mahzun had only met the man a few times, but his assistance had been instrumental in the liberation of Talas just a year earlier. While Mahzun was grateful for the help, there was something about the smiling face that reminded him of a weasel, ready to switch sides at the first opportunity.

"It's a pleasure to host Your Majesty and to celebrate our victory," Pavel said. "And I look forward to working with you as we turn the Empire's attention away from war and toward rebuilding."

"I have big plans," Mahzun replied, the knot in his stomach loosening at the words. "For Talas, Segova, and all of Einar."

"That is exactly what I like to hear," Pavel said, and he hesitated before continuing. "Could I beg an audience with Your Majesty? There are a few items of urgency I would like to discuss."

"I will check His Majesty's schedule when we return to the palace," Lorna said before Mahzun could respond. "He has only just returned, and the list of items requiring his attention has grown long. Expect a messenger later tonight."

"I was rather hoping we could have just a few minutes alone," Pavel said, shifting his gaze to Lorna. "After all, balls are a time for such things—unless our dear Emperor would prefer to enter the dance floor."

Mahzun held in a laugh at the look on Lorna's face.

"How dare you—"

"No, it's fine," Mahzun said, cutting off his sister's words. "I'm more than happy to give our distinguished host a few minutes of my time."

That smile flashed wider, and the man let out a breath before beginning.

"Nobody is more enthusiastic about the fall of the Heirs than I," Pavel began as his eyes focused in on

Mahzun's. "There is no doubt Einar will thrive under your leadership, and I very much—"

"If I wanted to dance, I'd be out there," Mahzun growled. Pavel's smile wavered before returning in force.

"I do so love the simplicity of a warrior. Well, to be blunt, I've been wanting to discuss your plans to destroy the Shajarat."

"On the morning of our victory celebrations, I will use the Eternal Blade to destroy it," Mahzun said. "What else is there to discuss?"

"I believe our dear host is trying to say he disagrees with your plan," Lorna cut in. "You'll need to learn that when a nobleman wants to 'discuss' an issue, it's because he holds a contrary view."

"I have been forced to rely on reports from the Atsada," Pavel continued, "as I was not present when Your Majesty called on the power of the Blade. However, I see your face—some may not notice a difference after all these years, but I know the toll heaped upon your body each time you to use the Blade."

"Are you honestly concerned about my health?" Mahzun scoffed. If there was one thing he had learned about the nobility—especially the members of the Elder Council—it was that their self-interest knew no bounds. If Lord Pavel was indeed worried about Mahzun, it could never be for altruistic reasons.

"With the Heirs gone, I grow ill at the thought of your untimely demise," Pavel replied in a hoarse whisper. "Without your iron will, I worry that Einar will shatter into a thousand pieces. The war will have been for nothing if our great leader dies before cementing his legacy."

"I've destroyed the seven Heirs," Mahzun growled. "I've spent ten years on campaign. Do you really expect a giant tree to pose a problem?"

"The Shajarat is not some overgrown piece of flora," Pavel said. "Read the histories—in the past three thousand years, there have been at least a dozen documented attempts to destroy that tree. Two hundred years ago, a group of magi took the city in a coup attempt. Over thirty of them died launching a wave of Destruction spells, and there wasn't even a scratch on the bark."

"I'm no simple mage," Mahzun said, folding his arms and leaning back in his chair.

"In the year 732, the Heir of Tagus tried to destroy the tree. His powers rebounded so hard that the body was never found."

"None of them had the Blade."

"The Blade is destroying you—can't you see that? I fear that using it to destroy a small kitten would be enough to damage you beyond repair. I can't sit by and watch you—"

"That's enough," Mahzun said, but Pavel didn't stop.

"—destroy what is left of my home. If you fall, everything that's been built will—"

"I said, *that's enough*," Mahzun shouted, leaping to his feet.

The words echoed throughout the ball, and both the orchestra and hum of conversation grew silent. Hakan Pavel's face transformed into a tight scowl instead of the forced smile, and there was a fire in those eyes. Mahzun cleared his throat.

"You will speak no more of this," Mahzun growled, trying to ignore the hundreds of gazes fixed on him. Without another word, he bounded down the stairs. Lorna scurried after him, but Mahzun refused to slow, even for her. His polished black shoes cracked with each step on the marble as he crossed the silent ballroom before finally reaching the exit.

He stopped at the top of the mansion's outer staircase and took in a breath of the cool night air as he scanned the host of awaiting coaches and drivers. His eyes found the only carriage with the Imperial seal on its doors—a griffin holding the Eternal Blade. Lorna's footsteps were pounding behind him as he sped off toward the waiting vehicle.

The driver was waiting with the professionalism expected of an Imperial servant, but his eyes grew wide as the Emperor approached. Before the servile being could descend from his perch to open the coach door, Mahzun leapt into the waiting vehicle.

Lord Dimitri sat in the opposite seat, his silent gaze tearing into Mahzun more than the hundreds of noble eyes had. Those eyes were dead, emotionless, and glassy. Yet there was something in them that made Mahzun feel open and ready to be judged.

"Do you think I should have handled that better, old man?" Mahzun shouted at the apparition. As always, Lord Dimitri failed to respond.

The door opened, and Lorna began climbing in without a word, followed by Sasha. She took a seat at Mahzun's side and placed a hand on his knee while the large cat settled into its place on the floor. A whip cracked outside, and the carriage took off with a lurch. Mahzun couldn't tear his eyes away from Lord Dimitri as the mansion grounds passed by in his periphery.

On the floor, Sasha growled at Mahzun, emulating the emotions that must be swirling through Lorna's soul. The connection between a mage and a soul-bound was so strange, as if stronger than the spell itself.

The carriage took them through the city streets, and after a few blocks, Mahzun finally unlocked his eyes from Dimitri's and rested his head against the window. Streetlamps gave off enough of a glow for him to see, even as the moon was covered by clouds.

"I'm never going to find peace, am I?" Mahzun finally said without turning to look at his sister or Dimitri's apparition.

He could feel his sister tense up at the words, even without looking.

"Not until you actually start looking for it," Lorna replied.

Mahzun gritted his teeth and turned to look at her. Lorna's skin was a full shade paler than usual, and her eyes were wide. Bags had formed underneath those beautiful orbs and a few wrinkles were making their way onto her face—those had been formed in his service. She had not suffered in the same way he had, but she had suffered. There was no reason to take out his anger on such a beloved and faithful friend.

"I'm sorry," Mahzun replied with a deep sigh. "It's just that...well, Lord Pavel may be correct. It doesn't take a seer to know what the Blade has done to me, and I'm not exactly a young man anymore."

"The truth can be more painful than a thousand blows."

"I understand that using the Blade again could do more damage," Mahzun said, trying to force his eyes to remain on Lorna, even as they were constantly drawn to Lord Dimitri. "But it's a risk that I have to take."

Lorna studied him for a moment, also directing her gaze to the other side of the carriage. He knew she wouldn't see anything, and the furrow in her brow and scowl made sense. It was obvious to everyone—Mahzun included—that his mind was fraying.

"Why must you take this risk?" Lorna asked, leaning in and placing a hand to Mahzun's scarred cheek. "I understand the Shajarat is a symbol of the old world. It reminds you and everyone else of the Heirs, but we could transform that over time. Symbols can be changed, co-opted. How can destroying a symbol possibly feel worth risking everything you have worked so hard to accomplish?"

"Because I believe it's more than just a symbol," Mahzun said, turning back to look out the window. The carriage was already approaching the Mount of Creation, and he could see the giant tree dominating the night sky. "It's the *draod*."

"The *draod* isn't a single thing," Lorna replied as if she were addressing a school child. "It's a power that's everywhere and nowhere. It fills the world. Saying one thing is the *draod* is like saying—"

"We've been taught that for so long that it's supposed to be common knowledge," Mahzun said. "But what if that's just a story? Pavel spoke of other attempts to destroy the Shajarat in an attempt to dissuade me, but it only validates my belief. Others must have known the truth; otherwise, what would be the point in destroying the tree?"

"Let's suppose you're not crazy, and the Shajarat is the source of all power and energy," Lorna said, the words coming out slowly as she was obviously trying to form the question. "Would its destruction be a good thing?"

"You've been in Talas for a year now," Mahzun replied, turning away from the tree to look back at his sister. "How many elite families are there?"

"Between ten and thirty, depending on your definition of 'elite.'"

"And what makes that tiny minority of the city better than everyone else? Is it their intelligence? Their wit?"

"Generational wealth has built up for hundreds or even thousands of years. You would have to take down the entire economic system of Einar to really stop that from happening."

"But what was it that gave them that leg up? What is the single thing that could vault a peasant into the highest rungs of society?"

"A *qilada*, of course," Lorna said, and she stopped as the word hung in the air.

"Exactly," Mahzun said. "The ability to use the *draod* is what separates the wealthy from everyone else. We obsess over these tiny relics from the First Heirs because they give access to unspeakable power. Imagine if that power was no longer accessible...or if it didn't exist at all."

"You're talking about removing the very foundation of our society," Lorna replied.

"I've been doing that for years. Killing the Heirs has been my obsession, but they were just part of the problem."

"So, if you really believe the Shajarat is the source of the *draod*, why didn't you destroy it years ago? It would have made the Heirs powerless, and we could have avoided a decade of bloodshed."

"There's a reason those other attempts to destroy the tree failed so spectacularly," Mahzun said, thinking back to the ancient texts he had read.

"And you've been able to figure out where they went wrong?"

"I think so," Mahzun said. "It's difficult to tell when reading the old tongues, but it appears the Shajarat and the Heirs are linked. The Heirs draw their power from the tree, and those powers in turn protect it. Once the Heirs are gone, however..."

"So are the protections," Lorna said, finishing his thought. For the first time, she wasn't looking at him like a petulant child. "How sure about this are you?"

"As sure as I've ever been about anything. I know that using the Blade will drain me yet again, and I have no idea how much I have left to give. But if I can remove the force that divides my people into artificial classes, I will gladly make any sacrifice."

"Maybe the people are right about you," Lorna said as a broad grin took over her entire face. "You really are mad."

Chapter 15

Zahara swayed in her saddle, her eyes trying to adjust to the grey light of dawn. While the trio had been on the road all night, the sun was just beginning to rise. After yet another full night of riding, Zahara's aching bones were ready to find a secluded grove for a day's rest.

Ahead, Farban slowed his mount and came to Zahara's side. The old hermit was smiling.

"It's beautiful, isn't it?" Farban whispered, pointing toward the horizon.

"What's beautiful?" Zahara asked, squinting against the sunlight.

"Oh, right—you probably won't be able to see it without a spell," Farban said.

Zahara focused, pulling on threads of Restoration and crafting them into a small tapestry. She slapped the spell over her eyes and looked eastward. A gasp leapt from her throat as her enhanced eyes took in the outline of branches reaching into the sky.

"The Shajarat," Zahara whispered, and Farban nodded at her side.

The tree grew hundreds of feet above any other structure, its branches growing outward enough to shade the Mount of Creation and massive portions of the city center.

"When we get closer, you'll see that the greatest paintings can't do it justice," Farban replied as Ekarath came up on Zahara's left.

"I wonder if the city will be as beautiful as it used to be," Ekarath said. "I'll admit that I'm looking forward to seeing the Shajarat again with my own eyes."

"If you'd like to stop, I could try teaching you the spell so you don't have to wait," Zahara said without taking her eyes off the Shajarat. "Though I'll warn you that it took me weeks to master."

"We can start going over it tonight," Farban responded. "It's best not to stop too much. I'd like to make it to the city as soon as possible. I'm sure news of the Atsada's fall is everywhere, and I don't want too many of our people giving up hope."

"Speaking of hope," Ekarath began, his voice catching in his throat. "I was wanting to talk about how we're going to tell people who...or what...I am."

"What do you mean?" Zahara asked.

"Well, I was thinking that if people know the Heir of Segova is just some teenage boy who doesn't even know how to do a single weave, they might be a little...disheartened."

"More disheartened than thinking all the Heirs are gone?" Farban asked with a chuckle. "I think you're underestimating yourself. You certainly look the part of a leader. I mean, just look at that jaw of yours."

"Farban does have a point," Zahara said. "For a lot of people, the magic of the Heirs isn't as important as their leadership. You may not know the *draod*, but you're a part of the *Hundiin*—and you're certainly not some little boy. You risked your life to save a dozen of your comrades."

Not to mention you're incredibly handsome, Zahara thought, but she didn't voice those words aloud. And she agreed with Farban about the jaw.

"Still, I can't help but think that during a time like this, when we're facing such a threat, that well...maybe we should tell everyone that Zahara is the Heir?"

"That's preposterous," Zahara shouted before bringing her voice lower. "I mean—I couldn't fool people like that. Besides, they would see my *qilada* and know that I still need it to use the *draod*."

"Listen—Dimitri meant for you to be the Heir, not me. There's got to be a way to make that a reality, some sort of weave powerful enough to take my powers and give them to you. So, in a way, we wouldn't really be lying. It's just that we need to figure out how to fulfill Lord Dimitri's wishes."

"Ekarath, I really don't think—"

"I'm a soldier, not a mage," Ekarath said, his gaze switching back and forth between her and Farban. "On top of that, Zahara can beat me in a physical contest without her magic, which makes her my superior not only in weaving the *draod* but in basic combat. There's absolutely no reason I should be the Heir of Segova. None."

Zahara couldn't find the words after Ekarath finished. Could she tell him the truth? That she used the *draod* in their physical contests because she was a sore loser? She looked down at her saddle, feeling the sway of her horse's gait.

There was also the fact that Ekarath was right. She really was supposed to be the Heir, and she couldn't understand what had gone wrong. Even after a few days to process the situation, the thought that Ekarath had all that power coursing through his veins sat in her stomach like a bitter pill.

"Except for the fact that *you* are the Heir of Segova," Farban said, his grisly voice cutting through the icy silence. "Did you know that Dimitri wasn't supposed to be the Heir, either?"

"What?" Ekarath asked in a shout. "That doesn't make any sense."

"If an Heir dies without a successor, the power goes to a newborn baby," Farban began. "The method of how the *draod* chooses that baby could keep philosophers arguing for weeks, so I won't go into it much. When Lord Paulus died, his successor had been dead for a week—he just didn't know. It took his magi three years to track down Dimitri, born to a fisherman and his wife. He didn't earn the title; it was given to him just as it was to you.

"So yes, maybe Zahara was supposed to be the Heir, but that's in the past. The fact is that you have the responsibility of leading Segova through the most turbulent chapter of its history. You can either step up and be the man we need you to be or you can feel sorry for yourself and get us all killed."

Zahara could feel the power of Farban's words, and she looked over to Ekarath. His gaze was directed at the horizon. She couldn't quite read his face, but she reached out her hand and grabbed his. He returned her squeeze and turned to her with a smile that looked more like a grimace.

"I will do whatever it takes," Ekarath said. "When we stop for the day, teach me...something, anything. The most basic weave you know. If Dimitri could do it, then so can I. I'm going to be the Heir we all need."

***

The trio sat around a small cooking fire, and Ekarath could feel the warmth of the rabbit stew filling his belly. It was amazing what a few days of hard bread and stale water did for the appreciation of real food. There was nothing particularly delicate about the chunks of rabbit, potatoes, and carrots, but every bite was a reminder of no longer being a prisoner.

"Okay, are you ready for your first lesson?" Zahara asked, turning to look at Ekarath.

"Ready as I'll ever be," Ekarath said with a shrug. "Where do we start?"

"Well, I think we should start with some of the basics. Farban, go ahead and chime in if you think I'm sending Ekarath in the wrong direction."

"Will do," Farban responded from the other side of the fire, though he already had a book open. Ekarath shook his head with a smile—the old hermit really wasn't used to dealing with people, at least not *young* people.

"Okay, so there are three basic types of power you can pull from the *draod*—Destruction, Illusion, and Restoration. Threads of Destruction are the thickest and easiest to deal with. Illusion is a bit trickier, and Restoration will take the most practice."

"Got it," Ekarath said. "I think I've been feeling the *draod* more since...well, you know."

"That's a good place to start," Zahara said. "Now, take a second to close your eyes and feel that power, feel the energy. Try to pull some threads into the mortal plane and describe what they feel like."

Ekarath let out a deep breath and tried to focus. His ears picked up the soft song of a robin, the chirping of some unknown insect. His mind went to the *sahali* that had almost killed them.

No, focus.

He felt for the buzzing energy of the *draod*, the feeling that had been in the back of his mind since becoming the Heir of Segova. It was like a vast ocean of power. One second it threatened to break through and crush him. The next, it was shy and elusive.

He moved his fingers, trying to summon that energy into useful threads. His heart skipped a beat as a single, hair-like tendril appeared. Zahara had told him it would be thick, but it was not much thicker than a hair. It felt warm, ready to destroy.

"I...I did something," Ekarath whispered, and he opened his eyes to see Zahara perk up. In that moment, the thread disappeared. "But now I lost it."

"Still, that's impressive," Zahara responded with a shake of her head. "My mother spent weeks working with me before I could even feel the *draod*, let alone actually pull in a thread."

"So, um...what do I do next?"

"Let's try to pull on some more threads. Then, if you can, let's do a weave," Zahara said, grabbing a stick. "This is one of the first I ever learned."

She began drawing a circle into the dirt. Within the circle, she drew a single triangle.

"This will create a flame," Zahara said. "If you were to make the circle with several threads, it would make the fire bigger. If you form the triangle with more thread, it will make the flame shoot further and faster. When you finish with a small knot, the weave will be done. Make sense?"

"I think so," Ekarath responded, scrutinizing the drawing. "So, for now, I'll just do one pass—no need to alert the entire countryside."

"Good idea. Now, take a moment to close your eyes again. Feel for those threads of Destruction and weave them into this pattern. And remember to be patient with yourself. Nobody's expecting you to get it on your first—or even your hundredth—try."

Ekarath closed his eyes and tried to, once again, clear his mind. This time, the threads poured out of the vast ocean, as if they were excited to be put to use. The more he pulled, the more the threads responded.

He focused on a single thread and formed it into a circle. Within, he wove the same triangle Zahara had drawn into the dirt. His body began to tremble with anticipation as he finished off the weave with a simple knot.

A fireball erupted from his hands, the force knocking him onto his back. The flame—well beyond the size of the Usurper's griffin—soared into the morning sky like a second sun.

As the flame faded, Ekarath's bones hummed with energy. He blinked hard, his vision nothing but a blur after the sudden burst of light. After a few seconds of blinking and rubbing his eyes, he looked over to see Zahara and Farban staring at him, mouths open.

"Did I do something wrong?" Ekarath asked, pulling himself upright and checking for any wounds.

"Not at all," Zahara said with a laugh. "That was...absolutely amazing."

"I think our boy will make a fine Heir, after all," Farban said, laughter in his voice.

"But that might be enough for today," Zahara said. "Like you said, we don't want to draw too much attention to ourselves; burning down the entire forest would certainly do that."

Chapter 16

E karath hadn't seen Talas since it had fallen to the Usurper. As a trapper in the forest, he never really needed to make visits to the metropolis, but it was sometimes helpful to sell items at their highest price directly to the nobility. He often used merchants passing through the forest or its surrounding villages to avoid the travel, but he had to admit that there was something intoxicating about the city.

He didn't know if it was the sheer amount of people packed into such a small space. Perhaps it was the array of markets that sold fruits and spices from all corners of Einar, including the Wilds. All he knew was that a trip to Talas was a treat well worth the journey.

Yet as he approached the city walls, that feeling was gone. The sun was beginning to set, casting an array of oranges and pinks on the white granite that formed the once-majestic walls of Talas. Formed over three thousand years ago by the First Heirs, those walls had stood strong, protecting the city's inhabitants.

Now, they showed signs of damage. Large chunks had been taken out from the Usurper's trebuchets. Some sections even sat in rubble, making the city gate feel rather pointless.

There was little traffic flowing into the city at this time of evening, though a steady stream of farmers, trappers, and peddlers were leaving the city after a day spent selling their wares in the markets. Most looked down, their shoulders hunched with a sense of exhaustion. Ekarath couldn't tell if it was just the physical exertion from the work or if news of the Atsada's fall had reached the city.

Ahead, Farban rode with a straight back, his resolution evident from the way he kept his gaze forward. Ekarath looked back to see Zahara doing the same—neither looked ready to give up. Ekarath stiffened his posture, trying to convince himself that all was not lost.

He felt again for the *draod*, its energy buzzing all around him. While he had been able to create a massive flame, his abilities still felt so limited. He could see the weaves placed on the walls—ancient and complex. There was no way he could ever replicate something so delicate.

The city's main gate was drawing near, and he could see the evidence of its destruction a year prior. While the portcullis had been repaired so that it could open and close, very little effort had been expended to fix the chunks of granite that had been knocked free.

A small contingent of the city guard stood at attention. For a moment, he wondered at their colorful uniforms that contrasted so sharply with the black of the Horde. However, the men looked tired, disinterested in the task of actually guarding the city.

Ekarath realized these men had stayed behind for what the Usurper saw as his greatest moment—they would certainly not be considered elite warriors. They might also be more loyal to the city than to the Usurper. Whether through ineptitude or apathy, nobody stopped the trio as they entered the city gate, and

Ekarath had to stop himself from letting out a deep breath as they passed the men.

The main street of Talas was wide, paved with white cobblestones infused with the *draod* to keep them pristine. With his new sight for such things, Ekarath could see the dizzying array of weaves put into place to protect the street from wear and tear. It sent a wave of nausea through him, and he forced his eyes to focus less on the tapestries.

So many complex patterns, he thought to himself. He hadn't expected the city to be so full of magic.

A park separated the wide road, creating a green space for pedestrians. Trees, shrubs, and fountains were intersected by walking paths, and even in the evening, there was a significant number of civilians meandering through the beauty.

Three-story buildings stood on both sides of the street. The bottom floors were generally made up of stores and restaurants, while the upper floors had the look of homes and offices. For a moment, Ekarath could almost imagine the city as it once was, or at least close to it.

As they passed a few blocks, the first of several large plazas met his gaze. Before falling to the Usurper, the vast square of cobblestone had been filled with vendor stalls selling pastries, produce, and hand-crafted treasures. Musicians had played for the crowds for spare coins, filling the air with a sense of magic that had nothing to do with the *draod*.

Now, a few dozen farmers were packing up shop with blank stares on their faces. The few customers still around were heading home, most looking over their shoulders as if they were afraid of being followed. The sun was setting, a soft twilight filling the air.

"Scouting reports said that the city's not the same," Ekarath whispered to Zahara. "But seeing it with my own eyes is something else altogether."

"I've heard similar things about Karajaan," Zahara responded in a whisper. "The country estate where I spent my childhood is nothing more than a pile of rubble and ash, and I have to imagine that it's not the only one. As much as I dream about returning home, I know it would break my heart to see what it's become."

Ekarath responded with a simple nod, knowing that Zahara didn't want to revisit the memories of her harrowing journey a year prior. He switched his focus to Farban as they approached the edge of the plaza. The old hermit led them toward the Mount of Creation.

"We're getting a little close to the Usurper's palace, aren't we?" Ekarath asked the old man.

"Remember how I said we need the right friends?" Farban asked, and Ekarath nodded in response. "Well, sometimes it's best to hide in plain sight. Some of those friends are the last ones you would expect."

Ekarath furrowed his brow, but the look on Farban's face didn't allow for more questions. He knew the spymaster had been running the guerilla war ever since Talas had fallen, but they were quickly entering the most affluent part of the city. He had expected a safehouse in the slums or a large warehouse.

The trio didn't speak again as they came up to the base of the sheer cliffs of the Mount. The sun was mostly set, with little more than a soft twilight competing with the white glow of the Shajarat.

Here, the streets were no longer lined with three-story buildings. Rather, exterior walls separated the street from the courtyards and mansions of the city's elite. It made sense that the nobility would try to be as close to the palace as possible, even when that palace was occupied by the Usurper.

Farban came to a stop in front of a pristine gate of gilded steel bars. The white light of the Shajarat bounced on the gold, and an elaborate crest depicting the head of a lion dominated the center. Through the bars, Ekarath could see a perfectly manicured garden, its trees endeavoring—unsuccessfully—to block his view of the mansion beyond.

Farban pulled on a chord near the gate, and a bell rang in the distance. The old spymaster held a smile on his face, as if he were absolutely giddy about their current situation. Within moments, a tall man approached the gate, dressed in a white suit and a dark dress shirt.

"Who approaches?" the man asked, his voice a strong baritone.

"Those who seek to restore holiness to Einar," Farban replied.

The man's eyes widened with the words, and a smile spread across his face.

"Ah, Master Farban—it's good to see you again."

"Likewise, Claudet," Farban responded as the man began opening the gate. "I trust Lady Ivana is in."

"You have come at a most convenient time," Claudet said. "My Lady is currently playing host to individuals of interest to one so esteemed as yourself. Would you like me to show you the way, or is your memory sufficient?"

"If you have other tasks, I don't need to distract you," Farban responded. "I'm assuming she is in her study?"

"You are correct, as usual," Claudet said, closing the gate behind them. "I will take your mounts to the stables, though I would prefer to accompany you. The look on My Lady's face will be a treasure of its own."

"I will be sure to recount every detail to you afterwards," Farban said, his smile growing larger.

Zahara looked to Ekarath, but he simply shrugged. The old spymaster certainly seemed to love his secrets, and he just held in a sigh as he followed the man.

He led them through the gardens, up to a front door crafted of heavy wood. The main building was three stories tall and wider than three or four of the townhomes they had passed. The exterior was covered in fine limestone that reflected the glow of the Shajarat and moon, and Ekarath could see the various threads of Restoration woven into the building.

Without stopping to knock, Farban opened the front door, revealing a grand entryway. The floors were polished marble, and the ceilings were coffered and gilded, with each panel containing a work of art. A massive chandelier hung from the ceiling, holding over a dozen *kura*.

Straight ahead, two staircases curved gently, framing an arched doorway that led to a ballroom. Ekarath couldn't see where the stairs led, but Farban didn't hesitate in picking the steps to their right.

The hallways on the second level were well-adorned, though the ceiling was much shorter. They walked past a number of closed doors, and Ekarath couldn't help but wonder what they contained.

The hallway ended at a work of art. A door of rich mahogany contained a carving of the Shajarat, the tree glowing with a simple weave. Again, Farban didn't bother to knock as he pushed the door open.

"I'm sorry to interrupt," Farban said to the room's inhabitants, who were largely blocked from Ekarath's view by the spymaster's frame. "But I've made quite the journey to see you."

Gasps sounded from the room, and Farban entered fully. More than curious, Ekarath followed.

The room itself was a work of art. A large table dominated its center, while a majestic window offered a view of the Mount of Creation. The glow of Shajarat illuminated the window, almost negating the need for lamps or *kura*.

While the table could easily accommodate a dozen occupants, it currently held only three. On the far side of the table sat a man in a dark suit, his red hair and mustache perfectly groomed. Across from him sat a young woman in a dress of green silk. Her blond hair cascaded past her shoulders in silky waves, and a set of bright blue eyes looked up at the newcomers.

A tall, willowy woman at the head of the table practically ran across the room to embrace the spymaster. She was older—late fifties or early sixties—but she moved and held herself with as much grace and beauty as Zahara.

Her blue dress fitted a thin frame, and her blond hair was braided into an immaculate top bun. Her neck held a diamond necklace, which hummed with power.

That's a rather fancy qilada, Ekarath thought. He still wasn't used to noticing the tools, which often masqueraded as mere accessories.

"We've been so worried," the woman said, her arms wrapping around Farban's neck. She didn't even seem to care that the old man was dirty and smelly after the journey.

"I'm assuming word has come of the Atsada's fall," Farban replied, wrapping his own arms around the willowy woman.

"We found out a few days ago," the nobleman said from the other side of the table, rising to his feet.

"Didn't you see the notices up all over the city as you came in?"

"We were a little preoccupied with avoiding suspicious guards," Farban said, still embracing the woman.

"It seems like both the town watch and the garrison have gotten less suspicious since the news arrived," the woman said, pulling away from her embrace with Farban. "Now that the war is over, they don't seem to worry about everyone on the street being a spy or saboteur."

"That just means we can operate with more ease," Farban said, his smile growing bigger.

"That's the kind of attitude we need right now, Master Farban," the woman said. "When we heard reports of the Atsada's fall, we feared the worst."

"The worst is most definitely upon us, but hope is not yet lost," Farban replied. "Apparently you lot agree, seeing as how you're still holding clandestine meetings."

"We plan to continue the fight, no matter the cost," the tall woman said, gesturing for Farban to take an empty seat before turning to Ekarath and Zahara. "And I'm sorry for my lack of manners. My name is Lady Ivana, Duchess of Cornellia and member of the Elder Council. Welcome to my home."

"Thank you," Zahara and Ekarath said in unison. He turned to his friend and smiled.

"You two are certainly a cute couple," Ivana said, her smile growing bigger before turning to the man with red hair. "Come on Maslov, be polite."

"I'm Count Maslov," the man said. "And I'd prefer to keep it at that with people I don't know."

"Oh, I can vouch for my traveling companions," Farban said, taking a seat at the foot of the table, opposite Lady Ivana. Zahara took a seat next to the spymaster, and Ekarath sat next to her. At his other side, the young woman looked him up and down. "You can trust them with anything you would entrust to me."

"Fine, then I rescind giving you my name," Maslov said, a smile coming to his face.

"Come now, my dear Count," Ivana said, shooting a glare at the man. "I know you have some strange rivalry with Farban, but that's no way to treat the Spymaster of Segova."

"There is no more Segova," Maslov said, shaking his head. "It died along with Lord Dimitri."

"Maslov isn't taking the news well," Ivana said, turning to Ekarath. "He's a nobleman, prominent merchant, and soon-to-be candidate for the Elder Council. It's only through his contacts that we've been able to purchase enough arms to keep our small bands equipped."

Ekarath wanted to ask more about that point. Who were these three dandies meeting so late at night? However, before he could ask, the young woman at his side spoke up.

"And I'm Lady Saren," the girl said, rising to her feet to give a small curtsy. Ekarath turned to really look at her for the first time.

She was about his age, with a petite nose and full figure. Even with a set of heels, she came no higher than his shoulder, but she carried herself with a quiet strength. There was something about her voice that spoke of confidence and poise.

"Saren is my niece," Ivana said. "She grew up in Marsalas, but her parents wanted her to experience life in the capital. She's got her own reasons to fight the Usurper."

"Alright, now that we're acquainted, how are people taking the news?" Farban asked.

"Mixed," Ivana said. "The Usurper has won over a lot of the common people—and a large chunk of the nobility—in the past year, so there is a fair amount of joy. However, the majority of the city is in shock—their adoration for Lord Dimitri knows no bounds."

"However, there's also a lot of relief, from both sides," Maslov said. "Mothers are overjoyed their sons no longer need to be conscripted into either army, and those boys are happy at the prospect of a long life in the comfort of Talas rather than dying on some forsaken battlefield."

"For us true believers, hope is disappearing fast," Saren chimed in. "So many of us signed up to fight for freedom, but it seems like that cause is lost."

Unless I can give them that hope, Ekarath thought.

Ekarath shook his head at the unspoken words. Despite the earlier conversation regarding the subject, he knew it would be worse for the people here to know they had another Heir—an Heir who couldn't even begin to use the Power of Creation.

He needed to make things right.

"But you haven't introduced your traveling companions," Saren said, her eyes fixed on Ekarath. "It's not exactly fair to keep us in the dark after we introduced ourselves."

"Fine, this young lady is Zahara," Farban said. "She's a gifted mage, and her skills are top-notch."

All three aristocrats nodded approvingly, while Ekarath furrowed his brow.

He didn't mention she's only an apprentice.

"The boy's name is Ekarath," Farban continued before Ekarath could dwell on the omission, "and as far as I know, he's the last surviving member of the *Hundiin*. Don't let their age fool you; these two took down a fully grown *sahali* on their own."

"A *sahali*?" Maslov scoffed. "On this side of the Jabals? I'm afraid the spymaster is losing his sanity..."

"We're honored to have you," Ivana cut in before Farban could respond to the incredulity. "Ekarath, you've got the look of the *Hundiin*. The Creator knows we need more well-trained soldiers to stiffen up our raw recruits. Zahara, we could most certainly use another mage—we lost one of our best three days ago in a raid. I wasn't sure how we were going to get along without him."

They're so much happier to have another mage in their ranks, Ekarath thought. *I'm just another sword.*

"Zahara was one of the most powerful mages in the entire Atsada," Ekarath said. "She'll end up being more valuable than you could possibly imagine."

Farban shot Ekarath a look, one that he interpreted to mean "please, shut up."

"I wish we could have beaten the rumors and official declarations," Farban said, shaking his head. "But I'm here to confirm that the Atsada has fallen. Lord Dimitri is dead."

"May his soul rest with the Creator," Ivana whispered. "It's still so hard to believe that after all these years, the Usurper has really won. The Wild Man killed all seven Heirs..."

"But the fight's not over," Farban interjected.

"Not as long as we have talented magi to cause trouble for the new regime," Maslov added, his smile directed at Zahara.

Ekarath squirmed again in his seat. He might as well be invisible—just another faceless soldier to be sent into battle. Zahara and Farban were trained magi with skills more valuable than a hundred soldiers.

"And what about you?" Ivana asked, her question directed at Farban. "Did you have any trouble getting out of the forest?"

"We did have a run-in with some Imperial soldiers, but we managed to escape."

"With two magi, a few legionnaires shouldn't be much of a problem," Maslov barked before looking at Ekarath. "Sorry, I know you're *Hundiin*, but that doesn't really compare to a pair using the *draod*."

Ekarath's stomach fell at the man's words, which confirmed the sentiment he had already picked up on, but he just nodded in response.

"Ekarath is more valuable than you can imagine," Farban replied. "In fact, he's the reason we were able to escape."

"Glad to hear it," Maslov barked, raising an eyebrow in disbelief before clearing his throat. "May I ask why you took such a risk to join us here? That journey from the forest can't have been easy, and it's hard to imagine a place more dangerous than the Imperial City for someone like you."

"Well, I was growing a little tired of playing the hermit," Farban responded with a wink. "But I do have more significant reasons for coming..."

"By the Creator," Ivana gasped, her eyes looking into Farban's. "Does our dear spymaster have a secret?"

"One that will change everything," Farban said, clearing his throat before continuing. "We come not just to lend aid, but also to seek refuge and counsel. What I'm about to tell you must not leave this room."

All three aristocrats nodded in agreement, their faces losing all trace of either disdain or levity.

"The news of Lord Dimitri's death is unfortunately true, but that does not mean all hope is lost. A few days ago, I saw a display of power that I've only seen a handful of times in my life. In fact, I've only seen it done by seven other people."

Ivana's eyes widened at the words, her mouth dropping open. All eyes moved to Zahara, to the *qilada* on her ear. Ekarath could feel their excitement—a successor to Lord Dimitri, a young woman trained in the *draod*. Their eyes were wide with excitement, and he knew the next bit would destroy any hope that was kindling in their chests. Ekarath clenched his jaw, making his decision. Before Farban could continue, Ekarath leapt to his feet.

"Zahara summoned a massive lightning storm," Ekarath blurted out, focusing on the three aristocrats and avoiding Zahara's gaze. "She killed the entire contingent of Imperial soldiers guarding us. Her eyes took on the color of molten gold, and light filled her entire being. Yes, Lord Dimitri is dead, but there is still an Heir in Segova."

Ekarath's heart pounded in his chest as his words hung in the air, and he could feel Zahara's icy glare at his side. Yet he didn't flinch, maintaining eye contact with Lady Ivana. He could feel her gaze scrutinizing him, and he resisted the urge to break away from the staring match. He could see the doubt creeping into her face, and he knew something else was needed.

Ekarath dropped to one knee in front of Zahara and withdrew his sword. Bowing his head, both to show reverence and to avoid Zahara's eyes, he offered her the blade.

I just hope she doesn't use it to kill me.

"Your Holiness," he said, the words barely making their way out of his throat. "As the only known surviving member of the *Hundiin*, I pledge my sword and my life in your service."

Zahara didn't respond, and Ekarath didn't dare look up. The seconds ticked by, marked only by Ekarath's breathing. A cold sweat broke out along his forehead, threatening to drip down onto his face.

"You'd better accept that oath," Maslov growled from his chair. "A member of the *Hundiin* is too valuable a tool to turn down."

"Of course," Zahara's voice sounded, and Ekarath could feel the ice-cold anger in those words. He had rarely felt it from her, but it was unmistakable. "May you serve me well."

Ekarath could feel the sword being taken from his hands, followed by the sharp steel tapping his shoulders, signifying that she accepted his oath. Without any further ceremony, he rose to his feet, and she handed the sword back to him, hilt first. He took it and slipped the weapon back into his scabbard without making eye contact.

"You have no idea what this will mean to...well, everyone," Maslov said, shifting his gaze from Ekarath to Zahara. "To know that this fight isn't over."

"While I share you your optimism, I just said this news can't leave the room," Farban cut in, casting a glare at Ekarath but regaining his composure. "Zahara is powerful, but no new Heir is just ready to take on the responsibilities that come with that title—especially in times like these. Before anyone can know, she needs time to practice and develop."

"There isn't time to keep her quietly hidden while the Usurper struts around unchallenged," Maslov said, his brow furrowing. "I've spent a fortune arming our soldiers, and they're beginning to lose hope. And it's not just the soldiers, but everyone—hope is being lost out there, and the longer we let it drain, the harder it will be to restore. It won't matter if this girl is the most powerful being in the history of Einar—if the people have given up, they won't fight."

"I understand what Farban is saying," Ivana cut in before the two men could escalate the situation. "And maybe we can find a balance? Her Holiness most certainly isn't ready to face the Usurper in open combat, but maybe we could tell the soldiers while she trains in secret."

"As soon as word gets out that there's an Heir, she won't be safe," Farban said, shaking his head. "All the hope in the world won't help if the Usurper runs her through with the Eternal Blade. The Creator has given us one last chance."

Maslov folded his arms and stared at Farban while Ivana's gaze switched back and forth between the two men. Ekarath didn't know if he should cut in, or what he would even say. He could feel Zahara's eyes launching daggers at his back, and he resisted the urge to turn around.

The silence that filled the room nearly smothered him, and his lungs struggled to fill with air. Ekarath could tell there was a veritable battle happening as the two men glared at each other. With a growl, Maslov unfolded his arms and leaned forward.

"Fine, I'll keep the girl's secret."

"As will I," Saren said.

"And now that we have Farban back," Ivana said, her smile growing wide, "we can start planning some real mischief."

"That's a capital idea," Farban said, a smile coming back to his face. "But I think that we should maybe wait until tomorrow to begin planning said mischief. We've been through quite a bit, and I would certainly like a bath and a good night's sleep."

***

Zahara sat in the spacious set of rooms she had been given. Unlike the tiny quarters she had occupied in the Atsada, she now had at her disposal a formal sitting room, complete with three sofas and a large desk. Behind the sitting room, a doorway led into a bedchamber, which held a four-poster bed draped in velvet. There was even a bathroom with a copper tub and a toilet that flushed waste into the city's sewers.

Though she assumed Farban and Ekarath had similar lodgings, something about the luxurious furnishings made her feel important.

Important? Ekarath told them I'm the Heir of Segova.

Her entire body still trembled at the thought. She knew Ekarath had plenty of self-doubt, but hadn't she and Farban done a good enough job explaining why this rouse was a terrible idea? Now there were three very powerful members of Imperial society who believed she was the Heir of Segova.

A knock sounded at the door, and she didn't have to ask who it was.

"Come in," she said, unable to hide the anger in her voice. The door opened, and that insufferably pale face covered in blond hair poked through.

"Are you sure I can come in?" Ekarath asked. "If you need some time, I can—"

"No, as Heir of Segova, I *command* you to enter," Zahara said, cutting him off. "We need to talk about this."

With an audible gulp, Ekarath slipped in and closed the door. Zahara pulled on the *draod*, creating a weave of air and placing it against the door. Hopefully, it would be enough to stop someone from eavesdropping.

"Now, I know what you're going to say," Ekarath began, lifting his hands in self-defense, "but really, I—"

"I thought we agreed that such a lie was pointless," Zahara snapped. "Like it or not, you are the Heir of Segova. Stopping the Usurper comes down to you. What happens when they send me out to fight him? Did you think about that?"

"I didn't have time to think of anything other than the severe disappointment that would come with the truth," Ekarath responded. "But Farban bought us loads of time—time that I'm going to use to figure how to make you the Heir. I understand that Lord Dimitri was born the son of a fisherman and that should help me feel better. However, he didn't have to immediately face an existential threat like the Eternal Blade. We don't have years to teach me how to weave, but we do have weeks to figure out how to make things right and make you the Heir."

"You have to know how upset this makes me," Zahara said, unsure how else to put it.

"I do, but I feel it's best for everyone that we tell this lie," Ekarath said. "And for now, you can teach me how to weave the *draod*—that way, I can actually give you my powers once we figure out how."

Zahara sat, chewing her tongue as she thought over his words.

"You're the worst. You know that, right?"

"That's all I've ever wanted to be."

Zahara held in her laughter, but a smile broke out onto her face against her will.

"Fine," she said. "Let's plan on tomorrow evening. There are a few things I would like to try out before I have to see your dumb face."

"Fair enough," Ekarath said, shaking his head. His posture almost melted, and he relaxed into the couch.

"Hey, you're still in trouble," Zahara said, wagging her finger. "But that being said, I would be a terrible friend if I didn't help you. The day will come when you tell the world the truth—I'll just need to make sure you're ready for it."

Chapter 17

The golden sunlight of dawn streamed through Mahzun's bedroom window as he found himself again in front of the gilded mirror. He had never brought one with him on campaign, and he didn't particularly enjoy the constant presence of his own countenance. This morning, the scars that snaked along his skin almost glowed with the sun, as if they knew of the pain to come.

He tugged at the violet robes of fine silk that had been tailored for his massive frame. The cotton underclothing was by far more comfortable than anything he'd ever worn, but the lack of armor weighed on his heart. He knew Lorna would prefer him to be wearing a dark suit to show his people that he understood the latest fashion, but for a moment as heavy as this, he felt the need to be connected to his roots.

Besides, suits were uncomfortable.

"You know what I'm talking about," Mahzun growled to the silent figure of Lord Dimitri standing at his side. True to form, the old man didn't respond. Those pale eyes just looked at him without the slightest hint of emotion. Still, the man wore his robes of green silk. He had probably never been forced to wear a suit.

"Today's the day," Mahzun said, checking his reflection in the mirror. The white turban bound his long hair, but it was not as tight as it could be—probably the best he could manage without a servant's help. His parents would likely be disappointed in his abilities with the traditional head wear, even if they would be immensely proud of him for, well...everything else he had done. He finished checking his appearance and turned again to Dimitri. "The final remnant of your corrupt rule is about to be destroyed. Does that make you want to say anything?"

Lord Dimitri didn't respond, but a knock sounded at his door before it swung open to reveal a scowling Lorna. She was dressed in a blue gown that flowed down her body like a waterfall, and her braided hair was wrapped around the top of her head like a crown. Overall, she was lovely, even if that scowl did take away from the effect.

Mahzun gave a scowl of his own as he felt the *draod* emanating from the clothing, as it was woven into every layer of the silk. It enhanced the beauty and durability, while adding to the sense of flowing water—he wondered what would happen once the power's source was gone.

"The Council is assembled, and the square outside is already overflowing with the people of Talas," Lorna said with a frown. "Do I need to tell you again that this is inadvisable?"

"You've spent the past week trying to get me to change plans," Mahzun said as Lord Dimitri disappeared into thin air. He focused his full attention on his sister. "You seem to lack faith in your younger brother."

"That's because my brother is talking about destroying something that's been around since the Creation.

Also, have you seen what the Eternal Blade has done to you?"

Mahzun strode out the door and motioned for Lorna to follow. With a huff, the woman pumped her legs to keep up with his long strides.

"I didn't wage a war that destroyed millions of lives—including my own, in many ways—just to supplant the Heirs," Mahzun said, trying to form the words that he'd been trying to express to his imaginary debate partner. "When I say that the old order is dead, I mean it—that includes the *draod*."

"And what if Pavel is right, and the Shajarat proves too powerful for you?" Lorna said. "You're taking a big risk by doing this in front of both the city's population and the Council. If you fail, it will be forever burned into their memories. This aura of invincibility you've built could be gone in an instant."

"I never wanted to be worshiped like the Heirs or the Creator," Mahzun snapped, stopping to look Lorna in the eyes. "I've spent the past decade talking about freeing the people of Einar. I've already given up my health, my face, and my youth to the Cause—if it means that I'm to make the ultimate sacrifice, I'm prepared to do so."

Mahzun spun on his heel and kept walking. A few seconds later, he could hear Lorna's hurried footsteps as she tried to keep up. The sun kept rising as he strode through the palace, cold fury coursing through his veins. The beauty of the palace around him only stoked those flames, a reminder of the splendor some enjoyed while others lived in squalor.

On the top floor, he reached an open archway, flanked on either side by guardsmen in their ridiculous uniforms. Their faces bore no emotion, though the tension in their jaws told Mahzun that Lorna wasn't the only one upset by what was about to take place. Somehow, he doubted that these young nobles' apprehension came from a fear for their Emperor's safety.

Without acknowledging the wooden salutes offered by the two guards, Mahzun stepped through the archway, emerging onto the large balcony that stretched along the entire top floor of the palace. There were dozens of chairs, all occupied by members of the Council and other aristocrats. Below, Mahzun could hear the sound of the commoners who were so disdained by those around him. The individual voices of thousands coalesced into a dull roar, but he knew that every conversation must be similar.

The aristocrats on the balcony rose to their feet as Mahzun entered, though he could feel only apathy and anger from them. His feet carried him through the sea of heavy perfume, and his eyes caught sight of the nearest noble—an old woman in a dress of white velvet. On her shoulder sat a small squirrel-like creature with long ears and grey fur, one of the most common soul-bound. While the woman stood tall, the *dreju* hissed and fidgeted.

Even if it weren't for the agitation shown by the soul-bound, Mahzun could see fear in the woman's eyes. She knew what was about to be done, and she knew what it meant for Einar. At least, the old woman thought she knew.

Mahzun forced his gaze away from the woman and all her compatriots, focusing his attention on the balcony's edge. He forced his eyes to avoid the Council and its cronies, though the hairs rose on the back of his neck under the weight of their glares. The thought of putting his back to such enmity made his stomach squirm.

A roar from the crowd below filled Mahzun's ears as he reached the balcony's edge, and he lifted both fists into the air. The roar grew as more and more of those assembled ceased their idle conversations and joined in. He could feel the warmth of their affection battling with the icy stares at his rear.

Mahzun lowered his fists, and the shouts and applause ceased, plunging the world into silence. A soft breeze whistled as it blew across the palace grounds, the only sound nature provided to fill the void. From somewhere deep in the crowd, someone coughed.

"I welcome you all—both friends and closeted enemies—on this historic day," Mahzun said, his voice filling the air and echoing throughout the palace ground. "For generations, we have been weighed down by a society that allows the Power of Creation to create divisions among brothers. The Heirs—in the name of their powerless god—did their best to ensure that we remained distracted by our differences, rather than focused on what brings us together. I come before you this day to celebrate the end of these injustices."

A roar erupted from the crowd below, and Mahzun reveled in the sound. The intensity of the fear and hatred from the Council escalated, and his back itched at the thought of ignoring his enemies. Mahzun lifted his hand and focused on the *draod*, summoning the Eternal Blade. His hand gripped the leather hilt, and the familiar weight threatened to bring his arm down.

"I present to you the tool of your liberation. The Eternal Blade has cut down each of the seven Heirs, destroying men and women who forced the people of Einar to bow down for over three thousand years."

Grey clouds began to swirl overhead, and a murmur broke out among the crowd. Thunder roared, and a sheet of lightning illuminated the sky. Mahzun's smile grew as his grip tightened on the Blade's hilt.

"Do not be afraid," he shouted, and his voice boomed above all else. "For now, I will use the Eternal Blade for a final time to destroy the last remaining symbol of the old tyrants. Welcome to a new age."

Mahzun opened himself to the Blade, and the raw energy rushed into his bones. Another flash of lighting filled the sky, followed by a boom that could shatter windows. Every muscle in Mahzun's body began to tremble, both from exertion and anticipation of the pain to come. His bones vibrated from the energy pouring into him, and his bowels groaned.

The acrid stench of burning flesh hit his nose before the pain shot through his body. He could feel the angry red welts rising up, could sense the small hairs on his legs and thighs curling up into charred bits. From the churning mass of dark clouds above, lightning flashed, and a bolt slammed into the extended Blade.

His grip tightened on the hilt as the muscles in his hand spasmed and locked into place. Anguish erupted from Mahzun's throat, and several of his bones cracked. Ribs popped out of place, threatening to pierce his lungs. His knees buckled as the power coursed through his body, uncaring of the damage inflicted on its host.

Gritting his teeth to keep down his screams, Mahzun turned around to face the Shajarat, extending out of the palace's center. He focused his mind on the white bark and branches—so delicate and yet powerful. He imagined the root system that extended for miles under the city. There was so much of it to destroy.

Raw power launched from the Blade—a streak of blue light flying through the grey sky—slamming into the alabaster tree. An electric blue light shot through the Shajarat, coursing along the porcelain bark and filling every branch and leaf. The Blade's power continued its destructive course through Mahzun's body, and his right shin snapped in two.

He forced himself to stay on his feet to witness the Shajarat's destruction. The power filled the ancient tree, and he could feel its protective barrier buckling under the weight. He gritted his teeth, forcing more of the raw energy through his body.

Just as had happened at the Atsada, a spiderweb of red light appeared where the bolt of lightning struck the tree. The veins of crimson began spreading across the bark, like blood on parchment. Even through the pain, Mahzun couldn't imagine a more beautiful sight. As if in anticipation, nature grew quiet as the wood moaned.

A flash of brilliant white shot out of the Shajarat, and the red light drew back in retreat.

The massive amounts of energy Mahzun had funneled into the ancient tree rebounded, fleeing from the power of the Shajarat and surging back into the Blade. Mahzun's shoulder popped out of his socket before the energy slammed him into the ground. His stomach flipped, and the Blade dissipated before his flight was halted by the granite railing that separate Mahzun from a fall to the ground below. His ears rang, and his vision was blurred as shouts filled the balcony. Those shouts grew quiet as Mahzun's vision grew dark.

I have failed. All is lost.

Another voice responded to his lamentation—thick, guttural, unlike anything he had ever heard before.

That's because you are a fool.

Chapter 18

Mahzun's eyes opened to the flickering light of an oil lamp. Incense burned nearby, giving off a sweet aroma. His body was supported by a soft mattress of down, and he blinked away the fog covering his eyes to see his bedroom. The curtains on his windows were drawn, showing the night sky, and moonlight streamed in through the glass. His eyes scanned the room in search of anything out of place. Other than the smoldering stick of incense on the nightstand, there was nothing unusual.

Biting his lower lip in anticipation of pain, Mahzun moved his right leg. Instead of shattered bones protesting his movement, the muscles responded with alacrity. He moved both legs and arms in a fluid motion—no pain, no sign that he had almost killed himself. Leaping out of bed, Mahzun ran to the gilded mirror.

He was dressed in cotton underclothes, though he could tell they were not the same ones he had worn that morning. His face was still covered in scars and puffy skin—no level of healing from a mage could undo the marks left by the Eternal Blade. However, there was nothing on his body to indicate that he had suffered from shattered ribs.

His eyes darted to a nearby chair, one that was meant for an evening of reading or quiet conversation. In the short time he'd occupied this room, Mahzun had never used any of the furniture except for the bed. Now, the pristine chair was occupied by a suit of black plate mail. A sheet of paper on top of the armor fluttered in the evening breeze that filtered in through the window. Mahzun left the mirror, grabbing the parchment in his hands and bringing it closer to the flickering lantern, squinting to read in the soft light.

Be ready

Those words were unmistakably written by Lorna's own hand. He had read countless reports written by her over the years as she managed the Empire in his absence. His eyes scanned the words again, and his stomach lurched.

His mind went back to that morning—at least, he hoped he had only spent a single day in bed—and his sister's words rang in his ears. Mahzun's failure to destroy the Shajarat would not go unpunished, whether it was by the Council or rebels within the city. Wherever she was, Lorna knew Mahzun would need his armor.

Without waiting for another invitation, Mahzun grabbed the various pieces and slipped them on. The years spent donning the plate mail every morning had taught his hands what to do, and they needed little instruction from his brain. In less than a minute, Mahzun's body was weighed down by the familiar heft of steel.

At the bottom of the pile sat a long sword in a simple leather scabbard. How long had it been since Mahzun had felt the need to carry a normal blade? His own fists were usually strong enough, and he enjoyed the sport of killing opponents with their own weapon. Yet he knew his sister had not included the mundane blade by accident. As he strapped the scabbard around his shoulder, the door swung open.

"Oh good, you're awake," Lorna said as she closed the door behind her.

She no longer wore the fine silk gown or head covering. Instead, Lorna was covered by a simple cotton dress of light charcoal—the same that would be worn by a servant. A leather satchel, bulging from its contents, hung across her chest. There was nothing about her that said she had any intention of staying the night in the palace.

"What's happened?" Mahzun asked, turning to face his sister.

"Nothing...yet," Lorna replied, shaking her head. "But my eyes and ears around Talas have been telling me for weeks that something is cooking. Your near-death is going to set it off."

"Wait, so you're ready to pack up and call it quits with nothing more than rumors? I can't believe you'd be so cowardly," Mahzun said, shaking his head and unbuckling the sword. "If there is work to be done, we should get to it."

"I'm not proposing we run very far, but something is going to happen," Lorna said, dashing across the room to put the sword back around Mahzun's shoulder. "I think it would be best if we leave the palace—just for tonight. After the assassins make their move, we'll be in a better position to counter their attack. Nobody knows that I healed you—everybody thinks you're in bed, a broken man. The hammer will fall, and I don't want to be in the palace when it does."

"Then let's stay here and spring the trap," Mahzun replied. "Sometimes the anvil smashes the hammer."

"And sometimes the anvil is shattered into bits," Lorna shot back. "Did you already forget what the

Shajarat did to you? Yes, I was able to heal the broken bones, but you can't possibly think to use the Eternal Blade again. If my spies are right, this isn't a single assassin—it could be dozens of magi and soldiers."

Magi.

"You know what this means, right?" Mahzun asked.

"That we need to get out of here."

"No. Do you understand why I failed? Why the Shajarat held under such a relentless assault?"

"Does it mean that Pavel was right? That the Shajarat cannot be destroyed?"

"It means there's still an Heir," Mahzun said, turning back to the mirror. "Somehow, one of them fooled me. Somewhere within the vast reaches of my empire, a viper sits, waiting to strike."

Lorna grabbed him by the arm, forcing him to look her in the face. Her eyes studied him, obviously looking for any traces of madness. Mahzun simply smiled in return. She didn't have to believe him.

"I know you certainly believe it," Lorna said, letting out a deep breath. "But you can't go off into the unknown, hunting after every whisper of a rumor. If there is an Heir, he'll make sure to hide on the periphery of the Empire. We need to focus on the enemies here and now—they won't wait to strike."

"I know—I'll focus on the current danger," Mahzun said, shaking his head. "There are enough vipers here to be dealt with. Whatever traps they've planned, we'll—"

An explosion knocked the two off their feet as the door caved inward. A ringing took over Mahzun's ears, and he shook his head in an attempt to clear it. He looked toward the entrance to see hooded figures streaming into the room.

A solid cushion of air formed around his body, lifting him upright. His recently healed shoulder screamed in pain, as did his legs, but he forced the feelings aside. He tried to shake off the binding, but the pocket of air only tightened, and the buzzing of the *draod* filled the room.

The hard crack of footsteps sounded in his ear, and the familiar face of Hakan Pavel came into view. His lips held a wide smile, and his eyes burned with a fire that could melt steel.

"Your speech this morning was quite inspirational," Pavel whispered. "And I admire a man who takes risks."

"That's good, because you're taking a rather large one at the moment," Mahzun growled as he again strained against the spell holding him in place.

"Oh, it's good to see someone who wants to attack every problem with brute force," Lord Pavel said, his smile growing wider. "Unfortunately, many of life's problems require finesse. A few decades on the throne may have eventually taught you that lesson, but I'm afraid your reign is going to meet a tragic end long before then."

Mahzun didn't respond, and Pavel's smile widened.

"In just a few hours, the entire Empire will enter into mourning," Pavel continued, patting Mahzun's cheek. "A new age has indeed begun, and we will forever revere Emperor Mahzun for the sacrifice he made to bring it about."

The golden *qilada* on the nobleman's finger began to glow a fierce red, and Mahzun didn't need to see the threads of the *draod* sprouting from the ether to know what was next. Yet he couldn't get his body to respond. Without the Eternal Blade, he was no match for a fully trained mage.

Threads of destructive energy began to wrap around his body. Pavel was clever—there could be no simple dagger used to bring about Mahzun's end. It had to match the self-inflicted wounds to convince the people that their emperor's death had been a tragic accident, a result of his own hubris.

Mahzun's skin again began to sizzle, though the pain didn't register. His mind grew fuzzy, and he could almost tell himself that he was settling in for a good night of sleep. He had defeated the Heirs. He had liberated his people.

"I will, reluctantly of course, take the mantle of emperor," Pavel said, rousing Mahzun from his thoughts. "And I will do my best to continue the great work you started."

A feminine scream sounded from behind Lord Pavel, and Mahzun didn't need his vision to know its source.

"You're nothing more than a monster," Lorna shouted. Mahzun could only make out the vague shape of her form, but she was definitely being held by two other blurs. "I can't wait to see you brought down."

"A new dynasty is a shaky thing, and I may well fall before long," Pavel hissed. "Fortunately, neither of you will be around to see it."

Mahzun again began to fade from consciousness. The woven threads of the *draod* were still moving across his body, and he knew it would not take much longer for his life to be snuffed out. The powers infused into his muscles and bones after using the Eternal Blade for so long were great, but even they had their limits.

A familiar, high-pitched scream sounded from outside, snapping Mahzun back into consciousness. He felt for the connection deep within his soul, and he could feel Aiya's anger as the wind whipped through her feathers. The floor trembled, and Mahzun could see his captors' eyes widen.

I have come for you.

The exterior wall shattered in an explosion of glass and granite, and Mahzun fell to the ground. His arms and legs flailed in panic, finally unhindered by the pocket of binding air. Mahzun opened his eyes, though the combination of darkness and dust blinded him.

Coughing to force the dust out of his lungs, Mahzun called upon the Eternal Blade. The familiar weight appeared in his hand, along with a surge of power that coursed through his veins. There was also a hint of warning—his body would not be able to withstand the power of a determined attack.

Mahzun rose to his feet, Blade in hand. Aiya landed at his side, her bulk taking up a large portion of the room. Mahzun grabbed onto the white fur with his free hand and scanned the room—at least, what he could see through the clouds of dust and debris.

Somewhere within the mess was the man who had tried to overthrow him. Unless the blast had killed him, Pavel would still be a dangerous foe. Yet Mahzun felt confident that with Aiya by his side and the Eternal Blade in hand, he could defeat the weasel.

His eyes scanned the rubble, searching for any sign of the nobleman. The dust began to settle, giving Mahzun's eyes increased clarity.

An inferno erupted from the rubble, but Mahzun sliced the woven energy with the Blade. As the spell unraveled, the flame died, the air humming with the *draod*. Mahzun's eyes found the source of the spell, and he leapt.

His hands grabbed Pavel by the throat, lifting him into the air. The man's eyes bulged, veins popped from his forehead as he struggled against Mahzun's grip.

"What? You have nothing to say?" Mahzun growled, squeezing harder. "I truly am the mad emperor, and I look forward to your face haunting my nightmares."

With his words hanging in the air, Mahzun slammed the Eternal Blade into the man's chest. The struggling ceased, the legs no longer kicked. As the life drained from those bulging eyes, Mahzun flung the corpse away.

Across the room, Lorna rose out of the rubble. Her head was bleeding, and she limped over to the Savior of Man.

"You are a lucky man," she wheezed before bending over Pavel's corpse. She pulled the golden ring off his finger—yet another *qilada* to be used for the Cause. A powerful relic no longer held by one of his enemies. A new ally that could be trained with the *draod*. Some good would come of this day.

"Thank you, my friend," Mahzun whispered, turning to pat Aiya. She purred in response, though he could feel her desire to leave the cramped space.

Your sister is correct, Aiya said. *You are lucky. Let's hope your luck won't betray us.*

Chapter 19

With a silver plate laden with fruit, bread, and chunks of roasted chicken, Ekarath made his way through a deserted corridor. The Usurper's failed attempt to destroy the Shajarat that morning had changed everything, and the uncertainty out in the city had made the hours feel like days. With the clock nearing midnight, his brain was filled with a dense fog, and there was just one person he wanted to see.

Saren popped out of an intersecting hallway, a smile on her face.

That's not who I meant, Ekarath thought, but he forced a smile just the same.

"Oh, hello there," Saren said, her smile growing even wider. "I was wondering where you've been hiding all day."

"I didn't think I was hiding," Ekarath responded. "Farban wanted to spend some time training."

The reality was that he had spent the day hiding—not from Saren, but from his responsibilities. Farban had spent a very unsuccessful hour training him, only to give up in a fit of exasperation. Ekarath had then spent the rest of the day in Ivana's library, searching for any hint of how he could give up his power without also giving up his life.

"Training? With the *draod*? I didn't realize you were also a mage. Do most members of the *Hundiin* weave?"

I need to be more careful with my stupid mouth.

"Not really, we mostly focus on physical prowess, but Farban thinks it would be good for me to learn," Ekarath said, lifting his hand to show the simple ring of silver that would have to make do as a fake *qilada*. "He says I'm so thick it will be years before I can do much of anything."

"Well, I think it's impressive. It's so good to learn as much as possible, don't you think?"

"Of course," Ekarath stammered before gesturing further down the hall. "I really should get going…"

"Oh, I'll walk with you," Saren replied, gesturing for him to keep going. "It's just been so long since I've had any real friends around. My aunt's a fairly influential player in city politics, and that's made for a lonely time. There are balls and parties nearly every week, but I've not been able to make many friends at them."

"I'm…sorry to hear that," Ekarath responded.

"It's okay, I'm just used to having friends—it wasn't a problem for me in Marsalas. My parents were wealthy and somewhat influential, but there didn't seem to be so many games as there are here in Talas."

"Well, now that Zahara and I are here, I'm sure we can keep each other company. After a year in the Atsada, I'm afraid Zahara might not be the best at talking to other girls. There weren't many our age…you know, with it being mostly soldiers and all."

"That makes sense. I'm just so happy to have you two here. I know Zahara is the Heir and I need to show her plenty of respect, but…I don't know, it just feels like we could be sisters."

Ekarath raised both eyebrows, but he quickly tried to hide his surprise. Zahara could be a bit guarded, and with the new stress of lying about being the Heir, she may not be the friendliest toward this aristocratic girl.

"I just hope I'm not too awkward around you," Saren continued. "I've only been in Talas for three months, and I already feel like I've forgotten how to speak with anyone but Ivana and the servants."

"Oh, you're doing just fine," Ekarath responded as they reached the door to Zahara's chambers. "Well, I'd best be saying goodnight at this point. Zahara wanted to work on a few things."

"May I join you? I absolutely love talking about the *draod*."

"Well, maybe for a few minutes, I guess."

Wow, this girl really is starved for friendship, Ekarath thought before knocking on the door.

A full minute passed, and there was no answer. Saren looked at him, her smile never wavering during the silence. Ekarath knocked again, his lips pursing without thought.

"Maybe she's asleep," Saren said. "We could go for a walk through the gardens. They're lovely on a summer's evening like this."

"Well, I'll just leave this for Zahara first," Ekarath said, hoping to avoid such a stroll. He pushed the door open and slipped inside.

Instead of a spacious sitting room filled with luxurious furniture, his eyes took in a dense jungle. Trees with obsidian bark filled his vision, thin shafts of sunlight streaming in through the canopy. Vines hung down from the branches, and smaller plants blanketed the ground.

In the midst of it all, he could see threads of Illusion.

"Zahara, this is amazing," he whispered, hoping she could hear him. To his eyes, it looked like the forest continued on for miles, though he knew that wasn't possible, no matter how luxurious her rooms were.

"Thanks, it took me all day," Zahara responded, stepping out from behind a tree.

"Reminds me of training with Master Kanu," Ekarath said, looking around. He wouldn't tell her that being able to see her weaves did alter the effect—even if Saren weren't at his side, it didn't need to be said. Nobody else would be able to tell the difference between the illusion and the real thing.

"Someday, I'll be that talented," Zahara responded. "There are plenty of flaws if you look close enough."

"Flaws?" Saren squealed. "I don't see any of those."

"Oh, hello Saren," Zahara said. "I didn't see you there."

"I ran into Ekarath on his way to bring you food," Saren replied.

"I thought it might be nice to bring you something," Ekarath said, offering her the plate. "Since you've missed breakfast, lunch, *and* dinner, I assumed you might be hungry."

"Thank you," Zahara said, taking the food. Yet her eyes were still focused on the forest around them. "Have I really been in here all day?"

"It's almost midnight," Saren said.

"Even Farban was starting to worry about you," Ekarath said, unable to stop admiring the jungle. "This illusion feels worth it, though."

"This isn't all I've been doing," Zahara said, a smile coming to her face. She set the plate down on the ground and disappeared behind a tree. Seconds later, she returned with a cloak in hand.

"First of all, will you verify that you can indeed see me?" Zahara asked, her smile growing wider.

"Of course," Ekarath responded. "You're standing right in front of me."

"What a silly question," Saren said.

"Thank you," Zahara said before throwing the cloak over her shoulders. As it draped around her body, she disappeared, leaving her head floating in the air. Ekarath's jaw dropped, and he struggled to force out a response.

"That...you—"

"It's a weave from Lord Dimitri," Zahara said, slipping the hood up and making her head disappear along with her body. "Very tricky. Making this forest was a breeze in comparison."

Ekarath squinted, looking for the weaves. He found the Illusion threads, but also something more. There was a faint outline of the cloak, but it was very difficult to make out.

"It's not true invisibility like in the stories about the First Heirs," Zahara continued. "But it's certainly close."

"You used Illusion threads to make the light bend around you," Saren said, her voice sounding serious for the first time.

"Exactly," Zahara replied, pulling back the hood to reveal her face.

"This is amazing," Ekarath said, trying to think through the possibilities. "And if you combine that with your other spell to silence your shoes..."

"We could move in complete secret," Zahara said, finishing his words. The girl pulled off the cloak, and Ekarath couldn't recall her ever smiling so much.

This girl has to be the Heir, not me, Ekarath thought, shaking his head.

"How's your training going?" Zahara asked, almost as if she could read his mind. Her eyes darted between Ekarath and Saren, obviously trying to weigh her words in front of the newcomer. "Sorry to abandon you all day, but I figured that Farban could teach you a thing or two."

"It's going...terribly," Ekarath said, and he could feel himself deflate at the memories. For a brief moment, he'd been able to forget his problems. "Remember how I made that huge fireball that almost burned down the forest?"

"Of course," Zahara responded with a chuckle. "I think my eyebrows are still singed."

"Well, now I can't even pull on any threads," Ekarath said. "I can feel the *draod*, but I just can't do anything with it."

"That's normal for a novice, isn't it?" Saren asked, her face showing genuine confusion at Ekarath's pain. "Don't tell me—you're one of those people who is just naturally talented at everything."

"Well, I—"

"Weaving is an art," Saren continued, cutting Ekarath off before he could articulate a single thought. "Just because you're talented enough with a blade to be part of the *Hundiin* doesn't mean you're going to be naturally gifted as a mage."

"You're probably just nervous," Zahara cut in. "It takes a lot of concentration to make the *draod* do what you want it to. Nobody just picks it up on their first try. Here, let's practice a bit."

Zahara's face scrunched up, and the finishing knot on her illusion came undone. A hum filled the air as the pattern unraveled, the energy returning to the ocean of power that surrounded them. The trees, vines, and undergrowth faded, leaving behind the sitting room.

"Didn't you say that took all day?" Saren asked, her eyes growing wide.

"It should get easier," Zahara responded with a shrug. "The point is to practice, not to make my rooms into a permanent jungle. Now, come on."

Zahara sat down on the nearest sofa, patting the spot next to her. Ekarath took a seat, followed by Saren, who nearly sat on his lap.

"Just close your eyes and feel the *draod* all around you," Zahara said, her eyes already shut.

Ekarath did as he was told and began feeling for the *draod*, though ignoring Saren nearly cuddling with him proved difficult. Pushing away all thoughts, he could feel the vast ocean surround him, but it resisted his touch. Instead of forming, the threads refused to give in. It was almost as if a barrier had been erected.

"It's…"

"Just focus," Zahara whispered. "The *draod* is like a wild animal. You can't hope to tame it. It needs to be coerced."

Ekarath couldn't help but think once again about the night before they had entered Talas. The *draod* had felt like an old friend, an ally eager to be of service. The threads had formed without much effort, almost weaving themselves.

At his side, Zahara began weaving another complex tapestry. His untrained inner eye could tell it was formed of Illusion, but other than that, he had no idea what she was doing. With a small knot, she finished the weave—a triangle with a veritable maze of threads throughout the interior.

A smile came onto his face as his mind latched onto the finishing knot. He tugged at it, and the threads unraveled. The *draod* hummed in his chest as the entire weave came apart.

Zahara's fist slammed into his shoulder.

"That took a lot of work," she hissed.

"Sorry, it was just too tempting," Ekarath responded.

"What happened?" Saren asked, and Ekarath immediately bit his tongue.

"Oh...nothing," Zahara responded before Ekarath could think of anything to say. "He just bumped me, and I lost my concentration."

"What were you working on?" Ekarath asked, trying to change the subject. "It looked...complicated. I mean, from the way you were focusing, it had to be."

"It was," Zahara responded. "I was going to put that invisibility spell on a new cloak for you."

"Oh, I like that idea," Ekarath said. "We could sneak out of here and explore the city a bit."

"I was actually thinking we could stir up some trouble," Zahara said. "You know, sabotage some buildings, steal weapons."

"Well, that's a much more responsible idea," Ekarath said with a shrug. "But I still like my idea better."

At his side, Saren's body stiffened, and he looked over to see her smiling.

"Just think of everything the three of us could accomplish," Saren said, practically giggling through the words.

Wow, this girl...

"We could attack the garrison complex, set fire to administrative buildings," Saren continued before her voice grew serious. "And then we could put a knife in the Usurper's back."

The room fell silent at the girl's words. Of course, they would all like to stop the Destroyer of Worlds, but the hatred in the girl's voice was palpable.

"Wow, I don't think that would be the wisest idea," Zahara said, breaking the silence. "I can make you invisible and silent, but an assassination attempt on the Usurper...that sounds a bit beyond my abilities."

Ekarath turned to see the girl's face going pale as she looked off into the distance. Just like everyone else, Saren must have experienced great loss—loss that was due to the Usurper.

Footsteps sounded outside the door, followed by a knock. Without waiting for a response, the knob twisted, and the door swung open to reveal Farban.

"Oh good, I was hoping to see you three together," Farban said.

"What's going on?" both Zahara and Ekarath responded in unison.

"There have been...developments," Farban said. "Ivana wants to talk to all of us."

***

Zahara took a seat around the large table, Ekarath at her side. Saren had taken a seat on the other side of the young man, scooting her chair to be closer to the *Hundiin*. Zahara resisted the urge to shoot her a glare, instead focusing her attention on Ivana.

The stately duchess stood at the head of the table. Though she held her head high, Zahara could see the woman struggling to keep her perfect posture. There were bags under her eyes, and her skin looked a bit paler than it had just the day before.

Count Maslov and Farban had both settled in on the other side of the table. The two men shot piercing looks at each other before shifting their gazes toward Ivana.

"It's been a strange day," Ivana began. "I've kept you all in the dark until the picture became clear, but now it's time to fill you in. After the Usurper nearly killed himself, Governor Pavel tried to launch a palace coup. Unfortunately for him and his co-conspirators, it failed. It appears that Pavel was killed in the fighting, and as of right now, the Primal King is moving swiftly, purging everyone he thinks was involved."

"What does that mean for you?" Zahara asked.

"Fortunately, I didn't have any part in the coup attempt—and I've been a vocal supporter of the Usurper in public. My secret dealings with the rebellion don't allow me to play the 'loyal opposition'."

"Not to mention that Pavel would have been a worse ruler than the Usurper," Maslov said, waving a hand in disgust. "Though he may have been easier to overthrow."

"So far, it looks as if the failed attempt to destroy the Shajarat will provide an abundance of danger and opportunity," Ivana said. "The fact that a snake like Pavel saw the Usurper as vulnerable should mean that others will soon believe the same. His rule could destabilize to the point that he could face rebellions in the other Heirdoms."

"And what are the dangers?" Maslov asked. "Beyond the fact that the Usurper could destroy the entire city in a fit of paranoia."

"My spy in the palace has heard that Mahzun has a troublesome theory about why he couldn't destroy the Shajarat," Ivana said.

"Other than it being an indestructible tree that dates back to the Creation?" Farban asked with a laugh.

"Apparently, the Usurper believes his failure was due to the continued existence of an Heir," Ivana replied, her words spreading across the room like a thick blanket.

Zahara didn't know what to say, and she resisted the urge to out Ekarath as the real Heir right then and there. If the Usurper suspected there to be an Heir, what did that change?

"Well, that could be good, right?" Maslov finally said, breaking the silence. "He'll comb the entire continent in search of the Heir, while she's hiding within sight of his palace."

"It could also mean increased vigilance," Farban said, shaking his head. "We'll need to take extra precautions when training Zahara. People may not suspect the Heir to be hiding in the middle of Talas, but a young, talented mage could draw suspicion."

"Exactly," Ivana said, looking directly at Zahara. "I'm afraid you shouldn't leave the manor for a while."

Great, yet another prison, Zahara thought.

"That makes sense," Zahara said aloud.

"And with this latest shakeup in the political landscape, I plan on taking the opportunity to cozy up to the Usurper," Ivana said.

Zahara's jaw dropped at the words, and she could practically feel the air pressure change in the room.

"Oh, not like that," Ivana said with a laugh. "Though I can see how you would interpret it that way. Fortunately for me, the Usurper is looking for a woman who can bear a child. Last week, I spoke with the Usurper's steward about our esteemed emperor accompanying young Saren to a ball."

In the corner of her eye, Zahara saw the girl visibly shudder at the words, but she quickly recovered. After her request just moments ago to stick a knife in the Usurper's back, there was no need to speculate why.

"Now that procuring a marriage and a scion will be of increased importance for the Usurper, I will be throwing a ball in three days. I have high hopes that I can convince the Usurper to be in attendance, with Saren at his side."

"What?" Maslov shouted before bringing his voice back to normal level. "I'm sorry, but it just doesn't seem wise to allow the Usurper into your home when you're hosting the Heir of Segova."

"Zahara will, of course, remain far from the ball-room," Ivana said.

"Is that really necessary?" Zahara asked. "I could attend and try to see what people are gossiping about. With Saren to distract the Usurper, I don't think we would even cross paths."

"That's far too risky," Farban said, shaking his head. "You're talking about being in the same room as the Usurper and hundreds of his supporters. What if someone recognizes you? The very fact that you were in the Atsada could be enough to get you executed."

"The only person who could possibly recognize me was just killed for treason," Zahara said, referring to Pavel. "I want to help—please don't make me sit around doing nothing."

"You will have plenty of opportunity to be of ser-vice," Ivana said. "But you are far too important for a menial task like spying at a ball. There couldn't pos-sibly be any information you could glean that would justify that risk."

Zahara sat back and folded her arms. She wanted to shoot Ekarath a look, but she knew that wouldn't do any good. Apparently satisfied, Ivana moved on, directing her attention to Saren.

"I know this won't be easy for you," Ivana said, her face softening as she looked at her niece, "but I do

think your age, gender, and beauty will be absolutely vital. The Usurper is concerned about passing on
the Imperial Crown, so he will be considering several
noblewomen for courtship. If we can get you close to
him—both physically and emotionally—I think it will
be the best chance we have. You can learn his secrets
and weaknesses."

"I understand," Saren replied. "With that knowledge—and Zahara's abilities—we will destroy him."

Chapter 20

Ekarath dropped a stack of books onto a table, kicking up a cloud of dust. At his side, Zahara coughed, waving her hands to dissipate the cloud and keep the particles away from her lungs.

"Are you sure this is the best way to spend our time?" Zahara asked.

"You heard Ivana," Ekarath responded. "It's not safe for us to leave the grounds. If we're going to be stuck somewhere, we might as well try to figure out how to make you the Heir."

"Even if I agreed with you—which I don't—do you really think we'll find a weave that will transfer an Heir's powers to another person? You have to be the first person stupid enough to even ask that question."

"I'm not saying we'll find a direct answer, but there has to be something that will give us a clue."

Ekarath lifted his arms, gesturing to the large library. The room was two stories tall, with shelves reaching to the ceiling. Thousands of books lined the walls, and thousands more sat in shorter shelves spaced throughout the room. Large windows on the east wall drank in the morning sunlight, and warm beams streamed in through the glass.

The table in the middle was large enough for a group to study, though at the moment, Ekarath and Zahara were alone. Fortunately, they had been able to avoid Saren and make their way to the library in secret.

"I can't just sit here and read old books until we wither up and die," Zahara said, sitting down at the table.

"It can't possibly take that long," Ekarath said, taking a seat at her side and opening the nearest book. It was a history of the first millennium in Karajaan, translated into common. "There has to be at least one Heir in the past three thousand years who's passed on his powers without dying."

Across the table, Zahara pulled out the book given to her by Lord Dimitri. By now, Ekarath could recite most of that opening message without looking, and it made his stomach squirm.

"Come on, you spent all day yesterday looking at Lord Dimitri's message," Ekarath said.

"I'm not just reading that first letter. The weaves described by Lord Dimitri are fascinating," Zahara said. "There's at least a dozen that I've never even heard of before. If you're interested, I think there's a lot more to learn in here than in that entire stack of books."

"I haven't been able to so much as touch the *draod* since our arrival," Ekarath said, trying to focus on the history book. "The sooner we figure out how to make you the Heir of Segova, the better."

Zahara didn't respond, and Ekarath turned his attention to the nearest book. His eyes moved over the same paragraph three times before looking back up at his friend. The girl's dark eyes were completely engrossed in Dimitri's writings, and Ekarath smiled at her brow furrowed in concentration.

"What's wrong?" Zahara asked without looking up. "Is your book a little boring?"

"Oh, uh..."

"It's okay," Zahara said, looking up at him with a smile. "I've been told my reading face is a bit comical."

"No, it was actually quite...yeah, comical," Ekarath finished. He wanted to say "beautiful," but he caught himself.

"Should I head back to my rooms?" Zahara asked. "I don't want to be a distraction."

"No, please stay," Ekarath said, lifting his hands for her to stay seated. "I have a feeling that studying all day in this library would get a little dull without you."

"I think you'll find those books to be a bit dull no matter who happens to be with you," Zahara said. "If you do get lonely, you could maybe ask Saren to come sit with you."

"Why would I do that?"

"Oh, come on—I saw the way she looked at you. From the moment she first set eyes on you, she couldn't keep her gaze away from your chiseled physique. She was practically sitting on your lap last night."

"Oh, I hadn't really noticed," Ekarath said, trying to think back to the time he had spent with the silly noblewoman before a smile leapt onto his face. "Wait, are you...jealous?"

"Jealous? Of course not," Zahara responded with a half giggle. "You and I are friends. Feel free to court anyone you'd like, though if everything goes according to plan, you'll be competing with the Usurper if you decide to go after Saren."

"I think I'll pass," Ekarath said. "Hard to really compete against the emperor of all Einar. Besides, I've never really seen myself courting someone like Saren—I'd prefer someone with a little more...depth."

Zahara gulped and looked back at her book. A silence engulfed the room, and Ekarath wasn't sure if he had said too much.

"Do you think we can compete against him?" Zahara finally asked, her voice barely rising above a whisper. "In addition to the Eternal Blade, he has the resources of all Einar to draw upon, and we have..."

"We have you," Ekarath said as her words trailed off. "You're intelligent, driven—there's no limit to what you can accomplish."

"But I'm not even allowed to leave this estate," Zahara replied. "This is just a gilded cage."

"That's just for now. I'm sure in a few weeks, you can join some of Ivana's rebels and cause plenty of mischief."

"I'm not even deemed worthy of going to the ball and spying. As long as I'm pretending to be the Heir of Segova, what makes you think anybody will let me do anything meaningful?"

"Is this the same girl who climbed to the top of the Atsada? Is this the same girl who tried to create a new *qilada*? Nobody lets you do anything—you just do it."

For a moment, Zahara just stared into his eyes, and he could see tears beginning to form.

"Thank you," Zahara said, shutting Dimitri's book and rising to her feet.

"Where are you going?" Ekarath asked.

"You're absolutely right," Zahara responded. "If I want to be useful, I need to take my destiny into my own hands."

With those words still ringing in the air, Zahara sped out of the library. Ekarath let out a deep breath and returned to his book.

I'm an idiot.

Chapter 21

Mahzun sat at the large table, trying to decide which was more bothersome: listening to the mixture of inane prattle or his suit. At his side sat a pretty, young thing—hair so blond it was nearly white, perfect skin, a petite yet full figure. Her dress was a rich vermillion, and her curves certainly filled it out.

She spoke plenty for the both of them, though he couldn't remember her name. *Niece of some member of the Elder Council*, he grunted internally. If that didn't make her a potential spy, he didn't know what else would. Yet he made sure to turn his attention toward the girl once in a while and at least grunt his acknowledgement.

Sitting once again atop a raised platform at the far end of the ballroom, he had a commanding view of the festivities. Dozens of tables were set up, all of which were occupied by lords and ladies in expensive silks. They laughed and spoke while drinking fine wines and taking delicate bites of gourmet food.

To his right, Lord Dimitri continued his silent vigil, the dead eyes boring into Mahzun's soul. The old man still refused to leave him be, and it was getting harder and harder to not return that glare. Yet he knew that acknowledging the apparition—in public, at least—would lead to problems.

At his side, Lorna spoke to the young woman forced to accompany him.

"It was most certainly an eventful evening, Lady Saren," Lorna said, the words pulling Mahzun out of his thoughts. "But His Majesty is not a man to be defeated by the likes of Pavel."

Ah yes, her name is Saren, niece of Duchess Ivana. I'll try to remember that.

"Killing that man was a pleasure," Mahzun replied in a low voice, the first time he'd done more than grunt in half an hour. "A traitor like Pavel can never really be trusted, even when his betrayal is beneficial. When he saw the opportunity to give up the city of Talas, he betrayed the Heirs. When he saw the opportunity to take the throne, he tried to betray me."

"Well, I know the entire city was overjoyed to hear of your survival," Saren said, a smile taking over her entire face. Yet there was something in her eyes, a mixture of emotions hidden behind a thin veneer. He could almost feel her hatred and revulsion bubbling to the surface.

A change came over the room, something he couldn't come close to identifying. It was almost as if a storm were coming, the imperceptible hum of impending thunder. Turning away from his date, his eyes moved toward the ballroom. At the edge of the festivities, he spotted another young woman.

She had the dark skin marking her as a native of Karajaan, and her tight braids were done up into an intricate pattern atop her head. A dress of dark blue silk embroidered in silver hung down to her feet. While the young woman was rather thin, she still managed to fill out the dress.

Yet it wasn't just her appearance—lovely as it was—that pulled in the Savior of Man. There was something about the way she stood, examining the room as if she were both above and separate from everything around her. Her head was held high, but it lacked the sneer that so often accompanied a noble countenance.

There was strength in that girl, a strength that filled every bit of her, down to the bones.

Her eyes moved across the dance floor, as if in search of something or someone. She stood alone, unaccompanied by either a romantic prospect or a group of friends. Something in her eyes said she preferred it that way.

"Now that the war is over," Lorna said at his side, "we have very big plans for the Empire."

Mahzun registered the words, and he knew that his sister wanted his attention. Yet he couldn't control his eyes.

"I know my aunt will want to discuss those plans with you," Saren replied, her voice losing a portion of its silliness. "And I would love to hear whatever you can share with me."

With all the willpower he could muster, Mahzun pulled his gaze away from the Karajaani beauty.

"Of course," Mahzun replied, forcing himself to look in his date's eyes. There certainly was a beauty to the blue orbs, but beyond the hatred held inside them, he found little depth. "I have plans—big plans—for all Einar. Without the squabbling between Heirdoms, we can now focus all our energy and attention to building roads, canals, markets—everything our people need to be prosperous."

"So much to look forward to," the girl said, her smile growing wider. "I have heard talk of a canal linking the northern farmlands and Talas. I can only imagine..."

The girl kept talking, but Mahzun lost focus as the orchestra began to play. Down below, couples transitioned from tables to the polished marble floor that dominated the center of the ballroom. He refused to look back at Saren, fearing she would expect an invitation to join those couples.

While he had been taking lessons—at Lorna's insistence—he knew that his skills were nowhere near ready. Instead, he just focused on the music, hoping the young girl at his side would understand.

His eyes once again caught the young Karajaani woman. She remained on the periphery, as if she had no desire to actually be part of the festivities. Yet he could see in the way she swayed to the music that she wanted to be part of the couples engaged in those orchestrated movements.

There's something familiar about her, Mahzun thought, but he couldn't place his finger on it. Certainly, there was no significant Karajaani population this far north. It had been five years since he'd conquered the southernmost province of his empire, and he'd not had a reason to return since then. Was his memory simply thinking of those campaigns a half-decade prior?

"Please, excuse me for a moment," Mahzun said, placing his napkin on the table and rising to his feet.

What am I doing?

Without pausing to assess his unvoiced question, Mahzun descended from the place of honor, ignoring the quiet protests issuing from both Lorna and Saren. The weight of a hundred eyes fell upon Mahzun as he crossed the ballroom, trying his best to keep to the outside edge of the festivities.

The young woman didn't notice his approach, her gaze focused on the dance floor. As he drew near, he cleared his throat. The girl jumped, turning with wide eyes.

"May I have this dance?" Mahzun asked, offering a deep bow to the girl.

"I—I—"

"I'll take that as a 'yes,'" Mahzun said, offering his arm. The girl continued to stare, but she managed to close her mouth before slipping her thin—yet surprisingly strong—arm through his. The weight of more eyes fell upon him as he led the young woman to the dance floor. The song ended, allowing for a change in dance partners, and they joined the existing couples.

She delicately placed a hand in his, and he put his free hand on the small of her back. Up close, her beauty was radiant: flawless skin that needed no makeup, eyes so deep he could see himself wandering through their depths for an eternity. His nose picked up the faint hint of clove and mint, a far cry from the heavy scents preferred by most socialites.

The orchestra started up again, and they began to move in time with the mixture of strings. While the girl had remained apart from the dancing, Mahzun could see no reason for it. Her body moved with a simple grace, making up for his lack of skill.

"Are you enjoying your evening?" Mahzun asked, trying to think of something to say. For the first time, the girl looked up into his face, their eyes making contact.

"It's lovely," the girl replied, breaking off her gaze and directing it upward. "Such a magnificent place to hold a ball."

"Agreed," Mahzun said, clearing his throat. "It's been a transition—moving from a life on campaign to one in the city. I've traded sleeping in the mud for a soft bed, and physical battles for political debates."

"Which one do you prefer?" the woman asked, her voice growing a bit stronger.

"They both have their charms," Mahzun said, his smile growing wider.

As he guided them through the basic dance moves, he became entranced by the woman's grace. She moved with the fluidity of a river, her muscles flexible. Yet there was a strength within her—one that came from more than just toned muscles.

"But I will admit, life in Talas has been harder than I would have thought," Mahzun said, the words leaving his mouth without permission. "I spent so long dreaming of the war's end. Now that it's here, I don't quite know what to do with myself."

Great, why don't you just start crying like a baby?

Yet the woman's face softened with the words, and he could feel her muscles relax, if slightly. Her eyes peered into his, no longer fixated on their surroundings. At that moment, he felt naked, as if this girl could see through his eyes and into his very soul.

"The war has been difficult for all of us," she said, the words coming out slowly, as if they contained a novel concept.

"I most certainly can't complain—my people have taken the brunt of the suffering. Now that the war has ended, they are the ones I'm most concerned about."

The music ended, though Mahzun wanted to keep dancing. Yet he could feel the weight of a hundred eyes falling on him yet again, and he knew the only proper thing would be to simply bow and allow the girl to resume her place on the party's periphery.

"Thank you for humoring a scarred old man," Mahzun said, giving her a bow.

"It was my pleasure," the woman responded, giving a curtsy.

Mahzun turned around and began walking toward Lorna and Saren. He glanced up at the table—his date watched with a dropped jaw while Lorna glared with enough power to kill a lesser man. When he reached the base of the stairs, he turned back to steal another glance at the Karajaani girl.

She was gone, nowhere to be seen.

***

Every muscle in Zahara's body trembled, threatening to spasm as she sped down the quiet hallway. Illuminated by moonlight and a few *kura*, her mind was occupied by a single thought. The skin on her lower back crawled, as if an entire colony of ants were making it their home.

Stopping at a large door, she pounded on the heavy wood. For a moment, she didn't know if she had reached the right room or not. She let out a deep sigh as familiar footsteps sounded from the other side, and the door swung open to reveal Ekarath.

"Good evening, Zah—are you okay?"

"I...I'm fine," Zahara stammered before shuffling into her friend's room. Unlike the entire suite of rooms she'd been given, Ekarath's quarters were much more spartan. Instead of a large, four-poster monstrosity, he had a bed barely large enough for his tall frame. There was a comfortable fireplace and a leather sofa, but it was much smaller than she had expected.

Ekarath was dressed in a nightshirt, and Zahara tried not to look at his bare legs. A pile of large books sat next to the sofa, and one sat open as if she'd caught him reading. For a moment, she considered leaving the young man alone.

"You are most certainly not fine," Ekarath said, grabbing her by the hand and leading her to the sofa. He sat her down and grabbed a pitcher of water, pouring her a glass. She gulped down the tepid liquid, and her muscles began to feel less tremorous.

"Now, what happened?" Ekarath asked, sitting down at her side. He grabbed her trembling hands and turned to look her in the face.

"Please don't judge me too harshly, but I...I snuck down to the ball," Zahara said, gesturing to her gown and styled hair before pausing to collect her thoughts. "I just wanted to experience it—maybe hear some gossip that could help Farban and Ivana."

"And?"

"...and I saw the Usurper."

"Oh dear," Ekarath said, wrapping her in his arms. Her muscles drank in the warmth, and her trembling—while failing to cease—lessened. There was no anger in his embrace, no sense of a coming lecture on the need to be obedient.

"I still think about that day atop the Atsada," Ekarath whispered. "Seeing him from a distance was enough to give me nightmares."

"That's not all," Zahara said, leaning further into the man's warmth. "He...he...asked me to dance."

Ekarath stiffened and pulled back, his eyes wide. He tried stammering a response, but Zahara pulled herself back into his arms, nuzzling her face into the cotton nightshirt.

"I don't think he recognized me, but I've never been so scared in my entire life. He held my hand in his and touched the small of my back. His scars..."

"It's going to be okay," Ekarath said, squeezing her tighter.

Zahara didn't know how long she sat there, completely enveloped in Ekarath's embrace. The clock on the mantel ticked off the seconds, and she didn't even try to keep count. For a minute, an hour or an eternity, the world felt still.

Ekarath pulled back and placed a hand on her face. She could feel his pulse, the beat a quick staccato. He leaned in, placing his forehead to hers. She could feel his breath on her lips, warm and sweet. That breath drew closer, and she could almost feel his lips graze her own.

What am I doing?

Zahara pulled back and looked around the room.

"I...I think I need to be alone," Zahara said, leaping off the sofa, heart pounding in her ears. "I just need some time to think."

"I'm sorry," Ekarath said, his face burning a bright red. "I didn't mean—"

"No, it's fine," Zahara said. "I...I'm going to go for a walk."

Zahara dashed out of the room, unsure of what she had just done. Or what she had just avoided.

Chapter 22

Despite the warm summer air, Zahara walked with her hood up, grateful for the weave that made her nearly invisible. Her muscles continued to shake as if the streets were gripped by winter rather than the soft summer breeze that tried to caress her through the hood. Images of the Usurper flashed through her mind, and she fought off a wave of nausea.

The wide avenue that circled the Mount of Creation was deserted at this late hour, the result of a strict curfew. The occasional noble carriage rode by, unaffected by the new rules, but Zahara's *draod*-enhanced vision didn't find any other pedestrians.

The empty streets were a welcome sight, and she took in deep breaths of the warm air to calm her nerves. As she turned onto Liberty Boulevard, she still didn't have a destination in mind. She just needed to keep moving, and the garden that split the wide road down the middle was preferable to anything else. The trees, shrubs, and fountains were not only beautiful, but they also provided further shadows.

After the events of the past few hours, she wanted nothing more than to hide.

Within five minutes, she passed the first set of fellow delinquents—a young couple engaged in a clandestine liaison. The sight of their passionate kiss sent Zahara's

mind back to Ekarath. She could still feel his lips on
her forehead, and for a moment, she longed for the
warmth of his embrace.

"This is no time for such thoughts," Zahara cursed
in a soft whisper as she strode past the couple.

She was in the middle of planning a rebellion against
the most powerful being ever recorded in the history of
Einar, and her desires to help were proving disastrous.
Zahara had not only ruined the evening for Saren, but
she was now in the Usurper's sights. Yes, there was the
physical revulsion she felt at being so close to the man
who was responsible for so much death and suffering,
but there was also the fear that her anonymity was at
risk.

Yet the worst part was that the evilest man in the
world had been drawn to her. What did that say about
Zahara?

Ekarath is also drawn to me, she thought. What did
that say about him?

Heavy footsteps sounded in the air, and Zahara's ears
perked up, yanking her from the thought. Just ahead,
a squadron of the town guards approached. Zahara
let out a sigh of relief upon seeing the bright, striped
uniforms rather than the dark leather and steel. While
the men held long pikes, there was little to fear from
the aristocratic dandies.

That couple a few blocks back may be in for a surprise,
Zahara thought, as she ducked into a shadow and waited for the soldiers to pass. The thought of surviving
a face-to-face meeting with the Usurper only to be
caught a few hours later by common soldiers for simply
breaking curfew brought a smile to her face.

Hoping to avoid another such patrol, Zahara moved
down the first side street she found. While the polished
cobblestone was still surrounded on both sides by tall

buildings, it lacked the gardens of Liberty Boulevard. Yet the glow of both the Shajarat and the moon created enough shadows, especially when mixed with her cloak.

She kept moving, her feet taking her along the smooth cobblestone while she allowed her mind to wander. She could still feel the Usurper's touch on her hand, on her back. Those eyes still bored into hers, and she could see the scars moving like worms.

His voice—so much softer than she had expected—echoed throughout her mind. There was certainly a disconnect between the man who had immediately shown humility, even vulnerability, and the monster who haunted her dreams.

The man is a murderer, she thought. Even if he hadn't held the sword, it was because of the Usurper that her father's bones sat amid the ruins of her childhood home. It was due to the hardship of their flight that her mother had died.

Because of him, she had lost everything.

I hate him.

Yet he didn't seem to feel the same way. While the Primal King's fascination with her was inexplicable by any standard, she knew it created an opportunity.

I can use that to strike him down.

Yet how? She wasn't strong enough to feel his touch again. What if he wanted to do more than just dance next time? She couldn't bring herself to do such a thing, even if it did mean the monster's downfall.

Shouts broke Zahara away from her reverie, and she looked around for the source of the commotion. Instead of the tall, well-kept buildings, she found herself in a much poorer section of Talas. Here, the buildings were squat, many of the facades badly damaged from time and vandalism.

An arrow flew through the air, sailing over her head.

Zahara slammed up against the nearest building and surveyed the scene with her *draod*-enhanced vision. Dozens of soldiers—real legionnaires in dark armor, not members of the guard—stood in a line, their backs to Zahara. They held large shields, protecting themselves from the barrage of arrows coming from further down the street.

Zahara shifted to get a glimpse past the wall of black leather and steel. Just a few hundred feet away, the road ended, blocked by a massive building. Near the dead end, a handful of archers stood behind a makeshift barricade.

With each salvo, the legionnaires moved forward. An arrow slipped past the shield wall, and a legionnaire let out a scream. He fell back, and his comrades—without skipping a beat—continued in their push. The men cornered at the end of the street continued to fire.

"For the Heirs and Einar," sounded one of the archers, and Zahara realized these were no simple bandits or criminals.

They were rebels.

Rebels fighting against the Usurper, possibly one of the bands under Ivana's command. Staying out of the fight no longer felt like an option. Cursing herself for a lack of weapons, Zahara checked the weaves on her shoes and cloak, ensuring she would be able to move both unheard and unseen.

Pushing off the wall, Zahara dashed into the street, toward the Imperial soldiers. Without making a sound, she launched her foot into the leg of the nearest legionnaire. With a sharp crack, the limb bent unnaturally, and the man fell to the ground with a shout. The men around him kept moving, assuming he had taken an arrow.

She grabbed a knife from the fallen man's sheath, ignoring his continued shouts, which were reducing to mere grunts. The soldier's eyes widened as his knife began to float in the air, and Zahara knew the effect it would have. With a smile, she flung the knife toward the man's comrades, the blade hitting another man in the back.

"There's a ghost," screamed the soldier whose knife she had stolen. The words echoed in the street, rising above the din of battle. Zahara launched her foot directly at the man's face, and he fell back to the ground.

Some of the legionnaires at the back turned, the realization dawning on them that they were under attack from the rear. Zahara pulled on threads of Destruction, creating a thick weave of fire. Her smile only grew as she finished the weave with a knot.

An inferno came to life, the mixture of orange, red, and blue careening through the air until it slammed into the soldiers. Shouts filled the street as the packed formation broke apart, spreading out in all directions. Several of the soldiers didn't move, instead falling to the ground with screams.

Zahara dashed toward the running men, grabbed the nearest soldier, and slammed her knee into his face with a sickening crunch. He fell to the ground and scrambled away, with blood dripping from his nose.

Aware of how it must look to everyone else, she kept up her attack. An officer tried to reform his men as they looked on in horror, their comrades falling from unseen blows. Shouts of fear began to accompany the screams of pain.

Zahara pulled on the *draod* once again, launching a bolt of lightning at the shouting officer. The force launched him backwards, his flight only stopped by the nearest building. The sight and sound broke the professional, hardened soldiers.

All around her, men fled. She let them go, thinking of her first victim's words. Soon, there would be rumors of a ghost protecting those who served the Creator.

Chapter 23

Mahzun took in a breath of city air as his carriage rumbled along the main avenue that ran from the Mount of Creation all the way to the main gate. While most streets of the Imperial City were wide and paved with smooth stones, Liberty Boulevard put the rest to shame.

Dressed in full battle armor, Mahzun finally felt at ease. The mixture of plate and chain mail weighed on his frame, but he had worn it for so long that it felt like a second set of skin. It was certainly more comfortable than the suits he'd been forced to wear in recent days.

The scent of urban life filtered in through his open window—a mix of charcoal fires and the spices used on the various meats and vegetables being sold by a nearby vendor. It mixed with the constant smell of too many humans packed into tight quarters, which Mahzun's nose had grown accustomed to after a decade in military camps.

Across from him, Lorna's scrunched up face said that she approved of neither the smell nor Mahzun's appearance. She was dressed in a regal gown of deep blue silk, and her hair was covered in a white shawl—apparel much more appropriate than Mahzun's ebony armor.

The dress reminded him of the young Karajaani woman, and his mind drifted to night before. He could still feel the delicate hand in his, could smell the faint aroma of mint and clove. He longed to stare into those eyes once again and lose himself, forgetting the problems of this world.

Focus, he growled mentally at himself, switching his mind back to the present.

If Lorna noticed his mood, she didn't say anything. Her eyes were focused on a report from some branch of government that Mahzun didn't really care about. Yet those eyes flitted toward him and the window enough to make her displeasure known.

The apparition of Lord Dimitri sat at her side, his gaze never wavering from Mahzun. The Emperor did his best to ignore those dead eyes, but they pulled at him like magnets.

Turning his attention away from the dead Heir, Mahzun smiled as the carriage approached the bustling marketplace. While luxurious carriages filled the streets, shoppers at the market stopped in awe of the only vehicle in the city carrying the Imperial seal. Many gestured to their fellow shoppers, pointing in the carriage's direction. Those faces projected a mixture of fear, awe, and worship—Mahzun could almost feel those emotions boring into him. He poked his gauntleted hand out the window and waved. A young girl near the market's edge returned his gesture with a grin, and Mahzun felt a smile of his own form on his lips.

"Don't get too drunk on their love," Lorna said. "For every citizen that's overjoyed to see you, there are two or three that want to see you dead."

Mahzun looked over to see his sister's gaze boring into him. While her hands still secured the report, her attention was now fully on him.

"I've sacrificed years of my life for these very people, even the ones who hate me," Mahzun replied, gesturing out the window. "They're the ones who are oppressed. They're the ones who need a champion. I hate that since returning to Talas, I've been forced to make nice with a bunch of aristocrats."

"That's because they're the ones with enough wealth and power to make the changes you want," Lorna said with a shake of her head. "It would be prudent to stay focused on staying in those aristocrats' favor. Besides, there's at least one noblewoman you didn't seem to hate."

Mahzun could feel the blood rush to his cheeks at the words, and he turned to face his sister. A wicked smile took up her entire face, and he let out a sigh.

"That was foolish of me, and I apologize."

"Lady Saren is the one who needs an apology. She was trying her absolute best last night, but I guess the heart wants what the heart wants..."

"There's something about that young woman," Mahzun said, shaking his head. "Couldn't you feel it?"

"Not at all. In fact, I thought she was a bit scrawny. Compared to Lady Saren, she was rather plain."

"Please tell me you know who the Karajaani girl is—you've spent an entire year getting to know the nobility of Talas."

"I've never seen her before," Lorna replied, pursing her lips. "Do you command me to find her?"

"Does it need to be a command?"

"Yes, because I think you can do better."

"There's something about her," Mahzun said, trying to figure out exactly what it was. "So yes, I'm ordering you to investigate. I need to know who she is and how I can see her again."

"As you wish, Your Majesty."

Mahzun ignored the sarcasm in the title and again looked out the window, this time to see the largest building below the Mount of Creation looming ahead. Originally built by the First Heirs and embellished over the centuries, the Great Hall of the Council was a monstrosity of white granite. The front was lined by tall columns that supported a covered portico. A tall dome dominated the center of the building, which had once housed a statue of the Creator. That statue was now nothing more than dust.

"Are you sure you want to do this?" Lorna asked. "You know the Council won't take kindly to your presence."

"They need to understand that I'm not just a replacement for the Heirs," Mahzun said, shaking his head. "I'm something new, and things have changed."

In the entire history of Talas, the Heirs had rarely attended the weekly meetings held by the Council, choosing to take a hands-off approach to governing. When they had attended, it was for special events accompanied by a formal invitation. The Elders—those who had survived Pavel's coup attempt—had no idea he was coming, and there was little chance they would accept his presence without protest.

Lorna responded with nothing more than a raised eyebrow, and Mahzun winced at her silent attack. At her side, Lord Dimitri's glare continued.

"Look, I don't really want to do this—in fact, I'd rather storm the Atsada a thousand times than face this pack of jackals," Mahzun said. "But the Council would much rather see me dead than anything else, and I need to keep them on their toes."

"Well, showing up unannounced and breaking a tradition that stretches back thousands of years will do the trick," Lorna said. "I just hope you're thinking all these things through. Duchess Ivana and the others are outwardly professing an undying loyalty, but they will always be scheming three or four steps ahead. I've spent the past year trying to coax them onto our side, and I'm worried you're going to unravel my efforts."

"Well, at least you're honest," Mahzun replied with a smile. "And I see what you mean, but you did what was necessary to help me win the war. Now it's over, and those old relics of the past may need to be discarded. Only time will tell."

Before Lorna could respond, the carriage came to a stop, and the driver leapt down from his perch. Mahzun cracked his neck to relieve the tension as the servant's boots sounded on the cobblestone. A rush of air attacked Mahzun's face as his door swung open.

"Your Majesty," the man droned with a bow. Mahzun just nodded in response as he stepped out of the vehicle, followed by Lorna. He didn't dare look back to see if the dead-eyed Lord Dimitri followed.

"Now that we're here, I don't hate your armor so much," Lorna said, gesturing to the black plate mail that weighed down Mahzun's gait. "It's good to remind the Elders that while they sat back in the Talas, you were out fighting."

"It should also remind them that I won't hesitate to keep fighting," Mahzun growled as they reached the steps leading up to the main entrance. His armored boots cracked on the marble, though the hinges of his armor were well-oiled, and they didn't make a sound as he reached the top of the stairs. Ahead loomed the entryway, which was blocked off by a dozen members of the town watch.

As their eyes fell on the approaching ogre, Mahzun could see their muscles tense. One of the guards—a young man with a strong chin and a feathered officer's cap—took a step forward and lifted a fist to his chest in salute.

"Welcome, Your Majesty," the officer said. "I'm afraid the Elder Council is in the middle of a meeting."

"And?" Mahzun barked without slowing. The young man's face deflated, and his eyes widened.

"If you'd like to speak to a member of the Council, I'd be happy to let you wait in an office," the soldier replied, his voice growing a bit higher.

"I'm going to enter," Mahzun said, stopping to look down on the noble officer who stood two heads shorter than his sovereign. "You can tell your men to open the door, or I'll do it myself."

"Of course, Your Majesty." The officer gulped before motioning for his men to open the door. "Sincerest apologies."

"None are required," Mahzun said as he strode toward the opening doors. "You were only doing your job."

The building's interior was meant to impress those with tiny minds. A large, square chamber was lined with statues of various historical figures sitting in alcoves that climbed up four stories. Marble figures at the top were twice the size of those on the bottom, distorting the sense of perspective to mere mortals. Above the statues, a gilded dome came together, drawing the eye skyward.

Yet Mahzun only had eyes for the members of the Council. They sat on stone benches in two aisles facing a podium at the far end of the room. The Elders were spaced out from each other to avoid whispered conversations with neighbors while official business was discussed. To Mahzun, it just made the room look empty.

Duchess Ivana stood at the podium, but her words died as Mahzun entered. The woman's face held neither a smile nor a frown, but he could sense annoyance in her eyes. That gaze didn't slow Mahzun's trek to the podium, and a smile took over his face as steel boots cracked on the marble floor.

"It is an honor to have Your Majesty's presence among us," Ivana finally said, her voice laced with a false honey. "But you must understand that this is no special event. We are only discussing mundane issues facing the city, things hardly worth the attention of our Dear Emperor."

"I'm glad you don't want to waste my time," Mahzun growled as he climbed the three steps to the podium. "However, now that the war is over, we have a lot of work to do. As emperor, I'm not some aloof tyrant, content to watch my city rot from the comfort of my palace."

Ivana forced a smile, one that didn't extend to her eyes, before turning back to the Council.

"It is now my honor to cede the floor to His Majesty," Ivana said before backing away and taking a seat on a chair behind the podium. Mahzun didn't like the idea of turning his back to the woman, but it couldn't be helped. He stepped up to the podium and cleared his throat, recalling the words that had spent the past few hours bouncing around his head.

"I'm not one for flowery oratory," Mahzun said, his voice bouncing on the marble walls. "But we must prepare for the new age that is dawning."

The Elders looked at him with blank faces, trying their best to hide the shock and hatred in their souls. After purging the men and women who had conspired with Pavel, their number was down from twenty-five to just nineteen. There would soon be elections for fill those seats, but until then, these were the people he had to work with.

Mahzun spotted Lorna standing near the front doors, her brow creased with worry. Dimitri stood at her side, the only person in the entire room who didn't display a single emotion.

"As the Age of Man is born, I look forward to working with all of you," Mahzun bellowed loud enough to make sure that everyone in the room would be able to hear him. "After millennia of oppression and a decade of war, all of Einar is in pain. The deeds needed to heal those wounds will require us to set aside our differences and work together. You can rest assured that I will not stop until this city—no, the entire empire—is a place where all may lead happy and glorious lives."

Instead of a polite applause, there was only silence from the men and women on the floor below. Their faces told Mahzun they were unhappy with both his presence and his message.

His eyes again found Lord Dimitri, but Mahzun forced his gaze away from the old man. Far too many rumors were circulating of his madness, and this intrusion would only create more. He couldn't let it be known that he regularly saw a dead tyrant.

"May I ask why you were elected?" Mahzun shouted at the silent aristocrats. "Does it soothe your egos to sit in this fine building while so many of your brothers and sisters starve on the streets?"

More than a few squirmed below, and the group of Elders went from impassive to hostile. Mahzun looked into the eyes of a frail old woman, but he saw the fire of a deep enmity. Next to her, a man in a fine suit of grey sat with a frown, his arms folded and brow set in a furious glare.

"While you sat here enjoying your little slice of power, I was out fighting to liberate the people of Einar from tyranny. For years, you fought against me, and I have magnanimously offered forgiveness. That doesn't change the fact that while you have been enjoying the city, eating decadent meals, and living in luxurious manors, I spent those years sleeping in the mud of the Arval mountains while clearing out mercenaries hired by the Heirs. I was forced to eat rats to stave off hunger while besieging Ulfa. My armor has been tempered by the blood of my enemies while you craft meaningless legislation in marbled halls."

As the words poured from his mouth, Mahzun could tell they weren't penetrating a single ear. These people were only here to puff up their pride and increase their wealth. Words were their weapon, and he was not able to turn that weapon toward them.

"As Emperor, I have promised to make life worth living for *everyone*," Mahzun growled. "The idea that you get to pass your lives in comfort and decadence while millions struggle to eat is one of the old age. I am inviting each of you into the Age of Man. Come willingly, and you will be partners in creating a world worth saving. Resist, and you will be swept aside just like the Heirs."

Mahzun descended the platform and strode through the building without stopping to make eye contact with a single aristocrat. His head began to spin as he exploded onto the street and took in a breath of the polluted air. The coachman startled, catching himself before falling from his seat. Mahzun just gave him a small wave and began walking up the street—now was no time to be confined to a carriage.

The sidewalk in this part of town was nearly abandoned, though the street was filled with carriages. He could feel the gaze of each that passed by, and he wondered how many recognized their emperor. Did they see him, or did they simply see an armored monster invading their paradise?

A screech filled the sky, and he looked up to see Aiya's wingspan descending. The griffin would have felt his anxiety rising over the past hour, and she would have made sure to stick close.

Are you in danger?

No, just human drama. I won't bore you with the details.

Thank you. Your kind tends to care about the silliest of problems.

Aiya's wings created a gale as she landed on the street before him. Shouts—both human and equine—filled the neighborhood as carriages came to a stop. Without waiting for any further invitation, Mahzun leapt onto the griffin's back and dug his thighs into the powerful frame. Her legs leapt into the air as her wings began flapping. Within moments, the two friends left the streets behind.

The air grew cool and delicious, away from the smog and human waste of the city. Below, the buildings grew smaller as Aiya's powerful wings took them higher and higher. Mahzun's stomach churned at the thought of simply letting go and falling through the air.

I know what you're thinking, and I advise against it.

"You really do know me too well," Mahzun said out loud as he nuzzled into the soft mixture of fur and feathers. "Take me somewhere without so many...people."

Aiya let out a screech in response as her wings settled into a glide. The wind whipped through Mahzun's hair and roared in his ears. It told him of times he'd been free, of times not spent in marbled halls. His heart ached for those days, but he focused his mind on the present battle instead of his old glory.

Below, the busy streets and mass of buildings were giving way to the fields and small woods south of Talas. He took in a deep breath of the fresh air, untainted by mankind. It tasted of maple and oak leaves, of decaying plant life and running streams.

His mind went back through those early years hiding in the Northern Wilds. The landscape below was relatively tame compared to that great wilderness—a place where every animal is ready to make you its next meal, where the very plants themselves want to end your life.

His heart ached for those simpler times.

His stomach flipped as Aiya began a steep dive, and Mahzun pulled himself out of those memories.

You're being too sentimental, her voice sounded in his head. *Just enjoy the moment.*

The griffin's pitch increased, and Mahzun let out a holler that was lost to the wind. Aiya shifted her wings just before they hit the treetops, pulling up and maintaining her flight just a few feet above the mixture of leaves and branches. The griffin pumped her wings, propelling them forward at a speed that transformed the trees into nothing but a blur.

The scent of smoke tickled Mahzun's nose, and he pulled himself away from Aiya's feathers to scan the horizon. To their left, a column of black smoke rose into the air—something told him it was not natural.

I see it as well, Aiya called out to his mind before she turned toward it.

Your first instinct is to run toward danger, Mahzun responded with a smile. *That's why we were made for each other.*

Aiya didn't respond as she hurtled toward the column of smoke, rising higher to get a better view of
the danger below. Fields of wheat and barley covered
the ground like a patchwork blanket, and a jumble of
dirt paths wound among small homes and orchards.
The exact name of this little outlying village escaped
Mahzun's mind, but that didn't make the trouble any
less important.

At the moment, this little hamlet was far from
peaceful. Flames devoured several homes built from
wood and thatch, and a half dozen bands of armed
men ran along the dirt paths after screaming women
and children. Mahzun's eyes caught sight of a hundred
villagers gathering in the central square, shouting at
the largest band of brutes. Men with clubs and swords
in their hands and murder in their hearts shouted back
as they approached.

Blood began to boil in Mahzun's veins, and images
flashed of such villains attacking his friends. The look
of pain on his own mother's face filled his mind's eye,
and he could still feel her blood on his hands. A feral
howl erupted from his throat, and Mahzun urged Aiya
toward the ground. The griffin didn't need much coercion, and she dove toward the gap between villagers
and thugs. Her soft paws barely made a sound as she
landed.

At ground level, the acrid stench of burning buildings and flesh was stronger, and Mahzun turned his
gaze toward the approaching bandits. They wore no
uniforms, and they lacked the coordinated movement
of trained soldiers—nothing more than a band of
thieves looking to take down easy prey.

Mahzun leapt down from Aiya's back, and his armor jangled as he hit the ground. His eyes scanned
the approaching thieves, each with a heavy weapon in

hand. The Eternal Blade called for him, but he ignored the desire to feel the leather hilt in his palm. Such mundane villains weren't worth that level of suffering.

Even without a sword in hand, he could see eyes widen. Unless they had spent the past decade under a rock, these men would recognize Aiya, and they would know what she meant.

The black plate mail identified him as an Imperial soldier.

The winged creature identified him as the Savior of Man.

With nothing more than his hands and a righteous fury, Mahzun leapt into the band of thieves. His mass slammed into a man armed with a short sword, burying a brittle frame in the dirt road. Mahzun grabbed the pathetic iron blade and leapt to his feet, swinging it through the leather armor of the nearest thief. Aiya screeched as she leapt into the fray, and her paws, talons, and beak made for invincible weapons.

With high-pitched screams, the mass of bandits melted like snow in the summer's heat. Faces that had burned with lust and greed seconds ago now lay on the ground with sightless eyes. Others were running at a full sprint toward the dark cover of the trees—Mahzun knew there was no amount of vegetation that could save these men from his wrath.

Weapons littered the ground, dropped both by the fallen and by men whose desire to escape outweighed their desire for loot. Letting out a breath, Mahzun began his chase of the routers, but the cries of joy emanating from his rear stopped his legs from moving. He turned to face the crowd of villagers that had been cowering only moments ago to see faces ablaze with smiles underneath a layer of dirt and grime.

As one, the adults dropped to their knees and directed their gaze at the ground, while the children simply
stared with open mouths. One little girl even let out a
giggle—it had a hint of relieved mania behind it, but it
was unforced laughter in the midst of carnage. Mahzun
didn't quite know how to react.

"All hail the Emperor," one man said, his voice trembling.

"Long live the Emperor," the rest of the adult villagers shouted without lifting their eyes. Mahzun's feet
took him back toward the square, though part of his
mind screamed that he should be chasing down the
infernal bandits who had caused so much havoc.

"On your feet, my friends," Mahzun replied, running
toward the group. "Will you explain what happened?
How could there be an attack like this so close to the
city?"

His words were met with a stunned silence. Some
of the villagers rose to their feet, while others stayed
put, apparently unable to believe their ruler would be
so informal as to call them friends. Mahzun turned to
the nearest woman who heeded his command to rise.

"We don't really know," the woman said. "One moment, we were working the fields, and the next we were
running for our lives."

Now that the woman was no longer bowing, Mahzun
could get a better look at her. She wore a patched dress
of old linen, and her face spoke of at least a couple
decades of working in the sun. A few chunks of dark
hair poked out from underneath her head scarf, and
her skin was covered in sweat and dirt. Mahzun had
no idea how much of that was from normal life versus
the horrific events of the past hour.

"Does this happen often?" Mahzun asked. "Not just
to your village, but to others around Talas?"

"We hear of rumors," the woman said, her gaze casting about for assistance.

"Well, now that I'm back, I'll do my best to make sure those rumors are put to the sword," Mahzun replied. "For now, I'll send a contingent of soldiers to investigate and hunt down the rest of those bandits. Look after your wounded, and I'll keep an eye out to make sure they don't come back."

Mahzun turned away to mount Aiya. Behind him, he could hear a young boy shuffle over to the woman.

"Who is that man?" the boy whispered, the words barely audible in Mahzun's ears.

"That's the Emperor—the man who has freed us," the woman replied.

"Why is he so ugly?" the boy asked.

Mahzun held in a laugh at the boy's words. He had heard that same question too many times to count.

"Because that's the price he paid for our freedom," the woman said.

The words made Mahzun stop, and he resisted the urge to turn back and embrace the woman. His throat began to constrict, and Mahzun leapt onto Aiya's back before the villagers could see the tears coming to his eyes.

Chapter 24

E karath let out a deep breath as he looked through yet another book in Ivana's library. How many hours had he spent here since arriving? He'd certainly lost count.

He looked down at the book, a dry history about the crisis of the tenth century. With so much chaos in such a short time, he had hoped there would be at least a hint of an Heir who had done something unprecedented. Yet so far, it was just a very dull recounting of what was likely a very fascinating period of history.

"Zahara should be here," Ekarath sighed. "Reading ancient tomes is supposed to be her area of expertise, not mine."

Just saying the girl's name made his stomach do a little flip. His mind drifted back to last night—the feel of her head nuzzled against his chest, the warmth of her lips brushing against his.

And then she just left.

He slammed his fist on the table in frustration, and a small yelp sounded from the other side of the shelf. Ekarath's blood froze at the sound, and he turned to scan the library.

To his right, the windows allowed the mid-morning light in. To his left, a dozen rows of low bookshelves not only held vast quantities of knowledge, but they also provided ample hiding space. Furrowing his brow, Ekarath rose to his feet to investigate.

"I'm sorry," a squeaky voice sounded before he could even peek around the first set of shelves.

"Saren?" Ekarath asked, and the girl popped out. The young woman was dressed in a blue gown that hugged her curves. She wore a string of pearls around her neck, a pair of diamond earrings, finished off with a set of silver bracelets. Her makeup was impeccable, as was her hair, which cascaded onto her shoulders in silky curls.

Quite the effort for a trip to the library, Ekarath thought, though he did have to admit she looked beautiful. While he had only known the girl for a few days, she certainly seemed the type to make immaculate preparations for an average day.

"Please don't be mad, I didn't mean to spy on you," Saren replied, her cheeks glowing a fierce red underneath all the makeup.

"Oh, I'm not mad," Ekarath responded. "And I'm sorry to scare you like that. Uh, may I ask what you're doing in here?"

"Believe it or not, I was looking for a book," Saren replied, placing hands on her hips. Ekarath forced himself not to smile—Saren didn't exactly strike him as the studious type.

"But then I saw you studying this pile of dusty relics," Saren continued, her voice softening. "Ever since showing up, you've spent all your time in here...what are you looking for?"

"I'm just trying to understand the *draod*," Ekarath responded, which was only a partial lie.

"You're *Hundiin*, I was hoping to see a little more action from an elite warrior."

"Sorry to disappoint," Ekarath said with a soft chuckle. "I seem to be doing that far too often as of late."

"I'm sure that's not true," Saren replied, putting a hand on his shoulder. "You've been through so much—escaping the Atsada, getting captured by Lord Pavel, becoming the Heir of Segova..."

Ekarath's jaw dropped at those last words, and he felt as if a mule had just kicked him in the stomach. Saren was a silly little aristocrat, a girl who ran around in dresses and too much perfume. How could she have figured it out?

"You aren't as sneaky as you think," Saren said, shaking her head with a smile. "Both you and Zahara have let things slip. Not to mention that she always has that beautiful *qilada* in her ear."

"Yeah, I guess we haven't been as careful as we should be," Ekarath said, unsure how to respond.

"But don't worry, your secret's safe with me," Saren replied, giving him a wink. "And I don't think Ivana or Maslov have figured it out. They haven't spent as much time with you as I have—they also expected a mage to be Dimitri's successor."

"That's the thing—Zahara was supposed to be the Heir. That's why I'm spending so much time in this library. There's got to be an answer somewhere."

"You really think that you can find a way to stop being an Heir of Creation?" Saren asked, raising an eyebrow.

"I have to," Ekarath responded with a shrug.

"Well, if nothing else, you have determination. Anyone else would be sleeping in after the night you had."

Ekarath's blood froze once again at the words. Did she know about his near kiss with Zahara? And that he'd been up most of the night, unable to sleep?

"What do you think happened last night? I was in bed long before your little ball even ended."

"Oh, really? Word has already spread throughout the entire city."

"What word? I haven't heard any rumors."

"You really should get out of the library more often. Everyone's talking about the ghost that attacked a whole squad of legionnaires. I figured with you being the Heir and an elite warrior..."

Ekarath's jaw clenched. Did Zahara include fighting a battle on her own in a walk around the city?

"I think we need to go speak with our friend," Ekarath whispered.

***

Zahara squared off against Farban as the old man's fingers moved in a blur. With a push, the hermit launched an inferno, the flames erupting from thin air and careening directly at Zahara. Her own hands moved just as quickly, creating a shield of air. She finished the knot, and the barrier sprung up just as the fireball crashed into it.

The inferno dissipated while the shield remained intact.

"That was good," Farban said from across the courtyard. "A warrior's first instinct would be to dodge a spell like that, but that would leave you vulnerable and exposed. A shield not only protects you from the initial strike, but now I have to account for it with my next move."

As the words left his mouth, Farban created another weave, and a bolt of lightning flew through the air. It slammed into the shield, leaving it cracked, the woven tendrils of Restoration beginning to fray. One more hit like that would be its end.

"The lightning weave takes longer, but it is exponentially more powerful," Farban said.

"Which means I can use that time to strike back in a way you won't expect," Zahara responded, finishing the spymaster's thought.

"I forget how experienced you already are," Farban said, shaking his head. "Sorry to bore you with the basics."

"The basics are everything. It's best not to get so lost in advanced weaves that you forget that a fight is often won by those who can create a shield of air or lightning bolt a split second before the other combatant."

As she spoke, Zahara readied another weave to launch back at Farban, but the sharp crack of heels on cobblestone caught her attention. Her weave dissipated as Saren—accompanied by a tired and surly Ekarath—rounded a corner.

Saren looked rather pleased, her makeup and hair the very essence of perfection. Her gaze switched back and forth between Zahara and Ekarath, as if she couldn't decide to whom she would rather give her attention.

Ekarath's face was stone, but she could see a quiet fury underneath the exterior. For a moment, she wanted nothing more than to lose herself in the boy's embrace, but from the look on his face, that wasn't about to happen.

"Good morning, Ekarath," Farban said, turning with a wave. "How goes your search in the library?"

"It's...going," Ekarath responded before turning to Zahara. "May I speak with you? In private?"

"Of course," Zahara said before turning toward Farban. "That is, if I may be excused."

"I don't think the Heir of Segova needs permission to have a private conversation," Farban said with a laugh, waving her off. Zahara smiled in response and allowed Ekarath to lead her away from both Saren and Farban.

"How was your walk last night?" Ekarath whispered, his voice cold as ice. Zahara could feel the weight of the question, and she knew it was no simple pleasantry.

"So, I'm assuming you've heard the rumors?"

"Saren just told me," Ekarath responded, his head shaking while a scowl took up his entire face. "She actually thought it was me. The rumors are everywhere—what happened to laying low? First you go to the ball and dance with the Usurper. Then you go out and get the whole city talking about a ghost. If that's not going to rouse the Usurper's suspicions, I don't know what will."

"I didn't mean to," Zahara said. "After the ball, I really did need to clear my mind, and I don't know of any better way than a walk. But I ran into a group of rebels pinned down by a whole platoon of legionnaires. What should I have done? Should I have sat by while they got slaughtered?"

"You can't go around risking your life. You know how important you are."

"You're the Heir of Segova, not me. Why can't you just accept that? Because you won't face your responsibilities, I have to stay cooped up. I'm going absolutely crazy, and you know what? It felt good to do something. Because of me, there are a dozen rebels who will live to fight another day."

Ekarath just responded with a sigh.

"Lord Dimitri chose *you*," Ekarath finally said. "Even if you're not technically the Heir, you need to be careful. If you die, who else could it be? I'm certainly not capable of it. Even Farban isn't as good as you."

Zahara sat, chewing on her tongue as Ekarath spoke. As he finished, an idea popped into her head.

"Listen, let's make a deal," Zahara said, holding out her hand. "Let's spar—no magic, just swords. If you win, I'll start helping you look through all those books in the library. If I win, you come clean about who you are, and you start acting like the Heir of Segova."

Ekarath glared at her, switching his gaze between her eyes and outstretched hand. She could see his mind working, weighing the cost and opportunity. He was still the better swordsman, but nothing was certain, even in practice.

"If I win, you also need to promise that you won't go out anymore without me," Ekarath said, grabbing her hand and shaking before she could object.

"You're the worst," Zahara said, pulling back from the handshake. She pursed her lips and thought about the extra condition. "But I agree."

Without giving Ekarath a chance to back out, Zahara turned toward the courtyard. Both Farban and Saren looked confused, but neither asked about the private conversation. She just hoped their words hadn't been loud enough to overhear.

"Ekarath and I are going to practice," Zahara said, moving to the edge of the training ground to pick up the two practice swords she had been using with Farban earlier in the morning. Spinning on her heel, Zahara tossed one through the air toward Ekarath.

To her annoyance, he grabbed the hilt, plucking it with little effort out of the air. Ekarath gave the wooden blade a twirl, the practice sword responding to his touch as if it were a masterpiece. For a moment, Zahara could almost imagine being back in the Atsada, training under the watchful eye of Master Kanu. Yet she knew there was no going back to those simpler times.

Ekarath leapt first, but Zahara blocked the blow. She backpedaled as the boy made three quick strikes, his smile growing wider with each. *Not a great start*, she whispered mentally. Clenching her teeth, Zahara struck back like a viper, and Ekarath's smile disappeared.

She jabbed, and Ekarath leapt backward before taking a swipe that Zahara parried. The crack of their swords filled the air, and sweat began to form on Zahara's forehead. The sun was out in full force, its rays beating down on her.

With a shout, Zahara brought her sword down in an arc, and Ekarath barely had time to bring up his own to block it. With teeth clenched, the two friends pushed.

But Ekarath was stronger than she was. A prolonged pushing match would not be in her favor.

Another set of solitary footsteps sounded from behind, the graceful staccato of a woman in heels. All around her, she could feel the spectators' attention shift. Yet she didn't dare rip her eyes away from Ekarath, even for a second.

"I think you two should take a break," Ivana's voice sounded. For a moment, Zahara didn't know if Ekarath would listen, but—at the same moment—the two friends pulled back. She gave Ekarath a nod of respect, which he returned.

"What's going on?" Zahara asked, looking toward the stately woman. She was holding a piece of parchment that had recently been held together with a seal of violet wax.

"I just received this from the office of 'His Imperial Majesty'," Ivana said, the last words laced with sarcasm. "Though it's really from his steward. She's asking me about the young Karajaani woman who attended the ball last night."

Zahara's stomach fell at the words, and the sweat on her skin turned to ice. For the briefest of moments, she had allowed herself to believe that maybe—just maybe—the Usurper would forget about her.

"There's not exactly a large population of Karajaani noblewomen in Talas, so I have to assume you are the woman in question," Ivana said. "I only stepped away from the function for a half-hour last night. Did you happen to make an appearance while I was absent?"

"I...may have snuck in for a little while," Zahara said before clearing her throat. "I just wanted to see if I could glean any information from your guests. The plan was to stay on the periphery and eavesdrop with enhanced hearing."

"Well, no matter what your plan was, it appears you've made quite the impression on the Usurper," Ivana said, handing her the letter.

Dear Lady Ivana,

Our esteemed emperor wishes to know the whereabouts and personal information of a young Karajaani noblewoman who was in attendance at your ball last night. He is quite taken with her, and he wishes to see her again. For obvious reasons, we would expect your help in finding her, as she left him with neither her name nor any other information.

Yours Truly,

Lorna, Steward of Einar

Zahara lowered the letter to see that everyone was now staring at her. She gulped, a lump in her throat nearly making such an act impossible.

What have I done?

"Well now, this is a rather interesting development," Farban said with a low whistle. "Here we were planning on Saren to catch the Usurper's eye. Without even trying, young Zahara has appeared to have accomplished that task."

"It was obvious he didn't care much for me," Saren said, her arms folded. "Personally, I think he was intimidated."

Zahara rolled her eyes but didn't let any of her thoughts escape.

"Trying to understand a man is difficult," Ivana said. "Trying to understand someone wracked by insanity like the Usurper is impossible. There could be any number of reasons why he is 'quite taken' with Zahara."

"Whatever the reason, this could be our way to infiltrate the Usurper's inner circle," Farban said before blushing. "Except that she's the Heir of Segova—I somehow can't believe that would be worth the risk."

"I think we'll need to discuss this further," Ivana said. "Especially because Maslov will be livid if he can't get his opinion in."

"How quickly can we get Maslov here?" Farban said. "This seems like one of those messages that can't wait days for a response."

"Unfortunately, I have some Council business that will keep me tied up until late," Ivana said, rubbing her temples. "The Usurper interrupted our meeting this morning, and it's thrown my entire schedule into disarray."

"What was he doing at a meeting of the Elder Council?" Farban asked. "That's certainly unprecedented."

"The Usurper doesn't give two figs about precedence or decency," Ivana said through a yawn. "For now, are there any objections to a midnight meeting? I would love to make it earlier, but..."

"Midnight will be fine," Farban replied. "We certainly need to plan how we can make use of the Usurper's feelings."

"We'll need to give her a bit of a makeover, but I think Zahara will do a fine job," Saren said, moving to grab Zahara's face. She batted the girl away and directed her eyes toward Ekarath.

He simply looked at her, his eyes wide.

"We'll figure that all out tonight," Ivana said. "Until then, be thinking—not just how you can burrow deeper into the man's heart, but how we can use that to destroy him."

Chapter 25

Zahara had made sure to arrive early, and she sat staring at the Shajarat. The clock above the fireplace told her it was nearing midnight—any moment, her thoughts could be interrupted.

She had spent the rest of her day studying Lord Dimitri's book, trying to learn a weave that would allow her to scale walls. So far, it was proving difficult.

"Good evening, Zahara," Farban's voice sounded as the old hermit entered the room. "I trust your day was fruitful."

There were bags under the spymaster's eyes and a smile on his face. The vermillion robes were clean, which must be a new sensation for the man who had spent the past few years in the woods.

"Just trying to learn new weaves," she responded with a shrug. "Lord Dimitri was very powerful, wasn't he?"

"He was the best. Don't worry though, I see a lot of him in you."

"But I'm not him," Zahara said, shaking her head. "Don't tell me you're starting to agree with Ekarath."

"Well, there is the fact that the boy can't seem to command the *draod*. We can't completely ignore the possibility of making you the Heir of Segova. It would fulfill Lord Dimitri's final wishes, after all."

Zahara began to respond, but footsteps sounded near the doorway, and she slammed her mouth shut. Count Maslov entered the room, the smile on his face disappearing as his eyes made contact with Farban.

Why do they seem to hate each other so much?

"Good evening, Your Holiness," Maslov said, turning to Zahara with a bow. "I hear you've been keeping yourself busy."

"I...yes, that's unfortunately true," Zahara responded. "Going to the ball was just meant to be a diversion, maybe a way of gathering some information. I certainly never expected the Usurper to notice me, let alone ask me to dance."

"Life has a way of surprising us," Maslov said as he took a seat next to Farban. She wondered if it was his way of not having to look at the old spymaster. Before Zahara could respond, more footsteps sounded, and she turned to see Ivana, Ekarath, and Saren entering.

Ekarath was dressed in a simple shirt and trousers, as if he were trying to force everyone—including the *draod*—to forget he was the Heir of Segova. Saren and Ivana both wore simple dresses, though Saren looked as if she had spent some extra time on her hair and makeup. The girl's eyes were practically locked on Ekarath.

"Good evening, Your Holiness," Ekarath said, giving Zahara a shallow bow before taking a seat at her side. Once again, Saren chose the seat next to the *Hundiin*, and she scooted as close as possible.

"I've spent the day trying to gather as much information as possible," Ivana said, taking a seat at the head of the table. "And I'm even more confused than I was this morning."

"What do you mean?" Maslov asked.

"In addition to catching the Usurper's eye, Zahara is the center of court gossip," Ivana said. "If they're not talking about the ghost that attacked a platoon of Imperial soldiers, they're talking about the young Karajaani girl."

Little do they know they're the same person, Zahara thought, though she didn't dare voice the words aloud.

"Nobody has ever seen her before," Ivana continued. "She just appears out of nowhere to capture the Emperor's attention and then disappears without a trace. Speculation is running rampant. I'm afraid that if Zahara were to make another appearance in public, she would be swamped by all the attention she would receive."

"So, what do we do?" Farban asked. "We never expected to have Zahara become a public figure. She has no backstory, nobody to back up any claims..."

"I've thought about this all day," Ivana said, shaking her head. "And I think that the chance to get close to the Usurper—while potentially useful—isn't greater than the risk. Zahara is the Heir of Segova, after all. We can't just use her as bait. She's far too important for that."

Zahara squirmed in her seat and shot Ekarath a glare. The boy should be able to accept his role so that she could at least do something useful. Saren also caught the look, and the girl smiled.

"Except for one simple fact," Saren said, her smile growing wider. "Zahara isn't the Heir of Segova. Ekarath is."

Silence thicker than a wool blanket settled over the room. Across from her, Farban suppressed a smile while Maslov and Ivana let their jaws drop. Zahara couldn't tell if she wanted to slap Saren or give her a hug.

"Did you really not figure it out, Aunt Ivana?" Saren said, breaking the silence. "I mean, it was pretty obvious to me, though I have spent more time with them than you have."

"Is this true, Farban?" Ivana asked, turning to the spymaster.

"Well, the secret's out," Farban said, shaking his head. "From what we can tell, Lord Dimitri intended Zahara as his successor. For some reason, the power went to Ekarath, and he was worried that everyone would be upset if the Heir of Segova was a man who didn't know how to use the *draod*."

"Zahara really should be the Heir," Ekarath said. "And I've been trying to figure out how to make that happen. So, it wasn't really a lie..."

"Yes, it was, Your Holiness," Ivana said. "But I won't focus on that too much. Besides, as the Heir of Segova, I am not really in a position to lecture you..."

"But this does change the whole discussion," Maslov piped up. "Because now we can consider Zahara...expendable."

"That's not a great choice of words," Ivana said, shooting the merchant a look.

"I appreciate your defense," Zahara said. "But I do believe Maslov has a point, even if he didn't make it very eloquently. Since I'm not the Heir, I can get close to the Usurper...learn his secrets."

"We would need to set up a whole persona for you," Maslov said from across the table. "You would need a backstory, a separate home—it would all need to be strong enough to stand up to scrutiny. And believe me, if you're going to be courted by the Emperor, there will be plenty of scrutiny."

"What if we just used my real name and identity?" Zahara asked. "I am a noblewoman from rural Karajaan, after all."

"It's so easy to forget that you're noble," Farban began, "because you don't really act like it."

"Being from the countryside of Karajaan, you could really act however you want," Maslov said. "The nobles of Talas don't really know much about the southern Heirdoms, and they'd certainly excuse any rough edges."

"And those rough edges could be used to your advantage," Saren said. "From the other girls I've talked to, it seems like those are the very reason the Usurper asked you to dance."

"What do you mean?" Zahara asked.

"Sorry—that didn't come out right," Saren replied, her cheeks growing a fierce crimson. "But the Usurper's well aware that everyone in the city is trying to get him to court their daughter. When he saw someone who was obviously not a fixture of the city's aristocracy, he knew there was an opportunity to throw a wrench in everyone's plan."

"So, I'm nothing more than a tool to make the city's nobility jealous?" Zahara asked. The revelation both stung and provided relief. Maybe there was nothing wrong with her after all.

"That's what I'm hearing," Saren replied. "Though it could easily just be jealousy—there are dozens of noble women in the city who would love to be Empress, even if it meant marrying the Usurper."

"Even if Mahzun is only interested in Zahara out of spite, we could still use this to our advantage," Ivana said. "I could tell the Usurper that I've taken you in as a refugee. You could begin courting, even if it is just part of courtly intrigue, you could still get plenty of information from the man."

Zahara's stomach squirmed at the thought, but she also felt giddy at the opportunity to be useful. At her side, Ekarath rose to his feet.

"This is absolutely unacceptable," Ekarath said. "Even if Zahara isn't the Heir of Segova, she is meant to be. Lord Dimitri chose her, not me. I won't rest until his final wishes are honored, and we can't risk sending Zahara into that monster's clutches."

"It's okay, Ekarath," Zahara said, looking up at her friend. "We all have to make sacrifices. If this is what I can do to stop the Destroyer of Worlds, then I'm willing to do it."

"But I'm not willing to let you," Ekarath said. "If I'm going to be forced into this role of Heir, I'm going to use some of that authority. I order this meeting to be adjourned, and there will be no further talk of using Zahara like this."

"But I—"

"I said it's an order," Ekarath shouted, cutting her off. "You've been wanting me to be the Heir of Segova, and that's exactly what I'm doing."

Zahara sat back in her chair and folded her arms.

"Well, I guess that's it for tonight," Ivana said with a sigh.

***

Zahara sat at her desk, eyes closed. The *draod* surrounded her, and she basked in the energy as she contemplated the next weave to practice.

Am I really nothing more than an Heir-in-waiting?

Her hands and brain worked in tandem, pulling threads of Illusion out of the *draod* and weaving them into a complex pattern. Before finishing the tapestry, Zahara opened her eyes and growled.

A knock sounded at the door.

"Come in," Zahara called out, ready to chew Ekarath's head off.

"I'm sorry to bother you," Saren's voice sounded from the doorway, and Zahara startled.

"Hello, Saren," Zahara said, trying to force down the words she had been prepared to hurl at Ekarath. "Come in."

"I just wanted to apologize—I shouldn't have told Ivana and Maslov about your secret."

"No, I'm glad you did. It's really Ekarath's secret, one that I've been trying to get him to free himself of. That boy needs to come to grips with his responsibilities instead of hiding from them."

"It's obvious he loves you," Saren said. "Do you return the sentiment?"

As if the words had been physical blows, Zahara felt the wind rush from her stomach. She tried to respond, but the words just didn't come.

"It's not always an easy question to answer," Saren responded, patting Zahara on the knee. "And I should apologize yet again. That was intrusive of me."

"I just don't think now is the time for love," Zahara finally managed to say. "The world is falling apart. I can't commit to living a normal life in a world suffering under the Usurper's yoke."

"Maybe that's the best way to resist," Saren replied. "We live the lives we were meant to live in spite of the Usurper. If we ignore the yoke of a tyrant, is he really able to bind us?"

"I don't know if that's possible. Can we ignore the power of the Eternal Blade? Can we just ignore the Horde?"

"Not completely, but we don't have to let the Usurper control every aspect of our lives," Saren replied, rising to her feet. "I'll bid you a good night. Thank you for letting me apologize."

"Thank you for coming," Zahara replied, rising to her feet. She gave the girl a hug. For a moment, she could feel Saren's confusion before she returned the embrace.

"Personally, I don't think anyone can bind you to their will," Saren whispered as she pulled away from the embrace. "Not unless you allow them to."

With that, Saren turned around and left, closing the door behind her. Zahara moved to the window, examining the glow of the Shajarat.

Nobody can bind me. Not the Usurper. Not Lord Dimitri. Not even Ekarath.

Chapter 26

Moonlight streamed in through Mahzun's open window, the soft light battling with the orange glow of a reading lamp. The curtains sat completely still on the quiet night, yet he hoped for a soft breeze to stir up the dead, hot air.

At Lorna's request, he was reading a novel—something she had recommended to distract his mind from both rebuilding Einar and finding the girl. While he had spent the past decade reading reports from his generals and aides, he couldn't bring his mind to focus on the printed words.

Seated in the chair opposite him, Lord Dimitri gave him his customary dead-eyed stare.

"Are leaders meant to read stories created for children?" Mahzun growled, lifting the book and tossing it to the corner. "I have a world to remake, a bride to court, and an Heir to track down. There's no time for such tales."

As expected, Dimitri made no response. Mahzun leaned back in his chair and folded his arms. It was better to sit and contemplate his problems than to get lost in such a ridiculous story.

The curtains fluttered, and Mahzun expected a gentle breeze to follow. Yet the night remained still. Rising to his feet, he moved toward the window to investigate.

"Why do you seek me?" a voice said from behind, and he spun to see the girl. She wore dark trousers and an obsidian shirt instead of a gown. Her hair was pulled back and secured by a leather strap instead of being intricately braided.

Somehow, the simplicity was even more beautiful.

The girl held herself with such confidence, such poise. The mere fact that she had been able to sneak in without a sound was proof enough that she was something special.

Mahzun's heart began to pound, and his head spun. He knew Lorna had made inquiries to Lady Ivana and a dozen other guests, and he trusted his sister to find the girl. But to see her here, right at this moment—it was too much. He took a deep breath and tried to put on his best smile, one that didn't make his scars move too much.

"My apologies if the search was inappropriate," Mahzun stammered, the words sticking in his throat, "but you disappeared before I could even learn your name."

"My sincerest apologies, Your Majesty," the girl said, taking a single step closer and dipping into a shallow curtsy.

She moves with such grace, Mahzun thought, unable to suppress his admiration.

"I was just a little...overwhelmed," the girl continued. "When I arrived at the ball, I had no expectation of dancing with anyone, let alone the Savior of Man. You must understand the effect you have on women."

"Usually, I repulse them," Mahzun replied, his brow furrowing as he took a tentative step toward the beauty. "But you—you seem to be made of something stronger than the perfumed ladies of Talas."

"You might be surprised at the steel core of many seemingly soft aristocrats," the girl said.

Footsteps sounded in the hallway, and Mahzun's door swung open to reveal Lorna's face. Her eyes were wide, and her skin had lost nearly all color.

"A messenger just arrived, Your Majesty. It's urgent."

"I'm actually a little busy at the moment," Mahzun said, gesturing to the girl. He turned to look at her, but she was gone.

"I know it's late and that you wanted the evening to rest, but this is important," Lorna said, striding into the room and grabbing Mahzun by the hand. "Please, you'll want to hear what this man has to say."

Mahzun couldn't bring himself to respond as his eyes scanned the room. There was no sign of the girl, no sound as she had retreated.

I still don't even know her name, Mahzun growled in his mind.

"Fine," Mahzun said aloud, shaking out of his sister's grip. It wouldn't be proper for anyone to see the diminutive woman literally pulling him through the corridor. Resisting the urge to keep looking for the girl, he followed Lorna out the door.

The corridors were deserted, and they didn't come across a single soul as they descended the main staircase to the bottom floor. Lorna didn't speak, though he could tell the news had left her agitated, at least enough to justify barging into his room in the middle of the night. At one point, he nearly stopped to make her explain, but he saw a glint in her eye that said she was enjoying his curiosity.

Lorna led him to a small room used for informal visits. While the furnishings were spartan by palace standards, the waiting soldier stood on his obviously exhausted feet. He certainly looked as if recent days had been unkind to him—much of his skin was burned, his hair completely singed away. His leather armor was tattered and filthy, and his right arm was in a sling, blood seeping through the bandage.

"Your Majesty," the soldier said, bowing to one knee.

"No need to bow, soldier," Mahzun said. "You look as if you've already sacrificed enough for the Cause."

"Thank you, Your Majesty," the soldier said, rising back to his feet and bowing his head. "I would have gotten here sooner, but my wounds slowed me."

"I have no doubt that you've done your duty to the best your abilities," Mahzun said. "Now, please take a seat and tell me what you know."

"I was part of a guard unit," the soldier began, planting himself on the nearest chair. "We were escorting some dangerous criminals from the forest back to the capital. One was the old spymaster of Segova...Farban, I think is his name."

Mahzun's memory stretched back—yes, he had received word that Farban had been captured. With everything else happening, he had not thought about that particular victory in days.

"What happened, son?" Mahzun said, trying to keep the impatience out of his voice. The man had obviously been through a harrowing experience, and he didn't want to appear angry.

"Well, once we got near some villages, one of the prisoners—a boy no more than eighteen—well, he went berserk on us. A whirlwind picked him up, lightning rained down from the sky. We tried shooting at him, but our crossbows were useless."

Mahzun's head spun faster and faster as the soldier spoke, and he struggled to remain on his feet. No mage could do what this soldier described. That meant this had to be the Heir that was stopping him from destroying the Shajarat.

And he was in Segova.

"There was so much death," the soldier continued, "so much screaming...the ground near me was struck, and I fell into a ditch."

The man stopped talking, his eyes looking upward as he recalled the memories. Mahzun placed a hand on his shoulder.

"Thank you," Mahzun said. "I realize the sacrifices you've made to bring me this information, and you've done the Empire a great service."

"Thank you, Your Majesty."

"I want this man taken care of," Mahzun said, turning to Lorna. "Get a mage to heal his wounds and get him some food. Wake one of the chefs if you have to—he deserves something better than day-old bread."

"Of course, Your Majesty," Lorna said before turning to leave the room. As her footsteps faded, Mahzun turned back to the soldier.

"Now, what did the boy look like?"

"Well, he was a pretty standard Segovan—blond hair, blue eyes, strong build. He had the look of a soldier about him."

"That doesn't narrow it down too much," Mahzun said, shaking his head while trying to keep the annoyance out of his voice. "How long has it been since the attack?"

"About a week," the soldier replied.

So, he can't have gotten far, Mahzun thought. *I'll need to get search teams north of the city—they'll be looking for a young boy accompanied by an old man.*

He thought about going personally, mounting Aiya and heading back out on campaign. A shiver of pure ecstasy ran up his entire body at the thought of escaping the viper pit of Talas. He could almost taste the inedible rations and stale water, could imagine himself bedding down in a field of alfalfa with Aiya by his side.

Except that would mean leaving the girl.

That's not important, Mahzun growled at himself. He needed to focus.

"Oh, and there was a girl with him, too," the soldier said, the words coming out of his mouth like molasses. "I know I've been on campaign for a long time, but she was real pretty."

"Okay, so we're looking for a trio of Segovans," Mahzun growled. "That should make it easier."

"The girl didn't look Segovan, Your Majesty. In fact, she looked like she was from the south," the soldier continued. "Maybe from Karajaan."

The last word coursed through Mahzun's veins like ice, and he turned back toward the messenger.

"What did you just say?"

"The girl? She had dark skin and long braids," the soldier replied, his voice trembling with Mahzun's response. "And she was a powerful mage—killed a dozen of our best men when we captured them."

Mahzun thought back to the ball. There had certainly been a hum to the girl's presence, a power unlike any he'd ever felt. Was it simply her connection to the *draod*?

"Her *qilada*," Mahzun began, leaning forward. "Do you remember what her *qilada* looked like?"

"Uh, I think it was an earring—silver with lots of jewels. It took up most of her ear."

Mahzun's stomach fell.

The key to finding the Heir of Segova had literally been in his hands. Without another word, he sped out of the room.

Maybe—just maybe—she was still within reach.

Chapter 27

Zahara sat in one of the chairs, tapping her fingers against the soft leather as she waited for the Usurper to return. Across the room, a tall, gilded mirror caught her eye, and she resisted the urge to examine her reflection.

The room, while luxurious and well-equipped, wasn't what she would have expected, either from a man with the power of an emperor or from a man with the reputation of the Usurper. She would have imagined more luxury, offset by prizes of war—suits of armor, exotic weapons, a rug formed from a creature of the Wilds. Yet it felt as if the room belonged to someone else.

What am I doing in here?

The thought came with the realization that she had just come—willingly, no less—to see the Usurper in his own palace. This was no pre-arranged social situation with a complete set of rules and niceties. In fact, she just now realized the implications of coming to the Usurper's bedroom of all places.

She was risking everything on his apparent infatuation, but what if Ekarath was right? They had come face to face atop the Atsada. The Usurper was insane, a creature of the Wilds more than a man.

I've made a terrible mistake.

She rose to her feet and approached the window. As she readied the hood, Zahara caught a glimpse of herself in the gilded mirror. The Destroyer of Worlds was enamored with this face. Somehow, if she left, it felt as if she would never have such an opportunity again. Zahara let go of the hood, studying herself in the large mirror.

The door burst open with a crack, and the Usurper leapt into the room, his eyes searching. As those eyes fell on her, he let out a growl.

"Where is he?" the Usurper shouted, dashing across the room. Before Zahara could react, his hand was around her throat. With inhuman strength, the beast lifted her into the air.

Panic seized Zahara's mind, and she gasped, clawing at the monster's hand. Her legs swung wildly, trying to hit the man's body, but they found only air. There was madness in the Primal King's eyes, a fury burning with the intensity of the sun. Yet there was also a sense of something else. Betrayal? Hurt?

"Where is the boy?" he shouted again. "Where is the Heir of Segova?"

Zahara tried to speak, but the man's grip was too tight around her neck. Without the fury is his eyes dampening in the least, the Usurper loosened his grip, just enough for air to pass through.

"I am the Heir of Segova," Zahara gasped.

The massive hand trembled, and Zahara fell to the ground in a heap. Her lungs gasping for air, and she could feel her throat beginning to swell with a bruise. The air was sweet, even as it burned going down.

Looking up, she saw fear and shock in the man's eyes. The Usurper's mouth hung open for a moment before turning into a smile.

"What an ugly lie to come from such a delicate mouth," the Usurper growled, bending low to bring his face close to her own. He placed a hand on her cheek, and Zahara resisted the urge to leap backwards, to jump out the window and escape.

The hand moved upward, away from her cheek and toward her ear.

"This is a lovely piece of craftsmanship," the Destroyer whispered as he caressed her *qilada*. The smile disappeared from his face as his fingers gripped with white gold and yanked it free.

Zahara howled as blood streamed from the three piercings. Placing a hand to her ear, she leapt to her feet and dashed toward the door. A strong hand grabbed her by the hair, pulling her to the ground. From her place on the floor, Zahara looked up to see the Usurper holding her bloody *qilada* in a scarred hand.

"You may not be the Heir of Segova," the man whispered, "but I know you're the key to finding him."

***

From his seat on the balcony, Ekarath leaned back into the plush cushion. His eyes were burning after so many hours of reading by the light of a *kura*, and he knew it was long past a reasonable time to retire for the night. Yet there was a hum in the air, and he couldn't help but think he was close to finding the answer.

I shouldn't have been so harsh with Zahara, Ekarath thought. His mind went through the midnight meeting, trying to decide if he had been out of line. Zahara and the others seemed so determined to take advantage of the Usurper's affections. Yet he couldn't bring himself to just throw her into that much danger.

Wishing he didn't have the authority to order anyone about, he turned his focus back to yet another ancient tome sitting on his lap. Like all the others, it had no mention of an Heir passing on the abilities without the necessity of dying. He leaned back, closing his eyes, giving them a moment to rest.

"There's a chance I'm never going to figure this out."

"Figure what out?" a feminine voice sounded, and Ekarath jumped, his eyes shooting open to see Saren standing in the doorway between his bedroom and the balcony.

"Don't...do that," Ekarath said, shaking his head. Adrenaline was already shooting through his veins, his body working overtime to react to the surprise.

"Sorry," Saren replied, taking a seat by Ekarath's side.

"Shouldn't you be asleep?" he asked, still trying to catch his breath. He must be exhausted for his body to be reacting this strongly to a small surprise.

"I could ask you the same question, but I won't. Instead, I want to ask why you're running from being the Heir. You have everything the people could want in a leader—you're strong, intelligent, handsome..."

"Maybe in a different time, I could learn to be the Heir of Segova," Ekarath responded, ignoring the girl's final word. "But we're facing a completely unprecedented crisis. There are no other Heirs, just me—a boy who can't even coerce the *draod* into doing a simple flame. The Usurper defeated seven of the most powerful people in existence—for some reason, I don't think my looks will be enough to defeat him."

Ekarath slumped into his seat, focusing his gaze on the book. At his side, he could feel Saren's brain working on a response.

"You love her, don't you?" Saren asked, and Ekarath popped his head up.

"Excuse me?"

"Zahara, you love her. It's as plain as day."

"I...don't...I—"

"Of course, the boy loves her," Farban's voice sounded as he moved onto the balcony. "And she loves you, too—even if she doesn't realize it yet."

"How does everyone seem to know I'm here?"

"You're on the balcony, not hiding in some dark, secluded room. I don't think any of us can sleep tonight, and I was out for a walk around the gardens."

Thunder shook the air, the balcony itself trembling. Looking toward the Mount of Creation, Ekarath could see dark clouds beginning to form. The stars disappeared, and the balcony grew a bit dim, as if the *kura* and lanterns were struggling to pierce the darkness.

Above the palace, lightning flashed, followed a second later by another low rumble. The sound echoed in Ekarath's ears, and his hands began to shake.

"This can't be good," Ekarath said, rising to his feet.

The shrill cry of an eagle pierced the night sky, rising above the thunder, the high-pitched call filling Ekarath's ears. He squinted toward the Mount of Creation, cursing himself yet again for being unable to pull on the *draod* enough to enhance his vision. Yet he was still able to make out a dot in the air, rising above the palace.

"It's the Usurper," Farban said at his side, and Ekarath looked over the see the weave across the spymaster's eyes. "And it looks like he has someone with him."

"That griffin never lets anyone but the Usurper on her back," Saren said at his side.

"Whoever it is, they're unconscious, laying across the Destroyer's lap," Farban said, dashing to the edge of the balcony and leaning forward. "Oh no, I think it's—"

"I have found the Heir of Segova," a deep, gravelly voice boomed. Louder than thunder, the words echoed throughout the city, the message reverberating until it faded into obscurity. "I hold her in my hands, ready to crush her bones to powder, ready to punish her for the crimes committed against the people of Einar."

Adrenaline coursed through Ekarath's veins, and he focused his eyes on the Usurper. Unable to do anything useful, his hands gripped the stone railing of the balcony until that deep voice again boomed through the air.

"At dawn, I will kill her with the Eternal Blade for all to see."

The blood froze in Ekarath's veins, and his heart dropped into his stomach. The words echoed throughout the city, repeating for everyone to hear. The Usurper's voice boomed once again before going silent.

"Only then can we truly be free."

Chapter 28

E karath dashed through the hallways, refusing to stop until he reached Zahara's rooms. The door was unlocked, and he forced his way in, hoping to see the girl either asleep in her bed or studying at her desk.

"Zahara," Ekarath shouted. "Zahara, where are you?"

Silence was his only response. The sitting room held no trace of the girl, and the bedchamber beyond looked as if it hadn't been disturbed in days. Near her desk, a window sat open, a gentle breeze wafting in from the storm brewing over the palace.

"She's gone," Ekarath whispered, a lump forming in his throat. "This is all my fault."

Ekarath stumbled toward the nearest sofa and collapsed onto its cushions. The tears began to roll down his cheeks, despite his attempt to push them back.

How could the Usurper have possibly captured her? Worse, how could the monster suspect her of being an Heir? Ekarath imagined a world completely under the Usurper's heel, a world devoid of happiness. A world without love. A world without hope.

It was a world without Zahara.

Images of that lovely face entered his mind. Even now, he could see her dark eyes bore into his soul. He could feel skin soft enough to be mistaken for down. He could almost hear her voice, mocking him for saying something moronic.

Footsteps entered the room, and Ekarath turned away. Whoever it was, he didn't want to be seen this way. He knew there were tears running down his cheeks—not a good look for a *Hundiin*, let alone for an Heir.

"She's not gone yet," Farban's voice sounded from the doorway.

"The Usurper has her," Ekarath responded, his voice cracking. He couldn't finish his thought. *She might as well be.*

"If I were the Usurper, why would I announce to the whole city that I have the last of the Heirs?" Farban asked, his footsteps and voice growing closer. "True, it will make a spectacle, destroying the Heir of Segova in front of the people. But he killed Lord Dimitri and the others without any ceremony. Unless I'm mistaken, this will be the first public execution of an Heir."

"Do you have a point?" Ekarath asked, still refusing to turn and face the spymaster. He just wanted to sink further into the cushions.

"My point is that the Usurper rarely does anything without a purpose," Farban said.

Ekarath could hear the old mage pick something up from Zahara's desk. A thud filled his head, and his vision spun.

"What—"

"This is no time to wallow in self-pity," Farban hissed.

Ekarath sat up and looked at what the spymaster had thrown. It was a simple book, bound in dark leather. He flipped it open to the first page, his eyes scanning the message written by Lord Dimitri.

My dearest Zahara,

The letter was written to her, not to him. It was just another reminder of how cruel the world could be. Zahara should have been the Heir, but instead it was him. Ekarath should be in chains right now, but instead it was her.

"Lord Dimitri also never did anything without a reason," Farban whispered.

Ekarath cleared his throat and turned the page. The next dozen held more instructions from Lord Dimitri—mostly the spells Zahara had been working on.

A brief flame of hope ignited in his chest as he scanned through the words. Was there perhaps a hint about giving up the power? Could he somehow give Zahara his powers before she was executed at dawn?

Ekarath didn't dare to breath as he flipped through the pages, scanning Lord Dimitri's writings. There had to be something, anything that would help him.

He reached the end.

There was nothing, no indication that the old man had ever considered the possibility of the wrong person becoming his successor. There was no cryptic message indicating further knowledge elsewhere, no invitation to search in another place. It just...ended.

"There's nothing in here but some spells," Ekarath said, resisting the urge to throw the book at the old man.

"Lord Dimitri was obsessed with secrets. Look again, but not just with your eyes."

Ekarath clenched his jaw, but he opened up the leather cover once again. At the end, he found it—a faint tapestry woven into the paper.

Ekarath pulled it toward him and squinted, examining the pattern of Illusion. The tapestry was thin, almost invisible even to the eyes of an Heir. Yet it was most definitely a complex pattern, one he could barely even comprehend.

Well, I might as well do the only thing I'm capable of doing.

His mind found the finishing knot and tugged at it. The entire pattern began to unravel, as if it had just been waiting for him to pull on the right string. A hiss filled the room as the energy dissipated, returning to the endless sea of the *draod*. An invisible hand grabbed him by the stomach, his entire body lurching into the air.

His eyes refused to open as he hurtled through space, his stomach tumbling with the force of gravity. After an eternity of falling, his feet landed on solid ground, and his eyes shot open.

Zahara's rooms were nowhere to be seen.

Instead of lavish furnishings, Ekarath was surrounded by a dense forest of aspen trees. The babbling of a stream filled his ears, accompanied by a chorus of birds. A breeze rustled the leaves, though Ekarath couldn't feel it on his skin.

The crunch of dried leaves sounded to the right, and Ekarath turned to see a young man with pale skin, blond hair, and a smattering of freckles bounding through the forest. He was in the awkward age between boyhood and becoming a man, when his limbs had fully grown, but his brain hadn't yet adjusted. His gait was awkward, and there were a few cuts on his face, likely from being unaware of his height while cutting through the dense forest.

Something about the boy's face was familiar, though he couldn't decide where he had seen it before.

The boy stopped at the stream and bent down to take a drink. He splashed the clear water on his head, embracing the simple joys of a life in nature. It made

Ekarath long for his own childhood, a life spent roaming the forest. Letting out a breath, he ran over to the boy.

"Hello, sorry to bother you," he said before reaching the boy. "I'm afraid I'm a bit lost."

The young man didn't respond, but he did find a soft patch of grass and fell onto his back. Without acknowledging Ekarath's existence, the boy just looked up into the sky. The stranger took in a deep breath, and his eyelids grew heavy.

"You must be tired, but I have no idea where I am," Ekarath said, scowling at his boorish behavior. No matter the age, a man shouldn't simply ignore a stranger like this. Yet he didn't stir, and his eyelids closed. The young man's breathing became shallow as he entered into a light slumber.

Not sure where that spell took me, Ekarath thought. While his knowledge of the *draod* was rather elementary, he knew that was certainly no normal tapestry. For five minutes, Ekarath sat and wondered what he should do next.

The footsteps of a small group sounded through the trees, coming from the same direction as the boy. Whoever was approaching, they had the sound of those experienced with the woods, and they made far less noise than the boy had. Ekarath's muscles tensed as two men and a woman appeared out of the trees.

All three looked Segovan, with the same pale skin and hair as the boy. The woman was thin, covered in sinewy muscles, and her face was sharper than the knife at her belt. Both men looked nearly identical—brothers, perhaps—with large frames that held an equal share of fat and muscle.

The woman held a bow with an arrow ready to fly while both men wielded heavy clubs that looked light in their over-powered arms. Their footsteps remained soft, even as their faces lit up with excitement, their eyes falling upon the boy. Those eyes belonged to hunters, but Ekarath could tell they searched for no ordinary prey.

One of the men leapt, and a shout erupted from the boy's sleepy throat, but it was stifled by the weight of his attacker. Though the boy was likely strong for his age, his arms looked as if they were pushing against a boulder rather than a man. The second thug ran up and smacked the boy across the mouth before gagging him with a cloth. Despite the boy's thrashing, the female withdrew a set of thick cords and began binding the young man's wrists.

Now silent, the boy was barely able to kick his legs as the first man lifted that thin frame onto his shoulders with a baritone chuckle.

"I'm sorry to do this, *Your Holiness*," the man sneered, and Ekarath's blood froze at the words. If this boy held that title, then he wasn't the only Heir left. "But the price on your head is just too much to pass up. You can rest, knowing that a dozen families will never go hungry again because of your sacrifice."

Ekarath ran after the trio with enough audacity to abduct an Heir. Whoever these people were and wherever he was, this boy was his only hope of getting some answers. With all the strength he could summon, Ekarath leapt onto one of the men.

He passed right through him.

The ground grew large in his vision as his face slammed into the dirt and fallen leaves. His vision swam, though the expected pain of careening nose-first into the forest floor was absent. With his head spinning, Ekarath picked himself back up to see the trio of criminals disappear into the trees.

The boy's muffled screams sounded again, and Ekarath took off down the trail. His eyes caught sight of the group in time to see the boy land a kick on his transportation's groin. A groan escaped the man's throat, and he fell to one knee.

While the man gasped for air, the boy scrambled off his captor's shoulder. Though his wrists were bound, his feet were free, and he took off down the trail. With a shout, the woman dashed off after him, leaping to tackle her quarry before he could get anywhere. Ekarath ran after them, catching up as the woman smacked a closed fist into the boy's face. He fell to the ground, and she moved onto her knees to launch another blow at his bleeding nose.

"This wasn't supposed to be so hard," the woman screamed, slamming her fist yet again into the boy's face. "You aren't even a real Heir yet."

The boy's face grew calm at the words, and a smile spread across his lips. Wheels began to spin in that young head, though Ekarath couldn't read his face well enough to know what the product would be. A breeze kicked up, and the *draod* began to hum as the boy's smile grew larger.

As the woman pulled back to deliver another blow, the wind wrapped around her arm, locking it in place. It picked her up with invisible arms, and she let out the gasp of someone struggling to fill lungs with air. With blood dripping down his nose and a bruise forming around his right eye, the boy rose to his feet and looked the woman in the eyes.

"I am indeed a real Heir," the boy said. "I am the Heir of Segova."

As the words left his mouth, a hum filled the air, and a light erupted from the boy's eyes. The chords around his wrists snapped, smoke billowing from the burnt edges. The two men yelled and ran back down the forest trail, while the woman let out a strangled gasp.

Fire leapt from the young man's fingers in needle-thin rays, slamming into each of the retreating bandits. Their shouts filled the air before cutting off as the flames tore holes through their bodies. The acrid stench of burning clothing, hair, and flesh assaulted Ekarath's nose, though he couldn't look away.

The boy took another step closer to the bound woman, waving his hand to loosen the air securing her. She took in a deep breath before letting out a sob.

"Go find whoever hired you to kidnap me," the boy said. "Tell them of your failure. Tell them that because of you, I am no longer a cowering boy—I am Dimitri, the Heir of Segova."

The declaration filled the air, and Ekarath could feel a power to it. The wind died, and the woman dropped to the ground. Without a second of hesitation, she dashed away, down the trail. Within seconds, she was lost in the density of the forest.

The same invisible hand from earlier now pulled Ekarath into the air, his stomach reeling as his vision blurred. His mind spun as he once again tumbled, though the knowledge that it would eventually end helped the eternity to pass much more quickly.

Ekarath landed hard, his boots cracking on the floor of Zahara's quarters. At his side, the book sat still, giving no indication of the feat it had just performed. As Ekarath gasped for air, his stomach squirmed, and the muscles in his legs wobbled like jelly. Yet the words of Lord Dimitri pounded in his head.

"Well, that was odd," Farban said, and Ekarath looked over to see the old man. "I thought I saw you disappear for a moment, but I must have just blinked."

"I've been gone for at least fifteen minutes," Ekarath said, his hoarse voice barely rising above a whisper. "Unless..."

"I told you Lord Dimitri loved his secrets," Farban laughed, shaking his head. "So, I can assume that something happened that's beyond my comprehension."

"I don't really know what just happened," Ekarath whispered, plopping down onto the sofa. "I do know one thing—I am the Heir of Segova."

The *draod* buzzed all around him with those words, and he pulled a handful of threads into the mortal plane. Above him, Farban's entire face lit up with a grin—whether it was from the words or whether the old man could sense that Ekarath was beginning to weave, he didn't know. Ekarath returned the smile with one of his own and began weaving the threads into a pattern.

Chapter 29

M ahzun stepped out onto the same balcony that had so recently witnessed his near destruction. Just as before, members of the Elder Council sat in attendance, and the odd mixture of various perfumes filled the air. Mahzun kept his gaze forward, determined to not let their presence mar his impending victory.

Yet he could feel the weight of their collective gaze, their eyes following his trek toward the balcony's edge. He felt their hatred, just as strong as it had been the morning he had tried to destroy the Shajarat. Mixed with that hatred, there was something else, something much worse.

There was hope.

Hope that the Savior of Man would undo himself again. Hope that the Eternal Blade would turn on its champion. Hope that they could somehow profit from the ensuing chaos.

Let them plan. Let them scheme. I am the Savior of Man, and I am about to achieve my final victory.

Ignoring the glares from those who had publicly pledged their loyalty, Mahzun approached the balcony's edge and rested his hands on the stone railing. With the sun peeking over the horizon, the white granite was cold to the touch. Mahzun closed his eyes and took in a deep breath, savoring the calm.

Opening his eyes, he looked at the crowd assembled below. Summoned by his nocturnal announcement, the plaza was brimming with his subjects—both loyal supporters and vehement opponents. While the noblemen at his back controlled the levers of power, the masses crowded onto the plaza were the true masters of Einar.

They just needed someone to help them realize that.

In time, they'll appreciate what I've done for them.

It might take decades, centuries even, for the world to appreciate his sacrifice. But the people of Einar would eventually realize what he had done for them.

The heavy double doors to the balcony opened, and the sound of footsteps caused Mahzun to turn away from the balcony's edge. A squadron of Imperial guards, their striped uniforms especially pristine for the occasion, marched forward. In their midst, the woman kept pace, though her arms were bound with heavy chains.

The three piercings that had held her *qilada* were mangled, though the skin was already beginning to scab over. Her face was a mask of polished obsidian, her posture unbowed. Even after a night in the dungeons, she still moved with unmatched grace, as if her muscles refused to believe they were beaten. While the guards tromped across the stone balcony, the girl floated, her feet barely touching the ground.

I still don't even know her name, Mahzun thought. The realization saddened him—a delicate flower was to be trampled underfoot, nothing but another sacrifice to the Cause.

"You look lovely," Mahzun said, placing a hand on the girl's face. "Believe me when I say that this brings me no joy."

The girl's eyes flared with a dark fire, her serene face suddenly pulsing with anger. That anger was something far more pure than the hatred emanating from the Elder Council. The girl's emotions lacked the same scheming and planning; it came without a desire for gain.

It was hatred, pure and simple.

"If death means I never have to again look upon your face, I greet it with open arms," the girl replied. "Give your speech, summon your blade, and be done with it."

"I pray that your friend will come for you. Once he's defeated, you will one day take your place as my empress," Mahzun responded. "If he proves a coward, just know that your sacrifice is for the good of all Einar."

Without waiting for her to cut him yet again with a response, Mahzun turned back around and lifted his hands. A cheer erupted from the people down below, though he knew that few throats made the sound with enthusiasm.

"A new era is about to dawn in Einar," Mahzun shouted, his *draod*-enhanced voice echoing in his ears. "In recent days, we have celebrated the end of the war, the end of the Heirs, and the end of oppression. Yet our enemies are clever, and we have been blind to their machinations."

Mahzun paused to clear his throat. Below, a heavy silence blanketed the crowd.

"But those who follow the Cause have reason to rejoice. Despite the best efforts of our enemies, we have apprehended the Heir of Segova, the successor of Lord Dimitri. Behold!"

The guards pushed the girl forward to a chorus of cheers, boos, and shouts. Closing his eyes, Mahzun called upon the Eternal Blade. Fire coursed through his veins as the hilt appeared in his calloused hand.

May this be the last time I call upon you, old friend.

"As we enter the Age of Man, remember that we must be a strong, unified Einar," Mahzun shouted, bringing the Blade to the girl's throat. "With the death of the girl, the world will finally be free."

The deep rumble of thunder sounded in Mahzun's ears, though it didn't come from the sky. Instead, it came from below his feet, the granite of the balcony shuddering. Shouts sounded from within the palace halls, and Mahzun smiled as the members of the Elder Council turned toward the noise.

"I'm glad to see the Heir of Segova is no coward," Mahzun whispered to the girl. She scowled, spitting on his face, but Mahzun only smiled in return before turning to the doors that separated him from immortality.

The large wooden doors shot open, revealing a young man with the pale skin and hair of a native Segovan. His eyes were a blue fire, his teeth bared. Mahzun couldn't help but laugh at the young man's indignation, even as the perfumed aristocrats scrambled for safety.

"I am the Heir of Segova," the boy shouted. "Unhand the girl."

"Of course you are," Mahzun replied, twirling the Eternal Blade in his hand. "I was hoping you would come."

The boy approached, his footsteps silent, his hands weaving a tapestry. Mahzun tested the weight of the Eternal Blade in his hands, bracing himself for the coming pain. Soon, it would be over.

"Ekarath, run!" the girl screamed at his side. "It's a trap."

Without taking his eyes off the boy, Mahzun back-handed the girl across the face, sending her to the balcony floor in a heap. A fire flashed across the boy's face, and his pace quickened.

"I think you're going to regret that," the boy growled.

"Maybe. Maybe not," Mahzun responded, his smile growing larger than his mouth. "I think you're going to regret—"

The boy leapt, his bulk slamming into Mahzun's chest. Together, they tumbled off the balcony, toward the plaza below.

Chapter 30

E karath struggled against the Usurper's bulk, trying his best to push the man away as they both careened toward the plaza. Time moved at a glacial pace, the wind roaring in his ears, the ground looming large. Without so much as a command, the *draod* wove itself into a cushion of air around both Heir and Usurper before they slammed into the polished cobblestone.

The force of impact ruptured the tapestry, the threads of energy exploding apart. A ringing filled Ekarath's ears, though the spell had softened the impact just enough to stop him from breaking every bone in his body. Ekarath forced his eyes open to see nothing but a cloud of dust.

Though muffled screams sounded in the distance, Ekarath couldn't see any sign of a plaza packed with onlookers. Instead, he was at the bottom of a large crater, its steep sides forming a shallow bowl. At the very center—no more than ten feet away—lay the Usurper, his grizzly form curled up into a ball.

It can't have been that easy.

As if in response to Ekarath's thought, the Usurper let out a deep groan. The sound echoed throughout the crater before coming to a crescendo. With the sound bounding on the crater walls, the Destroyer of Worlds leapt to his feet.

In one hand, he gripped the Eternal Blade, a soft blue light emanating from the ephemeral steel. Ekarath forced himself upright, unsheathing his own sword with one hand while the other pulled on tendrils of Destruction.

"I've killed seven Heirs, all of them with years of experience," the Usurper growled, tightening his grip on the Eternal Blade as a smile crept onto his lips. "Do you really think you pose a threat?"

Ekarath responded with a shout, launching a fireball toward the brute. A smile lit up the Usurper's entire face, and he casually swung at the oncoming firestorm. The threads of Destruction splintered at the Blade's touch, filling Ekarath's ears with a hum as the inferno dissipated. Clenching his teeth, Ekarath began work on another spell.

"You may think yourself powerful," the Usurper said, his heavy footsteps bringing him ever closer to Ekarath. "And in a normal world, that may be true. But you're no match for something as ancient as the Eternal Blade."

The Usurper lunged, bringing the sword down in an arc. Ekarath abandoned his weave and used both hands to lift his own sword to block the Primal King's assault. The ephemeral blade crashed into the mundane steel with bone-rattling force, knocking Ekarath back a step. Yet he remained firm, his arms unyielding.

With a shout, he pushed the Usurper back. The man's large frame stumbled as he backpedaled, but he quickly regained his footing. A scowl flashed across the scarred face, but it was quickly replaced by a grin.

"I'm glad to come across an Heir that can handle a sword," the Usurper said, twirling the Eternal Blade as if he were simply exercising. "All the others had such disdain for manual forms of fighting—they had no idea how to react when the Eternal Blade nullified their powers. Then, of course, there was Lord Dimitri—the poor man was so tired he didn't even fight back."

Ekarath couldn't bring himself to respond—his head was still pounding, and his vision was spinning. Only the adrenaline coursing through his veins was keeping him going.

That and his hatred for the monster standing before him.

Every word out of the Usurper's mouth stung like acid in his ears. Why did the man feel the need to speak while fighting?

"What's the matter?" the Usurper shouted. "Are you also spent? Too exhausted for the fight?"

As his response, Ekarath leapt at the man, his sword lunging at the Usurper's chest. With a laugh, the Primal King sidestepped and parried the blow, the crash of blades once again echoing throughout the crater.

Ekarath moved backward a few steps and readied himself as the Usurper attacked, bringing his sword down. With a grunt, Ekarath lifted his own blade just in time, though the force knocked him onto his back. As Ekarath scrambled to get upright again, an armored foot slammed into his ribs, knocking him back to the ground.

The Usurper placed his heavy boot on Ekarath's wrist, sending convulsions of pain throughout his entire arm and pinning his sword to the ground. While he continued to struggle, the Usurper let out a laugh that filled the crater.

"You cannot fight the rolling tide of history," he growled, standing over Ekarath with the Eternal Blade poised to strike. "The time of the Heirs is over. No longer is there a Segova, a Karajaan, or any other Heirdom. There is only a single, united Einar."

The Usurper lifted the Eternal Blade, but Ekarath didn't register his coming death. Rather, the Usurper's words rang in his head. While Ekarath may not like it, the other Heirs really were gone. Even if he could defeat the Usurper, things would never go back to the way they were.

There would never be another Heir of Karajaan or Heir of Tagus. Those powers were gone, severed by the Eternal Blade. Nothing could bring them back.

Ekarath was the last of his kind, the final link in a chain that extended back for thousands of years. He couldn't just serve the people of Segova, it wouldn't be right. All people of Einar were under his protection, and they needed him.

He was not simply an Heir. He was *the* Heir.

"You're right," Ekarath whispered, the words stopping the Usurper's blow. The monster's brow furrowed, and the Eternal Blade wavered. "I can't believe it, but you're right. There is no more Segova, Tagus, Karajaan. There is only Einar. I am not just a link in the chain of Heirs stretching back to the Creator. I am the *last* link in that chain. I am the last, the only, the *Final* Heir."

The *draod* roared in his ears with the words, and a cold breeze moved into the crater, swirling around him. The breeze turned into a stiff wind, whipping the Usurper's long hair into his face. Ekarath shouted as his vision filled with dust, but it was drowned out by the howling of the wind.

Raw energy surged through Ekarath's bones, threatening to shatter every part of his body. Images of that day—so long ago in his memories—just outside the forest flooded into his mind as the wind lifted him from the ground. His stomach flipped and tossed within as he hurtled through the sky, grey clouds forming around him.

Lightning struck the ground below, the heat cracking the air and rattling Ekarath's bones. Threads of the *draod* surged through him, and his hands began weaving faster than his brain could give commands. Darkness crept in, his mind threatening to give up consciousness. Yet he forced back the pure energy—whatever was going to happen, it needed to be done by him, not just the *draod*.

Out of the chaos, the shrill cry of the Usurper's griffin sounded, breaking through the rolling thunder. Ekarath looked down to see the griffin rising into the air, its wings pounding against the wind and dust. Sitting atop the creature's back, the armor-clad Usurper bellowed, Eternal Blade in hand. That triumphant smile was no more, replaced by a grimace, his teeth grinding in anguish.

With another shrill cry, the griffin lifted itself above Ekarath, avoiding a bolt of lightning that filled the air with a blue light. She rose higher and higher before levelling out and diving. The air filled with the howl of wind—mixed with the griffin's shriek—as man and beast dove toward Ekarath.

A powerful gust caught the griffin's wings, knocking her off course. The griffin screamed as she was propelled past her mark, the wind throwing her toward the city.

"You asked for this," Ekarath whispered. "Now it's time to be the Heir I was meant to be."

***

Zahara awoke to the rumble of thunder, her head pounding. She opened her eyes to see nothing but a grey blur, and she began blinking furiously. She moved to touch her face, only to find that her wrists were still bound with a coarse rope.

Her face stung where the Usurper had smacked her, and her ear was nothing but a dull ache. Yet her vision was already beginning to clear. Pulling herself upright, she looked around the balcony only to find that she was its only remaining occupant.

The plush chairs used by the nobility were empty, and many had been knocked over during the Council's evacuation. There was no blood, corpses, or any indication of a battle taking place on the balcony. It was simply deserted, Zahara forgotten.

Lightning illuminated the sky, followed immediately by a sharp crack of thunder.

Zahara looked up to see Ekarath once again floating at the center of a whirlwind. Unlike last time, there was no light shining from his eyes or hair—did that mean he was conscious? Or did it mean he was less powerful? There was still something wholly different about the boy, a power raging through his body.

The shrill cry of the Usurper's griffin sounded, higher even than Ekarath. A bolt of lightning struck the bird, but the Usurper lifted his Blade. The mass of blue light and energy hit the ephemeral steel, absorbing into the sword instead of striking down the Usurper.

"There has to be something I can do," Zahara whispered to herself. The dull ache in her ear was a reminder that her *qilada* was gone, but that didn't mean she could simply stand by while the fate of Einar played out in front of her.

With hands still bound, she dashed toward the broken doorway that led into the palace. Within the corridor, there were over a dozen guards laying prostrate, most with burns from the explosion that had destroyed the large doors. She looked from guard to guard until she found a man with a sword in hand.

Zahara began slicing her bindings on the exposed blade, each pass severing a few strands of the rough hemp. Another crack of thunder sounded from outside, and Zahara pushed herself. With a satisfying snap, the blade cut through the last of the rope, and she was free.

The fallen man's comrade held an Imperial crossbow in his hands, a single bolt already loaded. Zahara thought back to that morning—which felt like a lifetime ago—atop the Atsada. At the time, Ekarath had expressed his desire to at least scare the Usurper with a shot from his bow.

"Now, it's time for me to give that monster a scare," Zahara whispered, grabbing the crossbow from stiff hands before running back to the balcony's edge.

Lightning flashed yet again, filling the balcony with a harsh blue light as the bolt slammed into the Usurper's blade. The griffin hovered—her wings pounding the air—as the Eternal Blade absorbed the energy. With a deep breath, Zahara took aim with the crossbow and prayed to the Creator. As she let out a long breath, she pulled the trigger and let the arrow fly.

***

Lightning streamed through Mahzun's body, his bones threatening to shatter. His skin was roasting, adding another layer of scars. Yet he could only focus on the thrill of his impending victory.

A dull thud sounded near his legs, and Aiya let out a scream.

Something's wrong, she screamed in his head. *I've been hit.*

Mahzun looked down at the balcony to see the young Karajaani girl standing at the railing, crossbow in her unbound hands. A smile was on that impetuous face, one that gave no doubt as to her guilt.

Are you ready? Aiya called out, her words bouncing around Mahzun's skull.

"Looks like I have to be," Mahzun shouted. Without waiting for her to reply, he leapt off her back, Blade in hand. The wind's roar filled his ears, blocking out any terror that could try to seize him. He blinked away the water that sprang to his eyes, maintaining his focus on the boy and his shield.

Mahzun slammed the Eternal Blade into the weave of hardened air, and the world around him exploded.

***

Ekarath opened his eyes to nothing but dust—a cloud of grey and brown hanging in the air. A dull hum filled his ears, muting the sound of screams in the distance. As he tried to sit up, a fit of coughing racked his body, and he had to roll over onto hands and knees as his lungs attempted to expel the vile intruders.

His mind couldn't handle what had just happened. His bones ached from the impact, from the Eternal Blade piercing the woven threads of power. Yet he knew that he couldn't stay here—somewhere in the cloud of dust was the Primal King.

Two screams filled the air—one of a man, the other of a furious beast high above. Ekarath turned to see the Usurper charging out of the dust, blade held high over his head. His face was a mass of raw skin, a mixture of red and black char. His eyes were filled with a flame that spoke of madness—a madness that consumed his entire being, a madness that could only be sated by blood. Gritting his teeth, Ekarath called on the *draod*, pulling large chunks into the mortal plane.

At his command, threads of Restoration wove themselves around the cobblestone, shifting the ground at the Usurper's feet. The man fell from his berserker charge, toppling forward into a roll that was halted by the stones. With commands from both his hands and mind, the plaza's cobblestone and tile flew through the air, burying the Usurper.

Ekarath's jaw clenched as the power surged through his body, weaving a layer around the mass of stone, pushing on the Primal King and sealing the myriad pieces together. He could feel his foe's mass pushing back, straining for freedom. The desperate cry of an eagle sounded in his ears, and Ekarath turned his gaze away from the Usurper to see a set of talons a mere foot away.

His legs collapsed, bringing him to the ground as the talons brushed the top of his head. Without a finishing knot, the weave on the Usurper's stone prison dissipat-

ed. Ekarath pushed himself upright as the Destroyer of
Worlds burst out of the layers of rock and tile.

The *draod* surrounded Ekarath before he could even
summon it, the crash of cobblestones on hardened air
filling the small cocoon. With dust hanging in the air,
the shield faded back into the sea of energy. Through
the haze, he could barely make out the hulking shape
of the Usurper and the soft glow of the Eternal Blade
in his grip.

Without waiting for another assault to begin,
Ekarath's hands moved on their own, creating a complex weave. As he tied it off, a bolt of lightning
leapt from his hands. It flew through the air, casting
blue shadows on the dust as it careened toward the
bear-like figure. The Usurper lifted the Blade, and the
lightning slammed into the quasi-luminescent steel,
disappearing with a loud crack.

"You have some fight in you," the Usurper growled,
his voice deep and scarred. "More than the pathetic
weakling who came before you. He had no problem
letting his minions die in his stead."

"How many have you let die?" Ekarath responded as
the Usurper stepped closer. "Millions?"

The Usurper smiled in response and gave a little
chuckle. The fire in his eyes no longer blazed like an
inferno, but it still crackled and popped. His slow,
plodding steps echoed in the silence, muffled only by
the dust.

"I lost count decades ago," he responded. "But that
doesn't stop them from haunting me both day and
night. Even now, I see one of them looking at me,
playing witness to this defining moment in the history
of Einar."

Ekarath tried not to listen as he pulled on threads of
Destruction. The Destroyer's words made little sense,

but he could see the madness stirring in those eyes—it was growing, taking a stronger hold over the man who had usurped the Power of Creation.

"Soon, you'll join them," the Usurper continued, "your dead eyes reminding me of the sacrifices necessary to liberate mankind."

As the words left the man's mouth, Ekarath finished his weave and launched another bolt of lightning.

The Usurper lifted the Blade, the ephemeral steel absorbing the bolt. Sparks flew as Ekarath kept pushing, forcing more energy toward his enemy. A howl escaped the Usurper's throat, and Ekarath pushed harder.

That scream grew as the smell of burning flesh reached Ekarath's nose through the dust. The *draod* poured through him, using his body as a channel to push the raw energy into the Eternal Blade—slowly destroying its wielder.

Ekarath could almost feel the man's pain, could feel the bones shatter and the skin boil. In this moment, there was only the Usurper and the *draod*. All else felt small, distant.

"Ekarath, look out," a muffled cry sounded from above, pulling Ekarath from his focus. The words were followed by the familiar shrill call of a tortured eagle. He turned to see a mass of white feathers fill his vision before he was slammed to the ground.

The flow of the *draod* stopped as Ekarath crashed to the hard cobblestone, his head spinning. As if awakening after a long sleep, the world grew loud once again—the screams of the wounded, shouts from terrified civilians, the thunder rumbling in the clouds.

Warm breath tickled his face, and Ekarath opened his eyes. Instead of the grey sky greeting his vision, he saw only a set of dark eyes and a razor-sharp beak glaring down at him. Ekarath tried to move, but his entire body was pinned by griffin's talons.

Ekarath screamed and struggled, calling on the *draod*, but his head was spinning too much to grab on to the slippery threads. In the corner of his eye, Ekarath saw the Usurper rise and shake his head.

"I must be getting old," the man growled, bending over to pick up the Eternal Blade. He twisted his neck, and several of the joints popped. "Because you put up a much better fight than I was expecting."

Ekarath didn't respond as he called on the *draod*, but it again slipped out of his grasp. As if the Usurper could tell what Ekarath was trying to do, he placed the cold steel of the Eternal Blade to his throat.

"Thank you, my dear," Mahzun said to the griffin, who returned the words with a small nod. The creature's weight didn't shift as its talons kept Ekarath pinned. Along with the nod, the animal gave the Usurper a look, as if she were trying to communicate with him.

At that moment, a colorful weave flared up, extending from the griffin's chest to the Usurper's. Though his vision still spun, Ekarath squinted and directed his focus on the strange pattern.

It was old—decades, at least—and that time had strengthened the bond. The threads of Restoration were thick, heavy.

"And you," Mahzun said, turning back to Ekarath and pushing the Eternal Blade harder against his throat, "please leave the mortal plane with the knowledge that your failure has left Einar a better place."

The weave again flared, and Ekarath turned his focus back to the colorful strands of energy. Near the Usurper's chest, his mind found the finishing knot, and he yanked on it with all the strength he had left.

It resisted his fuzzy, addled brain. Yet he kept pulling, even as the Usurper thrust the Eternal Blade.

With a small pop, the knot gave way.

The Usurper's arms went limp, and his eyes widened as the weave unraveled. A soft hiss filled the air as the energy pent up for so long in the threads began to dissipate, the individual strands dissolving back into the sea of energy. The Blade shook in the Primal King's hand, and he took a step backward, lips trembling.

At the same moment, cries burst from both master and servant, loud and shrill enough to shatter glass. The griffin's talons loosened their hold, and Ekarath scrambled backward with trembling muscles. The howls grew louder as both the Usurper and his griffin fell to the ground.

The entire plaza shook as the griffin's tremendous mass rolled on the broken cobblestone. Ekarath could feel the tremors shake his bones, and he tried to call on the *draod*. Yet the exhaustion filled him as much as the anguish filled his enemies. For a terrible moment, Ekarath sat paralyzed, unable to comprehend exactly what he had just done.

Without warning, the griffin stopped its thrashing and cast its gaze on Ekarath. Those black eyes screamed of pain and hatred, and it let out another high-pitched howl. Instead of charging, it grabbed the Usurper by the waist and leapt into the air. Those powerful wings sent dust flying in all directions as the mass of fur and feathers lifted into the sky.

Ekarath could only stare as the griffin escaped with the Usurper. His entire body quivered at the thought of moving, his strength completely gone. He knew that he should do something, anything; yet movement was beyond him. Tears sprang to his eyes, and a wave of laughter erupted from his chest.

Chapter 31

E karath looked out the window of his rooms, the view different from the night before. Instead of viewing the palace and Mount of Creation, he now looked down on the city from those lofty heights.

His hair was still wet from the perfumed bath that had washed away the grime and dirt, though he still didn't feel clean, not on the inside. With smoke rising from some of the city's neighborhoods, he knew that defeating the Usurper this morning had done as much to end Einar's conflict as bathing had done to wash away the wounds.

The robes of green silk felt strange on his skin. Farban had suggested them to remind everyone of Lord Dimitri, as that had been his signature piece of clothing.

"There's nothing I can do about any of this right now," Ekarath whispered to himself.

The setting sun cast an orange glow on the city, amplified by the smoke. His muscles ached, not just from defeating the Usurper but from all the activities that took up the remainder of the day. They flew through his mind, the entire day a blur. And it wasn't over yet.

A knock sounded on the door, and Ekarath pulled himself away from the window. He checked his reflection in the mirror, ensuring that he looked presentable.

"Come in," he called out, and the door immediately swung open to reveal both Zahara and Farban. Both wore the vermillion robes of a mage, and Ekarath couldn't help but smile at the sight. Zahara had waited so long to leave behind her apprentice status, and the color certainly suited her. If nothing else, the robes would command respect, setting them apart from some of the nobles who had inherited *qiladas* without taking the time to become fully trained and dedicated magi.

"You two look great," Ekarath said, leaving the window to greet his friends. "Am I really so far behind?"

"You're the Final Heir—you're allowed to be a bit late," Zahara said. "Let the Council sweat it out a bit."

The Elder Council—those who hadn't fled the city—would soon be officially recognizing him as the Heir of Segova. Ekarath saw the wisdom in keeping the wealthy aristocrats running the city, but he knew it was going to be a fine line. Just because Ivana could be trusted didn't mean the others could.

"This is the beginning of a long power struggle, after all," Farban said. "The elders will gladly be your ally, but they'll need to be kept in line."

"I'm going to be the best Heir that I can," Ekarath said, shaking his head. "Though I'll admit I'm more than a little worried about finding the Usurper. I'd rather focus completely on creating a stable Einar, but I'm worried that monster is going to mess everything up again."

"We're here for you," Zahara said, taking a bow. "I've already dispatched scouts to look for him. We've also sent messengers out to the other capitals announcing your victory—only time will tell how the other Heirdoms will respond."

"Now, we should probably get going," Farban said before Ekarath could respond to Zahara. "We want to keep the Council waiting long enough to be annoyed, but we should show up before they begin to worry."

"Of course," Ekarath said before taking a deep breath. The battle was won. The war was just beginning.

***

Mahzun let out a shout as Aiya dropped him on the ground near the edge of a grove of ancient trees. His soul groaned with each passing second, and his entire body protested every movement. Broken bones, burnt skin—all of it shouted as a reminder of his failure. Worse than the physical pain was the hole left in his soul where once Aiya had resided.

He pulled up to the nearest tree and leaned against the rough bark. His heavy armor weighed down his broken ribs, and he moved a trembling hand to release the leather straps that held the mail in place. With a growl, he felt the extra weight fall off his chest, and he let out a sigh.

Aiya screeched, and Mahzun looked up at the griffin. She pawed the ground before curling up at Mahzun's side. He leaned against that mixture of fur and feathers, drinking in her warmth. He was hungry, but they both needed rest.

Standing above him, the silent apparition of Lord Dimitri appeared, intent on providing Mahzun with his usual stare filled with apathy. Yet there was something in those eyes that gave Mahzun a chill that had nothing to do with the breeze filtering in through the forest.

"If you're going to stare at me, you could at least give me some help," Mahzun growled. "A bandage for my ribs, perhaps."

Dimitri didn't respond. Those dead eyes continued boring into him with something akin to emotion—was it hatred or just a greater sense of apathy? Mahzun shook his head and returned to inspecting his broken body, forcing the silent apparition out of his mind.

"How could this have happened," he grunted, leaning further into Aiya's fur. "I'm broken, possibly dying. I don't even have any idea what to do next."

As the words left his mouth, Dimitri took a step forward, and Mahzun looked up at the ghost. The old man's mouth turned up into a smile, and a fire ignited in those eyes. For the first time, the old man's mouth stretched open, filling the air with a deep, grating voice that had most certainly never belonged to the real Heir of Segova.

"Poor, simple, unworthy servant," Dimitri said. "You're looking for ideas? Fortunately for you, I have several."

The adventure continues in *The Fallen Usurper*

About the Author

J on Monson is an American epic fantasy author from Salt Lake City, Utah. He is known for his Sun and the Raven trilogy, which won the 2019 Best Indie Book Award for Fantasy.

Jon is happiest when immersed in the fantasy worlds he so lovingly creates. When he pulls himself back into the real world, Jon loves spending time exploring the wilderness of southern Utah where he lives with his wife and two daughters.

To hear more from Jon, join the mailing list at jon monson.com.

59756191R10191